BN1

The Baynes Gang:
Book One

Montana Horseman

Also by John S. McCord

WALKING HAWK

The Baynes Gang:
Book One

Montana Horseman

John S. McCord

A DOUBLE D WESTERN
DOUBLEDAY
New York   London   Toronto   Sydney   Auckland

A Double D Western
PUBLISHED BY DOUBLEDAY
a division of Bantam Doubleday Dell Publishing Group, Inc.
666 Fifth Avenue, New York, New York 10103

Double D Western, Doubleday,
and the portrayal of the letters DD
are trademarks of Doubleday, a division of Bantam Doubleday
Dell Publishing Group, Inc.

Library of Congress Cataloging-in-Publication Data

McCord, John S.
  The Baynes Gang book 1 : Montana horseman / John S. McCord. — 1st ed.
    p.   cm. — (A Double D western)
  I. Title.
PS3563.C34439B37   1990
813'.54—dc20   89-71500
CIP

ISBN 0-385-41102-2

To Joan, who puts shade and cool water on every trail

The Baynes Gang:
Book One

Montana Horseman

PROLOGUE

WHEN MY FATHER was a young man, he was in a duel in New Orleans. Took him two months to get well, but he never got over it. The incident marked him for life, not just with the bullet scar but with an iron-hard will that such would never again happen to him or his.

Pa wasn't exactly from New Orleans. He was a planter and horse breeder, also raising hogs and cattle, with land miles and miles north and west of there. He was visiting the big city to run his horses in a big race when he found trouble.

Seems another fellow had set his sights on my mama. She was a beautiful young woman of good family, had just had her "coming out" party, and was attracting serious attention from the well-off bachelors around town. Pa dallied in New Orleans to pay her some serious attention too, and he got himself shot for it.

Most folks figured Pa won out in the end. After all, he ended up with Mama, although they had to elope to get away from her fancy family, and his horses ran off with bundles of New Orleans money. But Pa never forgot lying in his own blood while the other man walked off laughing. He must have told me and my brothers a hundred times that being right doesn't help a bit if a man is slow.

Pa practiced with a pistol for a year before the second duel, which put that other fellow in his grave. That's another thing Pa taught us, never to be forgetful of debts to be paid.

All of that has nothing much to do with me and my brothers, except to explain why we grew up slow to argue and quick to shoot. No son of Darnell Baynes could have lived to manhood without being fast and sure with pistol, knife, and rifle, plus being able to do two days work in one. Pa would likely have drowned us if we'd been either slow or lazy.

Mama felt the same way about it. I can still hear her saying, "A proper lady expects her man to be her protector. She expects him to look after her and not have to ask for help doing it."

She and Pa were always of one mind. My brothers and I were shocked to hear other folks talking about man-and-wife arguments. We never heard such in our house. There were some mighty long talks about this and that, but once they decided something, Mama and Pa stuck to it with no wavering or blaming if things didn't go smooth.

Practice with guns was an everyday thing, same as the prayers before meals, and books every evening. All of that, mixed with back-breaking work from dawn to dark every day but Sunday, will either make a man tough or kill him. That's how we lived on a quiet plantation and horse breeding stables in the backwoods of Louisiana. My pa didn't hold with bondage, so we never learned to sit on the front porch and fan ourselves like the slave-owning gentry.

A family such as ours could live for a hundred years and never bother a soul, but we weren't lucky. Some folks can't stand to leave well enough alone. My pa had no patience with talk of war, secession, and the like. Talk kept getting rougher and louder and tougher as time passed, since the war wasn't won overnight the way some expected.

There were wild rumors about us helping runaway slaves. That was true, but none we helped got caught, so there was no way for anybody to know—they had to make it up, same as a lie. Nobody knew the woods and swamps like the Baynes boys. We could have hidden those Negroes till judgment day if need be, but we had friends to help move them on.

A bunch of town men got together and rode out to the farm, thinking they were going to burn us out and force me and my brothers at gunpoint to join up in their war against the Yankees.

Even then, nothing much might have happened if we hadn't spent the day burying Mama. Shortly after dawn on that terrible day, we boys were standing at the door to the bedroom when she stopped her feverish rambling. Her voice was clear and sweet when she took Pa's hand and pulled him down for a kiss. She said, "Oh, Darnell, my love, what will you do without me to tend to you?" She looked at us over Pa's shoulder and said, "All my fine men." Then the Lord snuffed out the candle behind her eyes, and she was gone.

Probably Pa would have talked sense to those fellows on any other day, and that might have been the end of it. Lots of hot talk had cooled in the face of Pa's reasoning. Fact is, most of our neighbors looked up to him. But that day, with his eyes red from grieving, Pa said, "There won't be any loud talk here. No talk of war. There's grief in this house. Our lady just passed."

A big, red-faced deputy sheriff said, "Sorry, Baynes, but that and you being rich don't make no difference. There's a war to fight. We come to do a job."

Seems to me those men should have known that a short road to hell would be the only result from trying to force a Baynes to do anything he didn't want to do. If they hadn't misjudged Pa's soft voice for weakness, if they had come any other day than the one we buried Mama, or maybe if they just hadn't been drinking, perhaps it wouldn't have happened.

They rode onto our property that evening full of whiskey, carrying torches and yelling about us being nigger lovers and such. Still, I suppose it might have come to nothing if that stupid deputy hadn't said what he did and hadn't thrown a torch onto the front porch. I guess that must have been the signal for all of them to start pulling guns. All six of them fell within ten steps of the front porch.

Pa grabbed the torch off the porch floor and held it high, looking around at each of us. "You hurt, Ward?" he asked with his eyes on me.

"No, sir."

"You, Luke?"

"No, sir." My oldest brother was reloading and didn't look up to answer. The tallest and broadest of us, Luke never had much to say, but he was the best singer of us all. Even at twenty his black beard reached the third button of his shirt. He claimed that shaving was idle foolishness, a waste of time.

"Milt?"

"No, sir." The next oldest of the three of us at eighteen, Milton was more like an Indian. Slim, dark-skinned, clean-shaven but wearing his black hair long, he could move through woods as fast and quiet as a buzzard's shadow. He was still watching the downed men. Milt was always a suspicious sort, never taking anything at face value. He was ready to shoot again if he saw anything move.

Pa said, "I only got the deputy. You boys did some fast shooting, I'd say, to get the other five so quick."

Luke answered, "I just had time to get one, Pa."

Milt said, "Me too, sir." That's when they all looked at me, realizing that I had brought down the other three.

I didn't say anything. Instead, I bent over the porch rail and put my supper into the dust.

Pa's voice was gentle when he said, "Sometimes being a grown man is a harsh burden at only sixteen, son." He and my brothers were looking at me mighty solemn when Pa went on, "After something like this, a youngster as fast and certain as you can never be a child again. You'll be a surprise to the unwary. They won't expect the youngest cub to be the most dangerous."

We packed that very night and were miles away by dawn, leaving those men lying where they fell. We spent the night riding hard and trying not to look back. Pa called one brief pause in Natchitoches to have a lawyer write out a Power of Attorney to one of Mama's brothers to handle or sell our land and stock. Then our noses pointed west, and we showed our heels to the south.

That was the origin of the infamous Baynes Gang and the start of more lies than should be told in a civilized world. From that day and for years afterward, everything with a bad odor that happened in Louisiana and eastern Texas was laid at our door. Not a word of any of it was true. Not true unless you believe the Baynes boys couldn't tell the difference between a man and a horse. Along the way, until we got on into West Texas, we had some men take after us on a couple of occasions. We shot the horses from under them, that's true, but we didn't shoot a single man.

If you think a Baynes with a good rifle could hit a man, except maybe in the leg, when shooting at the horse under him, you have a severe gap in your education. The very idea makes me laugh. Shooting horses is enough to make a man cry, but we had to do it, that or shoot the men. My preference would have been to shoot the men, but Pa wouldn't allow it.

We didn't know anything about all the lying until later, and it wouldn't have made any difference to us anyway. We were long gone, heading west. Any man who says a Baynes robbed and killed and raped and stole—he's just a gossiping, lying, ignorant fool. We left home on June 5, 1863, and rode almost straight west, allowing for detours around the worst of the bayous. Take it from a man who was there. Anything happening in Louisiana after that date can be laid at somebody else's door; the Baynes family was not involved.

June 5, 1863, is easy to remember—nothing uncertain about it.

That was Pa's forty-fourth birthday, my mama died, and I killed my first three men. It's an easy date for me to call to mind.

Pa said that the West was far from both North and South, and we wanted no part of a war being fought over things that didn't concern us. Secretly, I think Pa was glad to go; he didn't want to see signs of Mama everywhere around him. Besides, I believe he'd grown restless with the idea of working his life away in one place.

He'd never gone anywhere except New Orleans, and I think he wanted to see some different country, to find new things to ease his mind. He told us boys, "I've never seen a mountain. I want to see if there is a place in the world where there are no mosquitoes."

We saw mountains, valleys, forests, deserts, plains, and the Pacific Ocean. There was talk with Sioux, Blackfoot, Crow, Apache, Spaniard, Mexican, soldier, sailor, trapper, and settler. We met the Comanche, but that was all gun talk. We never stopped for long, taking four years to ride over most of the western part of the North American continent.

When we came riding into Montana Territory, I was twenty, had killed two more men, not counting Indians, and was over having it make me sick. I had grown out of childish concern for men who came at me or my kin with guns or knives or bows and arrows or whatever. The choice between killing and being killed offers only one option for a man of sound mind. No sense in having nightmares or stomach upsets just because you elect to stay alive.

Four harder, tougher men couldn't be found. Oddly, Pa looked younger than when we left Louisiana. At forty-eight he looked hardly over thirty. Luke's full beard and square, hard-muscled body would have fit a pirate better than the soft-spoken, quiet man he'd become. Milt looked more like an Indian than ever, wearing his long hair braided and preferring to wear moccasins instead of boots.

Me? Everybody said I was the smallest, the meanest, and the fastest, the only real outlaw in the family. Some said, while admitting I handled horseflesh with rare talent, I was sick in the head, cold-hearted, crazy, vicious. If I was, they made me that way, but that doesn't make them wrong, nor does any of it make me ashamed. No matter. I never learned to give a damn what they thought, except for one petite little girl with hair black as the devil's shadow and eyes big and blue as the Montana sky.

ONE

When Pa said, "Boys, Montana Territory is as pretty as anything we've seen, in its own way," his voice was like a signal for a spatter of shots to echo through the mountains. I couldn't help but chuckle as we scrambled into the woods, darting for cover like scattering quail.

The frying pan hung where Pa left it in midair for a second or two before dropping to the ground beside the fire. That skillet fell straight down, landing flat on its bottom, not spilling a strip of bacon nor a drop of grease. Pa never was one to waste food, but I'll bet he couldn't do that trick again in a hundred tries.

Reflex action, that's what made us hop away from our breakfast fire. Like when you make a feint at a man's eyes, he'll blink unless he's dead. The shots made us dive for cover, but by the time we hit the ground we all knew they weren't aimed at us. No matter, in 1867, a man hearing gunfire that close had better jump first and figure out later what's going on, doing his thinking behind a rock or a tree.

"Damn close, Pa. Just over the ridge, I'd say." Milt was talking, his tone the same as if he was saying, "It's cold this morning. I'll do the milking."

Pa answered, "Indians maybe. Probably got a couple of prospectors treed. What about it, boys? Do we try to help or tend to our own business?"

Milt answered without hesitation, "Let's help." Milt admired Indians, copied their ways, and got along with them better than the rest of us, but he liked fighting them most of all.

"Yeah, let's help, if we can." Luke voted with a tone of voice that was a match for Milt's. They both spoke as if rushing into a gunfight was daily routine for the Baynes family.

Pa chuckled when I said, "Six or half a dozen." Fact was, I didn't see where it was any of our affair. Pa and my brothers felt any white man in trouble with Indians ought to be helped. I generally disagreed, didn't particularly care who won, honestly didn't give a damn either way, and my kinsmen knew it. But they also knew I'd go along with them if that's what they felt was the right thing to do.

Pa said, "Luke, you stay with me to pack up. We'll get ready, in case there's a need to do some running. Ward, you and Milt go take a look over that ridge. We'll come along slow and careful behind you." Pa shook his head and grinned at me when I folded bacon into a piece of pan bread before slipping into the woods behind Milt.

He knew I was just showing I felt no need to spoil my breakfast to rush into somebody else's trouble. I made my hideous, snarling face at Milt when he swung around, grabbed my bread and bacon, and took a huge bite. He stood there grinning and chewing for a minute before he handed what was left back to me and moved on up the hill. Younger brothers get used to being the butt of tricks like that from older ones.

The top of the ridge was hardly more than a hundred yards from our fire. We were camped by the water on one fork of a sweet little stream. The other fork flowed on the far side of the ridge, probably providing as good a place to camp as our own location.

Indians were most likely shooting at gold hunters, prospectors just like us, who were liable to be found most anywhere in Montana Territory, although in small numbers. Still, there were enough of us that the Sioux, Nez Percé, and Cheyenne were feeling crowded and short-tempered. Fur traders got along with Indians. Gold hunters didn't.

Milt, like always, was eager for a fight but didn't show it. He moved at a trot till we came almost to the top of the ridge, then did some cautious crawling to the crest and settled down for a long, slow look. I moved about ten steps to Milt's right, cresting the ridge behind a lightning-killed tree.

The first thing I saw was a downed horse, in the open, right at the edge of the creek, not more than a hundred yards from me. A saddled mount stood about twenty steps away from the dead animal, with four pack-laden mules standing nearby.

A soft morning breeze came rolling down from the mountains, setting everything in motion, carrying the clean smell of melting snow and fresh green growth. The little valley below my lookout point was lightly wooded, with lots of thick underbrush in spring bud with leaves beginning to open. It seemed deserted except for the horses and mules. Nothing showed of the men who had done the shooting.

They must have settled down into a waiting game, because it was obvious the show wasn't over. Somewhere down there were two riders, one for each of those saddled horses, and they must not be dead yet or the Indians would be swarming all over those mules. I never met an Indian who wouldn't walk all day for a mouthful of half-cooked mule meat.

A half hour passed, changing the soft, misty morning light into the clear, hard brightness of a mountain day. Pa and Luke brought our horses and mules through the woods and stopped about fifty yards behind Milt and me. I saw Milt slip back to them. He'd draw everything out on the ground with a stick, giving them the layout of things on the other side of the ridge.

Same as when we were hunting, Milt liked to be on the move, for he was almighty good at it. Stalking either men or animals came natural to him. Me, now, I was happy waiting, being the brother with the most patience. Sitting in ambush met my preference, especially in a situation like this one where I hadn't the vaguest notion what the fight was all about.

I could lie there happy and grinning until the leaves started to fall, if need be. What's a day or ten, here and there, to a young traveling man in Indian country? Nothing. Nothing at all, if he wants to keep traveling. Impatience can make a real homesteader out of a man, planting him in one place forever.

During the next thirty minutes or so, Pa and Luke slipped up to the crest of the ridge and did their own study of the situation. Pa passed close behind me and asked, "Any ideas?"

I whispered, "Yes, sir. Let's rush down there and get our asses shot off."

Pa gave me one of his grins with the corners pulled down and said, "That's white man's equipment on the stock. It's been still as a graveyard down there for a long time. You think the Indians have pulled out?"

"No, sir. I'm not even sure Indians emptied those saddles. If white men were shooting at each other, which side are we gonna be on anyhow? Nobody's moving down there, no talking, no nothing. Maybe everybody but the wives are dead."

"What? You see women?" Pa's whisper was puzzled.

I gave him a tiny, cautious shrug and kept a poker face. "Didn't you used to tease Mama that the best wives were women who were neither seen nor heard, Pa?"

He slid back a ways from the crest of the ridge before he answered in a chuckling whisper I could barely make out. "Ward, you're a pinhead."

The horse and mules were grazing like they hadn't a concern in the world. About all that told me was, either nobody was nearby or the animals weren't wilderness bred. Still, sooner or later, I knew I'd catch them staring and cupping ears if anybody got close.

I nearly jumped a foot when somebody below shouted, "Thackery."

After a minute or so, he hollered again, "Thackery, if you're still alive, ride out. You and the girl can go. We don't want you nohow. Just leave the mules and ride out."

Now, that was enough to make a man thoughtful. Big Mouth had told us five important things. One, his bunch was the attacking side, the ones who started the shooting. Two, they wanted those mules, or what they were carrying, bad enough to burn powder. Three, his bunch was willing to shoot even when a woman might be hit. Four, his "we" indicated that he wasn't by himself. And five, by speaking up like he did, he told us his general location. That's the bad thing about a man who likes to talk. He ends up saying more than he intended.

I couldn't see him yet, but his first move would probably be his last if I decided to make it so. At about a hundred yards, I can hit a man, running or still, anytime I take the notion, given a good rifle in hand and one second to aim. If I need to hit him in a special place, give me two seconds, and I'll still make that brag good.

That little speech was helpful of Big Mouth, and I appreciated it because when he made his first move, I saw him. Well, I didn't exactly see him, but I saw his rifle barrel move. Unless he fired a rifle from a different angle than the rest of the human race, I figured he was almost in a straight line behind that barrel. Whether left- or right-handed, his head would be close to the rear sight.

Then I saw a flicker; a hand moved in a place across the creek and up a ways from Big Mouth. That's the way these things usually go. Everybody gets restless and impatient about the same time when things start happening.

She was clever about it, but I was above her, being up on that ridge, and she had no way to know that. She moved her hand just a bit to brace her body so she could turn to look behind her. I got a good look at her face when she turned. The second I saw her face was the instant I lost doubt about which side I was on. Even at this distance, I could tell that was a face to launch a thousand ships, or at least that's the way they would say it in books.

Smart girl! She smelled a trick; she was turning to look in the opposite direction from the man who did the shouting. And sure enough, another man was moving in on her from behind.

That fellow was on her in three or four jumps, fast as a cougar. Even so, she would have shot him home to his ancestors if her rifle hadn't caught in the brush when she tried to swing it around. That rifle must have been longer than she was, but she was handy. She almost got it done, but he knocked her rifle away and landed on her like a cord of wood. Even then, the fight wasn't over. That little ol' girl was all over that fellow like a hair shirt, biting, scratching, and kicking. He was so surprised he turned her loose. She was on her feet and wading into him before I could blink.

It was a hell of a good fight for quite a spell. He swung a couple of haymakers that would have dropped a mule, but she ducked both times and came up kicking. I'll say this, she didn't quit, and she knew where to kick at a man to put caution in his mind.

Then he got tired of it and pulled a knife. I figured the fun was over, so I shot him dead center. Then I swung on the fellow behind the rifle barrel, the shouting man, and put a bullet where I figured him to be behind his weapon. I think my shot came just in time. It looked to me like he'd just about got lined up on the girl.

Not wanting to push my luck, I did a backward crawl off the crest of the ridge that would have made a crawdad proud. After all, I figured I'd scored twice from one place, which was one too many times to shoot from the same spot. Besides, I had kinfolk all along that ridge who were more eager than I was to get into this fight in the first place.

I gave Nadine a friendly pat or two on the butt and fed two rounds to her. She sulks if I don't keep her spanking clean and her magazine full. While I was at it, I pulled Jesse from his holster and took a look at him. I didn't want him to get dirty by accident, what with me crawling all over that ridge.

About then Pa hollered from somewhere off to my left, "Hello, down yonder. Don't shoot at me. I'm Darnell Baynes, and I'm friendly. My boys and I heard shooting and came to see about it. One of my boys just shot a man who was fighting a woman. He fired twice, so I guess he shot at somebody else too. How many people are after you, girl?"

She answered up loud and clear, "I think there were three of them, Mr. Baynes. Your boy killed one of them. Be careful. I don't know where the other two are, but my father is wounded. He needs help."

I was just taking a cautious look over the ridge when I heard a horse gallop downstream toward the fork. By the time I swung toward the sound, Milt fired. And a pretty good shot it was too, considering it was at a man about three hundred yards away on a horse twisting and turning among the rocks and trees. Milt knocked him right out of the saddle, but the fellow got up and staggered out of sight. That fellow ran with one shoulder drawn up high, and he held the arm on that side close to his body.

Luke spoke up. "I see the second one Ward shot at. His head's all bloody and he's lying dead still. I think he's lost interest, Pa."

Pa yelled, "Boys, cover me. Girl, I'm coming in, and I'm gonna be talking all the way. Boys, stay away till I get there. I don't want that girl shooting at you just because she doesn't know who you are."

He walked right out in plain sight and kept on talking. "Ward, you're the best shot. Stay where you are in case somebody shoots at us. Milt, see if you can find the horses those men were riding. Luke, bring our gear down here and get out our medicine bag."

Luke brought our stock over the ridge, and Milt came in with two unfamiliar horses and another pack mule before Pa waved to bring me down off the ridge. I came walking into camp all unsuspecting and looked right into a prettier face than I ever expected to see, even prettier than I'd been able to tell from up the hill.

She came running to meet me, stuck out her hand like a pint-sized man, and said, "I'm Kathleen Iris Thackery, and I want to thank you, Ward." Her eyes were so blue and her hair was so black she looked more like a picture somebody painted than a real girl.

Everybody has quirks. One of mine is I don't like to shake hands with women. Men shake hands. Women shouldn't do men's things. Mama taught me to bow and kiss a woman's hand, and I can do it as well as any, having been made to practice. But it still felt almighty prissy and silly to me.

I shifted Nadine to my left hand and jerked my hat off with the right. Ignoring her outstretched hand, I said sternly, "Pa must've told you my name. Did he tell you anything else about me?"

Her eyes widened and she jerked her hand down, showing she got the idea. Backing off a step, she said, "Why . . . why no, he didn't."

"Good. How's your father?" I turned abruptly and walked toward the man lying beside the fire with Pa seated by him.

She trotted a few steps to catch up before she said, "He was shot twice, but your father bandaged him and stopped the bleeding. Your father says he'll be fine."

"That's good news. I'd like to meet him. Is he up to it?"

"Yes, I think so. He asked to meet you as soon as you joined us."

By then we came up to Pa and the downed man. I dropped to one knee beside them and said, "Mr. Thackery, I'm Ward Baynes. How are you feeling, sir?"

"Ward, just call me Joe." Thackery lay stretched out, partly covered by blankets, but I could see bandages on both his left arm and leg. His icy blue eyes were clear and alert. Most men take on a vague, inward-looking expression shortly after being gunshot. This was a tough old wolf.

Wiry lean, with the cool look of a man accustomed to command, he went on, "We might as well go straight to first names. I don't feel the need for formality with the men who saved my life and my daughter's as well. And I feel like I've been shot twice, thank you." He raised his right hand and gripped mine with surprising strength.

I noticed the girl's rifle swung just a bit toward me when her daddy shook hands. The muzzle dropped toward the ground when Thackery's right hand slipped back under his blanket. It's a marvel what a man can see out of the edges of his eyes if he's in a watchful mood, but I wondered if I was making a lot out of a little. All of it had been smooth, casual, accidental-looking. Still, I'd bet a day's work Thackery had a shortgun under that blanket, and he had the hard eye of a man who wouldn't hesitate.

A suspicious man might think that girl was covering her daddy while his gun hand was occupied. I decided then and there that these two were a team, and they made a point of looking after one another.

Joe Thackery looked me up and down for a moment before he said, "My daughter tells me you killed two men in about two seconds, that you shot one clean through the heart and the other through the head. She says one man had her by the hair with his knife ready to strike when the bullet took him. She felt the bullet go by—it was that close. That's cool and accurate shooting for a man who looks about seventeen years old."

I answered shortly, "Close doesn't win prizes. She needn't have worried. I hit what I aim at."

Pa said quietly, "Ward's a bit touchy about being smaller than his brothers and looking younger than his twenty years."

Thackery never seemed to blink, keeping his gaze fixed on me. He said flatly, "Both of those things used to bother me too, back when I was young enough to be excused for being a damn fool. Are you still young enough, Ward?" He waited for an answer, but I didn't want to follow Pa's lead into a conversation about my bad points, so I changed the subject.

"Your daughter was being very ladylike and modest when she told you all those things about me, sir. She's giving more credit than I have coming to me. Actually, she whipped that poor man something awful. I was embarrassed for him, to tell the truth."

"What? What are you saying?" The girl stepped closer.

I glanced at her. "No offense, ma'am. I know you wouldn't deliberately be untruthful with your father or anything like that. You were just being modest."

Kneeling on one knee was becoming tiresome, so I eased to the ground and sat cross-legged. "Fact is, sir, your daughter swarmed all over that poor man. She whipped him so bad he was trying to cut his own throat when I shot him. It was an act of mercy, sir, that's what it was."

Pa said, "My son has an unusual sense of humor."

Joe Thackery finally blinked. I thought there was a pleased glint in his eyes for a moment, but it could have been a flicker from the midmorning sun off the ripples in the nearby stream. In the silence, the sound of tumbling water seemed louder.

From him, when they came, the three words had an ominous ring. "Yes. Very unusual."

He was obviously sizing me up, and I didn't like it. He was looking me over like I was a horse he might or might not buy. I was talking to a hard man, a man flat on his back from two fresh wounds but who looked as helpless as a motionless rattler. There was something coldly indifferent about Thackery, something that said he'd be a very dangerous man to have for an enemy. He seemed to be pushing, testing me, and I wondered why. Goaded by irritation, I decided to do some testing of my own.

I realized a silence had fallen when Thackery spoke again, sending a chill up my back when he said, "He's working up to something important. He'll get to it, in his own time."

Kathleen stepped around the blanket and stood facing me, looking me square in the eye. Pa backed away a couple of steps, like he was giving me space, or like he was stepping out of the line of fire. At least, it seemed that way.

Using my best go-to-hell grin, I said, "I decided something the minute I walked into this camp."

Thackery nodded, a very small movement.

"I decided to try to court that girl, that Kit. You ought to know about that right away, it seemed to me."

She snapped, "Don't talk about me like I'm not even here."

I gave up on our little staring contest for a moment when I swung my gaze from her father to speak directly to her. "Seemed Kathleen was a heavy load for a little bit of a girl like you. I figured your initials fit better. Kathleen is mighty pretty, but it's too big a saddle for a dainty filly, not even full grown."

She said, "I'm big enough to pull my own freight," but her voice didn't sound quite as snippy.

"Interesting coincidence," Thackery said. "Nobody but her mother ever called her Kit. About this decision of yours, I think you're joking again, and the joke's in poor taste."

I hesitated, my mouth going a little dry. "Maybe I'm reaching for more than I can carry, but I'm not joking, sir. I must have looked like a joke when I walked beside her on the way over here. I never saw anything so pretty in my life. You must have thought me a fool, the way I was trying to walk sideways so I could keep looking at her."

He waited, flat on his back, about as relaxed as a crouched panther.

"I feel I better make it clear. My intentions are honorable. It's important you understand that."

"Your concern is justified. If Kathleen rejects your attentions, will you respect her wishes?"

"I will."

"If I tell you to stay away from her, will you respect my wishes?"

"No, sir."

"Then why are you discussing this matter with me?"

"I wanted you to understand my intentions, sir. It would grieve me to have to kill you because of a misunderstanding."

"How many men have you killed, Mr. Ward Baynes?" Joe Thackery asked the question calmly, the same way another man might have inquired about my age.

Now, that wasn't a friendly question, but I kept my face blank while considering my answer. Nobody said a word while I was thinking. Everybody seemed willing to wait. Thackery's face told me nothing. He looked like a man waiting for an answer to a casual question, nothing more, nothing less.

If I came out with the straight of it, some men would mistake my answer for bragging. Others would wrongly take it as a sad confession. I finally decided Thackery would interpret the truth simply as the truth. So I gave it to him straight, without sugar.

"Seven, not counting Indians."

"I thought so. You don't act like a man who's new to it."

I had read him right. His tone was satisfied, almost smug. In that instant, something changed about him. His next question came out in a tone that was merely curious, like the big test was over and now the talk was to be more relaxed. "Why don't you count Indians?"

"Because no man can know such a thing, not the way they fight. They don't believe in running off and leaving their wounded and dead. If every man who thought he'd killed an Indian was right, all the Indians would have been gone long ago."

A trace of a smile crossed Joe Thackery's face when he turned his head slightly to look at Pa. "Your son is a most unusual young man, Darnell. He may be more unusual than you and his brothers realize. Ward knew at once how necessary it is for men like us to understand each other quickly. He's very observant for such a young man."

Pa nodded, his opinion safe behind a poker face.

Thackery spoke again. "Gentlemen, if you don't mind, I'd like to rest awhile. For some reason, my wounds have started to give me hell. Kathleen, would you bring the bottle from my dead horse?"

I came to my feet quickly. "I'll get it for you, Kit."

I had a little trouble stripping the gear from the dead animal. Luke, with his great strength, could have done it with one hand, but jerking the stirrups from under that horse was a job for me. Finally, sweating a little, I dropped everything beside Thackery without comment, leaving it for Kit to find his bottle. I had no intention of intruding on that iron-faced man's privacy by opening his saddlebags.

Pa said in a low voice, "Drag that dead horse half a mile or so downstream and back into the brush. When you're done with that, come help your brothers bury those men."

"Yes, sir."

Kit spoke quietly, "He'll have a cup of coffee and a minute's rest first, Mr. Baynes. Then he'll come right along."

Pa said, "That'll be just fine, ma'am," and turned away.

I took a couple of sips from the cup she shoved into my hand before it dawned on me what had happened. My Pa was a generous, loving, wonderful father, but nobody, I mean nobody, stepped between him and his sons when he was giving orders. I couldn't even remember my mama ever trying to do such a thing. Kit, hardly more than a girl, just told Pa, in effect, "Ward'll be along when I think he's ready," and he accepted it without even blinking. Now that was something to think about, but not for long. Pa had put habits too deep in me. Sitting and thinking over a cup of coffee came after the work was done.

I mounted up, dabbed a loop on the dead horse, and pulled it away from camp like Pa wanted. When I rode back, I went to where Luke was digging. The dead man was wrapped in a blanket, a man I'd never seen except for his gun barrel.

Luke said, "Try not to shoot anybody in the head, Ward. That's the most awful thing I ever saw." He shuddered. "Don't look under that blanket."

After about three hours of hard digging in the rocky soil, the hole was deep enough, so we lowered the man's body into it.

I asked, "Did you go through his pockets?"

Luke said, "Yeah, didn't find much. I gave it all to Pa."

"Good." I threw a shovel-load of dirt into the grave.

Luke hesitated. "Shouldn't we get Pa to read the Book over him?"

I was tired and dirty, sweat trickling down all over me. For some reason, I found myself shaking and having trouble breathing all of a sudden. "To hell with this bastard. Who cares about a swine who'd shoot from ambush at an old man and a woman. Let's get this over with. Pa can come up and read later if he has a notion. I had almost no breakfast, looks like we won't get any lunch, and flies are stinging me. Let's finish and be done with this."

Luke grabbed my arm. The power and weight of my oldest brother was never more obvious than when I tried irritably to twist out of his grip and failed. The rage rising in me suddenly vanished when Luke spoke gently. "I can finish this. Would you go help Milt? He's been working all by himself. Pa's back at the camp watching the horses and all."

I reached across with my free hand, patted the huge hand holding my arm, and felt my brother's grip loosen. "I'm fine now. I just can't abide the idea of standing here pretending I wish this man any good luck. Far as I'm concerned, the devil can have him for firewood."

Luke said, "You had to do what you did. Don't let it bother your mind. Thank God you had the eye and the quickness. It's a blessing. Me, now, I couldn't have done it."

Luke leaned on the shovel. The laugh wrinkles deepened around his eyes as he looked at me. He went on, "I saw it all, but I was too scared I might shoot that girl. You stayed cool and did everything right. And you did it fast. Don't let it trouble you. What you did was righteous."

A moment later, with my shirt draped over one sweaty shoulder, the shovel across the other shoulder, and Nadine in my free hand, I looked into Luke's face again. "I'll tell you what upsets me something fierce. One of those bushwhackers got away. He was wounded and running, and it didn't make sense to push that fight any farther, but I wanted to catch him and kill him so bad it's still giving me the shakes. I'd track him down and kill him if it was up to me."

"You got it to whip, Ward. There's too much hate in you."

I walked away from my brother's troubled expression.

Milt was nearly finished when I joined him. Acting like a big brother again, he took the opportunity to rest for a while, just long enough for me to finish the digging. When I rolled the body into the hole and started shoveling dirt down onto it, he did his share of that task without comment. Then he stretched and asked, "You willing to stand guard while I get wet?"

"I'll trade off with you."

"Good, let's ask Luke to come along."

When the three of us came back into camp after bathing, Kit poured my tin cup full of coffee and brought it to me.

"How'd you know which cup was mine?"

"Your pa told me."

"Been talking about me, have you?"

"Just to pass the time. I remembered you asking if your pa had talked to me about you. It seemed to worry you."

"Uh-huh. What'd you find out?"

"He didn't say anything bad about you. He did say he was surprised at the way you talked to my father."

"That a fact? Well, he and my big brothers never miss a chance to tease me. They never miss a chance to make me look like a pinhead."

"Is that so? A pinhead is a dumb person? Isn't that what you mean? They make you look dumb?"

I nodded.

"Seems to me you don't need their help. You're pretty direct. Maybe I ought to be offended, but I didn't even think about that when you were talking to my father. I was worried about you. My father is a proud, short-tempered man. Your pa did tell me you'd never showed much interest in girls before now."

"Hmm. Well, I never saw one could fight like you. You won my heart. I guess I been looking for a fierce female."

She pointed at my cup. "Want some more coffee?"

I shook my head.

She said, "Give me the cup. I'll wash it out for you. Supper's to be just before dark." Kit skipped away a couple of steps and then turned back to face me. With a wide grin, she said, "Oh, yeah, your pa told me one other thing about you."

"What?"

"He said you're a pinhead sometimes, but you aren't such a bad fellow."

I asked, "You interested?"

Kit stood in front of me, showing me a half-grin, half-smirk. "Haven't decided yet."

I nodded solemnly. "Well, if you do get interested, be careful."

She tossed her head. "You don't scare me."

"I don't scare anybody. I'm shy. You're the one has to worry. You don't want to go scaring me off. Don't rush me."

She gave me a little curtsy and said, "I'll try to control myself." With that, she turned and walked off toward the fire.

The prettiest thing in the whole world is the way a woman walks when she knows an interested man is watching.

TWO

ANOTHER SADDLED HORSE wandered in shortly before dark. Milt put a rope on it, stripped off the gear, and hobbled it with our stock. When he came back into camp, he told Pa, "Nothing in the saddlebags but odds and ends. The saddle's cheap and worn-out, not worth keeping. The rifle boot was empty."

Pa nodded. "Sad thing for a man, wounded and set afoot in empty country."

Milt answered, "Sad for us if he has a rifle and is circling back at us. He might have hard feelings. His rifle went flying when I winged him, but he might have sneaked back for it. I figure to look for it in the morning."

I said, "The man is more important than the rifle."

Pa turned to me. "You want to try to help that fellow?"

"Yes, sir. I'm eager to ease his pain."

Pa said nothing, just sat quiet, waiting for me to speak my mind, the way he always did with his sons.

"Once started, a thing should be finished, seems to me," I said. "I didn't want to mix in this affair at the start, but I was wrong. Now we have a man out there somewhere who hides and shoots at people. It's getting dark, so I think we ought to put out the fire. I say we track him down in the morning and put him out of his misery. But maybe I'm wrong again."

"You boys may not know as much as you think." Pa took a stick and spread the fire so it would die out. "That third man might have just been holding the horses. He was a good distance away when Milt wounded him. Maybe he wanted no part of this. Maybe he didn't know what-all was going on up here and just wanted to get away."

I glanced in Thackery's direction. Pa'd wanted him to be out of the firelight, so we'd moved the fire rather than move him, not wanting to start his wounds to hurting again. Confident he couldn't hear our talk,

I asked, "What was on Thackery's mules to make those men so eager to go to shooting?"

Pa answered, "The girl took the packs off, wouldn't let us touch them. I'd say the packs of three of those mules are loaded with gold. She couldn't lift them, had a hard go of it dragging them, but they didn't look full."

"Doesn't make sense," I said. "It's barely spring. Nobody's crazy enough to be panning gold up here in the winter."

Without looking up I could tell by his voice Milt was grinning. "Maybe your pretty girl's daddy is crazy. Maybe you're gonna have crazy in-laws."

Pa's voice came sharp. "Milt, I won't have that. It's not fitting. Ward made it clear he set store by her the minute he saw her. I'll not have my sons teasing about a serious thing like that. No joke is worth risking bad trouble in the family. Show respect for your brother. I don't want to speak about this again."

I nearly fell over backward when Milt said, "I'm sorry, Pa. I wasn't thinking. Ward, I apologize. I won't joke about the girl again. I mean it."

I tried to remember Milt ever apologizing to me before and couldn't. I put my hand on his shoulder and said, "Thanks, Milt."

He put his hand over mine and gave it a brief squeeze.

Luke, so quiet as usual we could almost forget he was there, spoke, "Things change when a woman mixes in, especially a pretty one, but that little Kathleen seems mannerly, not a trouble-making sort. Her pa may be different. I haven't been around him much, but he seems touchy to me. He's a watchful man. I don't think he takes to joking much. You better be real careful with him, Ward. I think we all better be."

Pa said, "That's good advice."

Milt laughed and said, "Luke just used up all his words for a whole week."

We all chuckled when Luke made like he was going to reach for Milt, who backed off quickly.

Pa glanced at me. "You worried me today, son. You spoke up mighty serious for such short acquaintance. Did you know he had a pistol under his blanket?"

"No, sir, but I figured he did. Did you notice Kit when I shook his hand?"

"No. What'd she do?"

"I'm not sure, Pa, but it looked like she got her rifle ready to cover her daddy while his gun hand was occupied. They aren't trusting people. Maybe them having mules loaded with gold explains it."

Milt snickered. "Yeah, that and getting shot at and hit."

Pa came to his feet. "Luke, bring the stock in closer. I don't want anybody moving around tonight. Everybody's nervous. We'll spread out, but I want all of us to know exactly where the others are. Boys, we'll sleep around the Thackerys. I'm going over to talk to them before it gets too dark."

Milt chuckled when I said, "I'll come along, Pa."

Pa spoke in a low tone when we drew near in the gathering darkness. "Darnell and Ward Baynes coming in to talk."

Kit answered quietly, "Come."

She was wrapped in a blanket, rifle across her knees, sitting with her back to a tree, hidden so well in the shadows we almost stepped on her. Meanwhile, she had us outlined against the evening sky. That girl knew how to handle herself.

Pa asked, "Where's your dad, Kathleen?"

"He's already asleep."

"We'd like to know where. We're drawing in close, and we need to know where everybody is. You mustn't walk around tonight. My boys will shoot at anybody moving. If you need anything, get it now, or let us get it for you, so you can keep still the rest of the night."

Her voice sounded stubborn when she answered, "He doesn't like for strangers to know where he sleeps. That's why he moved after you shifted the fire. I'll tell him what you said."

Strangers! The word hit me like a slap in the face. The minute I heard it, I got mad. What a way to describe men who'd saved your life, killing two men and wounding another in the process. That single word exposed a thankless, suspicious, and insulting attitude. If we'd wanted to take their damned gold, we'd have it by now. In about two seconds I was mad clean through. Strangers, indeed.

My voice sounded half strangled when I said, "That's it, Pa. She got our message. We strangers better back off before this woman shoots us." I turned and walked away. Pa could stay to try to make sense of such foolishness, but I'd had enough.

Milt met me and showed me where he and Luke were going to bed down. They'd picked spots for Pa and me too. I spent most of the night backed against a tree, boiling mad, hoping somebody did try to sneak into our camp. I was sure enough primed to shoot.

At first light, I started a new fire and put two pots of water on to heat for coffee. Pa joined me in time to drop ground coffee into one of the pots. He pointed to the other and gave me a questioning look.

I said, "Just being neighborly. I figured she'd want to make their own coffee. We strangers might poison them."

Pa said gently, "Slow down, son. Ever since you saw that girl you've been going too fast. Let's reason together. You up to some cool thinking this morning?"

"Spent a good bit of time on it last night, Pa. Seemed as straightaway an insult as we ever stood still for."

He nodded. "Seemed so to you. Didn't to me."

"I'll be damned if I see why not."

Pa raised a hand. "Now don't go to cussing. I can see you're still wound up tight. Think of it this way. Does this little Kathleen seem like a good girl to you?"

"I don't see how you can ask me that, Pa, after what she said. She's suspicious, thankless . . ."

"You think she's a decent young woman, son? You think she is a woman of good character?"

"Well, now, I don't think . . . uh . . . what're you getting at, Pa?"

"Do you think she's likely to do what Thackery tells her to do? Does she seem like the kind of young woman who'd respect her father? Does he seem like a man who'd demand that?"

I poured my coffee and sat quiet, holding my cup while it cooled a bit. Pa did the same, waiting for me to speak. Finally, I said, "I reckon."

Pa didn't look at me. He kept his gaze fixed toward the woods behind me. "Figure she's a scared girl. Figure she's trying not to show it, with a wounded father and night coming on. He tells her what to do, to keep him hid from us, and to stay on guard most or all the night. Have you made her trust you enough to have her disobey him? You expect that after her knowing you less than one day?"

I liked to see myself as a thinking man, saw it as my way to measure up in a family of bigger, stronger men. Still, once in a while Pa made me feel like a half-wit. I'd spent most of the night stewing in my own juice and pulling at a hard knot instead of untying it. Pa was trying, like always, to help a son see a mistake without shaming him. All he did was ask questions. He made me come up with the answers. Still, Pa took me down about four notches, left me feeling small and petty, and that mood was in my voice when I answered him.

"I suppose not."

Kit said, "Might take a whole day. Maybe two. Would that be all right, Ward?"

Pa had watched her come up behind me without giving a hint. I didn't look around. "It's unladylike to creep up and listen to private conversations."

She came past me to pour coffee for herself. "I'll practice being ladylike if you'll practice controlling your temper."

"I don't have a bad temper unless I'm pushed."

"My father said to watch out for that from you. He said he was the same way when he was younger, that most men of small stature are quick-tempered, always trying to prove something."

"Soon's your pa's awake, I better talk to him, tell him I've thought it over and changed my mind. I think I'd better stay away from you. All you do is keep me mad with one insult after another."

She gave me a sad look and said, "I think it's too late for that. He'd probably shoot you for trifling with my affections. My father is a very old-fashioned . . . gentleman." Her pause before the last word drew a little blood. Women can be devilish clever about cutting a man and then hiding the knife.

I copied her sad expression. "He'll understand. I'll tell him I found out how you snoop around eavesdropping so much you can't have breakfast ready till noon. He seems a practical man. He'll be sad you missed your big chance."

Luke walked up and looked at the dribble of coffee left in one pot and the boiling water in the other.

I said, "Don't fool around with that hot water. I put stranger poison in it."

Luke's sleepy expression changed to comical confusion. He drew back from the pot and asked, "Stranger poison? What's that? What's he up to now, Pa?"

Pa just grinned, shook his head, and looked away.

I went on, "Stranger poison's deadly stuff. We're going to trick Kit into making coffee with it for her and her daddy, since she made it so hard for us to sneak up on them in the night."

Kit smiled at me and jerked her head toward the woods, giving my oldest brother the same signal. Luke and I followed her to her father. Between us, we supported him while he limped to the fire. Luke could have picked him up and carried him easier, and he made the offer, but Thackery wouldn't allow it.

When he was seated and looked comfortable, he said, "Good morning, everyone. No, not everyone. Where's Milt?"

Pa answered, "Milton's the restless one in our family, Joe, our gypsy. He's out looking around. He most always circles our camp in the mornings. If anyone is near, Milt finds them, or their sign. We're men of habit."

Thackery said, "Men of good habit, I'd say. By heaven, coffee smells good this morning. I drank both our canteens dry last night, never had such a thirst."

"Losing blood causes thirst," Pa said. "You aren't in bad shape, no bones hit or anything. But you bled a lot before we could tend to you. Barring infection, you'll be all right in a few days. That leg wound is a problem, though. Being shot through the thigh like that, you'll be at least a week, probably longer, before you can sit a saddle. Otherwise, you'll just hurt yourself and start the bleeding all over again."

Thackery said, "You've been most helpful. My daughter and I are obliged to you, but you have your own affairs. We needn't be a further burden. I think we can do fine now."

Pa said, "Of course. On the other hand, we're in no hurry. If you don't mind, we'll camp here until you get your strength back."

Thackery made no reply. We all sat watching Kit cook. She made coffee with my hot water and brought me the first cup. After a couple of swallows I pretended to be getting sick, but she handed a cup to Thackery and refilled Pa's, paying me no mind.

When Thackery looked at me, Pa said, "Don't be fooled. Nothing wrong with him. He's just deviling that girl. Don't be surprised if she hits him with a skillet."

Kit brought breakfast to Thackery and Pa. With a jerk of her head toward the two older men, she said to Luke and me, "I respect my elders. You two come get your own."

After I filled my plate and sat down to eat, she looked at me and said, "It isn't noon yet."

I nodded and said, "If you slice the bacon thicker and cook it slower, it won't curl up so much. Some things can't be hurried."

She nodded back and said, "I'm glad you know that."

Thackery asked, "What have I missed? What's important about noon?"

Giving me a mean grin, Kit turned to her father and said, "Mr. Ward Baynes gets hungry for breakfast shortly after midnight, Papa Joe. Maybe he still needs a night feeding. Maybe he's even younger than he looks."

Ignoring her, I couldn't help but grin at Thackery and say, "Papa Joe. I like that."

Thackery put on a sheepish grin, Pa chuckled, and everything changed in our camp at that moment. The whole feeling of things went from stiff to friendly. I figured there'd be no more talk of strangers.

Suddenly, Milt came staggering out of the woods and sank to his knees near Kit, clutching at his middle and groaning. Kit gave a little scream and dropped her plate when she jumped up. Milt, his face twisted in agony, extended a trembling hand toward her and whined, "Hunger. I'm dying. Help me. Please help me."

Kit screamed, "Oh! That's awful! Why, you . . . Don't you ever do that again. You scared me to death, you . . . you . . ." She picked up her tin plate and threw it at him.

Milt ducked the plate and turned to me, still on his knees. "See, Ward, she's hard, hard clear through. No pity at all, not even a sense of humor." He jumped to his feet and walked to the fire, saying, "Anything left for me?"

Kit turned to me, just beginning to laugh, and said, "Oh, Ward, how do you put up with him?"

I shrugged. "Pa warned you about us being men of habit. He does that mighty near every morning. You'll get used to it. Besides, I guess blood's thicker'n bacon grease."

Milt, filling his plate, said, "Found me a nearly new rifle this morning. Nice piece of equipment. Couldn't find the man who belonged to it, though. Mmmm. Pan biscuits. Who made biscuits this morning?"

Kit said, "I did."

"Thank you, ma'am."

Pa asked, "Did you try to trail him?"

"No, sir, not really. We didn't decide last night what to do about him. So I didn't want to find him, not knowing whether you wanted me to kiss him or kill him. I just tracked him for a little peace of mind, just enough to see if he turned back this way. He didn't."

Milt took another bite of biscuit, chewed, and swallowed before adding, "I don't think that fellow went much farther anyhow." He looked suggestively at Kit, then to Thackery, then back to Kit.

Thackery said flatly, "Kathleen, go wash the dishes."

She jumped up quickly, gathered the plates, and headed for the stream without saying a word.

Milt said quietly, "The way I read the trail, that fellow wasn't just hit in the arm or shoulder the way it looked when he ran off. He was either throwing up blood or coughing it up, lots of it. No doubt in my mind, he's either lung shot or gut shot. He probably didn't live through the night. The only point in tracking him would be to bury him."

Milt ducked his head toward the stream in Kathleen's direction. "Thanks, Mr. Thackery. No need to spoil the lady's breakfast, hearing such as that."

Thackery spoke quickly, "The thanks are mine, sir. I appreciate your thoughtful signal. I shall apologize to her later. She isn't accustomed to that tone of voice from me."

Pa said, "That poor man died alone. Sad. Didn't even have a blanket."

After a brief silence, Luke agreed, "That's a hard thing, a pitiful thing."

Milt glanced at me, and we both looked at Thackery. Without words, we understood each other. The vote was three to two. Three of us figured that man got what was coming to him. It may have been sad, but it was just, and that was more important. For the three of us, nothing was so feared and despised as a man who shot from ambush. He'd bled and died from a wound in the back, a wound suffered while running away from a fight he and his partners had started. We'd as soon feel sympathy for a scorpion.

THREE

A FEW DAYS LATER, Kit came up to me while I was working. "What kind of men are you anyway?" Her tone was impatient, and she was slapping a little stick against her skirt.

I looked up from scraping a deer hide and shrugged. How could a man make sense of a question like that? I nodded to the grass near me. "Regular kind, I guess, Kit. Come in the parlor and talk awhile. Something make you mad?"

Kit gathered her skirts and sat down. "You talk about everything under the sun except yourselves." She had a way of looking directly at me with those blue eyes. I found it most agreeable.

"We aren't keeping secrets. Just ask."

"Papa Joe says asking isn't acceptable. He says people out here don't do that. It makes men mad if you do."

"Then you'd better not do it. You already know how short men like me fly into rages. Short man, short temper, right?"

"Aren't you supposed to tell me about yourself? Aren't you supposed to do that when you're . . . uh . . . courting me?"

"Don't think so. I'm supposed to tell you I admire your beautiful eyes. I admire your beautiful eyes. I'm supposed to say your dress is becoming. Your dress is becoming. You're supposed to serve me tea and cookies. Where's my tea and cookies?"

She sat smoothing her grease-spotted garment, probably the only dress she had. Certainly, it was the only one I'd seen her wear. "Where would I get tea and cookies out here? Besides, I've cooked almost every bite you've eaten for the last five days. Doesn't that count?"

"Yes, ma'am, that counts. You boil beans as well as anybody in the world, but that's regular meals. We're talking about courting fare."

"Well, you'll just have to do without cookies and tea, so stop talking about it. You got fighting mad when I called you a stranger that first night. You'll stay a stranger to me if you don't tell about yourself. All you do is joke, like you're doing now. Either that or you do strange things."

"What strange things?"

"You sit around reading a book printed in Spanish. Milt reads a book in French. Mr. Baynes reads a book of English poetry, and Luke usually reads the Bible. Your family doesn't seem to care what language it is, you just read it, or you pretend to read it. I find that strange."

I shifted the hide so I could work on another spot. "Have you seen any anthills close to our camp?"

"Yes, why?"

"Soon's I finish scraping, show me where one is. The ants will finish cleaning this skin for me. That's a great trick I learned from the Indians."

"You're dodging. You aren't going to tell me anything, are you?"

I stopped working and looked at her. "I just told you something. You aren't listening. A man feels irritated when his woman doesn't pay attention to him."

"I'm not your woman yet. What did you tell me?"

"That I learned a trick from the Indians. That tells you I've been associating with savages, maybe even living with them. You're supposed to become suspicious and jealous and ask me if I had anything to do with Indian girls, and I'm supposed to lie and say, 'Oh, my heavens, no. How could you think such a thing of me?' Then I'm supposed to look prissy and offended while I sip tea and nibble a cookie you're supposed to serve me."

She jumped to her feet, her face flushed. "Is all that true?"

I turned my gaze to the hide and went back to work. "Only some of it. Can you tell what's lies and what's true?"

"Is that part about Indian girls true?"

"Can't you tell?"

Kit answered sharply, "No."

"So now you know I'm a great liar. See how fast you can learn when you pay attention?"

"If you won't be serious, if you won't be nice to me, I'm going to walk away."

"Miss Thackery, will you please sit down? I feel this great urge to tell you my life story. Actually, I'm only going to tell you the serious parts. It's obvious if I try to tell you the funny parts you'll become angry and walk away."

She hesitated for a moment, then gathered her skirt with that grace-ful little move of hers and sat down.

"Now, Miss Thackery, I was born in . . ."

"You may call me Kit," she said primly and giggled.

I started again. "Now, Kit, I was born in Louisiana. We left there in the middle of the war, since none of us wanted to be soldiers. Some men tried to recruit us at gunpoint. My mama died early that very day. It was the worst time possible for those men to start an argument. They lost the dispute. We left all six of them dead, and I think Pa has taken such a liking to travel I doubt he ever wants to stop. At least, it seems so, since that's mostly what we've been doing ever since we left home."

I dropped the knife on the hide and turned to face Kit. "Mama was Spanish. Her maiden name was Maria Solita Dolores Margarita de la Cartilla y Silvana. Pa says she was a 'woman of quality.' She spoke English and French as well as Spanish, and she taught us her lan-guages. Matter of fact, all of us except Pa have Silvana for a middle name. We don't mention that much since it sounds like a girl's name in English, but we're proud to carry it.

"Pa says he vowed to Mama before they married, as long as he could influence their children, he'd have them read something every day. Pa takes promises seriously.

"That's the story. You made me tell everything, no mystery left to make me seem romantic. Now you'll be bored." I bowed my head, looking up at her with a sad expression.

Kit's voice came in a rush. "My mother died during the war while Papa Joe was gone. He fought for the Confederacy. We lived in Vir-ginia. When Papa Joe came home he worked all the time, night and day. But he had trouble with carpetbaggers, who finally stole all our land. I think he shot a man, maybe more than one. He took me out of school the night before graduation. We rode and rode, changing horses several times. I had to leave all my clothes behind, everything. Then we came out here." She stopped like she'd run out of breath.

Before I could say anything, she burst out again with another gush of words. "I'm eighteen years old, and I've never had a suitor before. If I do anything to displease you, please tell me and I'll stop. You saved my life. You're my white knight."

I couldn't have been more surprised if she'd shrieked like a moun-tain lion and sprang for my throat. After she blurted all that out she became still, eyes locked with mine, like a small statue, except I could see her fingers twisting together in her lap. Finally, I managed to speak.

"I'm a poor excuse for a white knight, Kit, but I'll try my best. You wanted me to be serious. You get your wish. You have my word. I'll do the best I can for you. I want you to come to have an affection for me. I've never been called on to talk serious to a woman before, except for Mama. Maybe I do joke too much."

Kit came to her feet with a beautiful, effortless movement. She stood over me for a moment before she said, "I don't like your short-man jokes. You're handsome. Please stop complaining because you aren't big and ugly like your brothers. And don't tell me about Indian girls. I don't think it's proper for me to know about that."

She turned on her heel and started walking away. After only a few steps, she spun around to face me again. "I like your brothers. They're wonderful men. But they're not good-looking like you. Did you mean it when you told Papa Joe that first day that I'm the prettiest thing you ever saw? Was that one of your jokes?"

Feeling like I was trying to stay on a runaway horse, I answered, "I meant that. I sure did."

"Thank you. Maybe you'll be my last suitor as well as the first. Wouldn't that be nice?" Without waiting for an answer she walked back to the fire.

I kept my knife sharp as a razor. Pa believed in keeping tools of every sort in working condition. A man in my state could lop off fingers without noticing, so I walked away from the hide I'd been cleaning. I found my way to the creek, cleaned the blade, washed my hands and face, and sat peering into space. Pa came by and gave me a puzzled look.

I said, "Pa, I'm taken with that girl more than ever."

He nodded and left me alone, left me sitting on my butt as if paralyzed, in broad daylight when there was work to be done. I guess Pa figured my condition was a form of sickness. He never asked us to work when we were ailing.

Then, that very night, she put food on a plate and brought it to me, just to me, since Thackery was getting around better and helped himself with the others. I thanked her and sat looking down at my food for a minute or two. When she served her own plate, she didn't go to her usual place beside Thackery. She sat close to me while Pa said grace. Women have wondrous clever ways to make a man feel chesty.

I thought nobody but me noticed anything or paid attention. But when I looked his way, Milt winked, and his hands flickered briefly in the evening light. Milt, if so inclined, had it in him to make bright and shining music with Indian sign language. He gave me a sign, the sign for big heart.

FOUR

ABOUT A WEEK LATER Thackery said to Pa, "I'm feeling fit enough to ride. I'll pay you five hundred dollars if you and your sons will ride to Bannock with me."

Pa didn't look surprised, nodded like he'd been expecting just such an offer. "Seems high pay for not much of a ride. I think that's too much money, unless you have more than ordinary reason to expect trouble."

Thackery answered, "There was no particular reason for me to expect trouble before. I didn't expect to get bushwhacked like I did. I don't think I have any enemies out here, but maybe loaded mules like mine attract too much attention in gold country."

His glance drifted to Kathleen rinsing the breakfast plates beside the stream. "Besides, I have the girl to think about. No telling but what those men were after her as much as what's on my mules. Anyway, it's worth the money to my way of thinking. It'd take a big gang of thieves to take on all five of us. Seems to me we'll have enough men to make anything but a fairly big war party of Indians think twice. We should have no trouble unless we get careless."

I felt awkward, like it might be better for me to keep my mouth shut, but I said it anyway. "Think back on it. One of those bushwhackers called you by name, Joe. Remember?"

Thackery's eyes narrowed when he glanced at me. "You're right, Ward. I forgot that."

He turned to Pa and said, "There's another indication to show how cool this young man is when about to get into a gun battle. He remembers every word, like a lawyer."

Turning his eyes back to me, he went on, "Your reminder doesn't help, though, Ward. I didn't know the man's voice, and I didn't get a look at him before you men buried him. I've hardly spoken to anybody in Montana Territory except store clerks when I bought supplies. Even then, I don't remember mentioning my name. That's odd, very odd, and most upsetting. I shall give that more thought."

"We talked it over the first night," Pa said. "My boys and I figured you had three of your four mules loaded with gold. You must have made a big strike."

When Thackery made no comment, Pa went on, "We've heard a lot of talk since we rode into this country. Seems many a man makes a strike up here and then can't hold on to it. A man alone has problems, both fighting off claim jumpers and getting his gold safely to town. The idea came to me that you could use some partners. Have you given the idea any thought?"

Nodding, Thackery answered, "Might be an advantage. What kind of a deal do you have in mind?"

"Fifty-fifty," Pa said without hesitation. "You already know where the strike lies. You work with us, and the girl cooks and washes. You and the girl get half, and my family gets the other half. We split all expenses, starting after the partnership makes its first shipment. Before the first shipment, you outfit us from the gold you already have. You've seen the way my sons eat, so I expect that'll make you hesitate, but you haven't seen them work. When you see that, the food cost won't bother you. On the other hand, given time for it, my sons are probably the best hunters in the territory. We'll have fresh meat if anybody does."

Pa paused to light his pipe. "Another thing, seems to me each of us ought to file a separate claim, including the girl. That way, our partnership can include six claims. Whatever we take from any of the claims goes into the partnership. We'll contribute four claims to your two, but you found the strike. Without you, we could ride around these mountains for no telling how long without finding enough gold to pay decent wages."

Thackery answered, "Done," and stuck out his hand. While he and Pa were still shaking hands, Thackery added, "No offense intended, but I'd like to put everything in writing when we get to town."

"No offense taken," Pa said. "I figure the partnership decisions will be made by you and me, with the young folks having no vote." Pa kept a perfectly straight face when he went on, "But if we disagree, we can let Kathleen and Ward fight it out to see which way it goes."

I said real quick, "Wait a minute, Pa, I already saw her whip a fellow bigger'n me. If you and Papa Joe here start disagreeing, I might not be fit to work if she's being turned loose on me all the time."

Thackery looked at me with a glint of humor in his eyes before saying, "I don't think her heart would be in it, Ward." Then he glanced back with a raised eyebrow at Pa. "Darnell, that remark from you clears up the question about where Ward and Milt get their unusual style of joking."

Pa said quietly, "Yes, I see myself in my boys, the way I was once." Then he added, "I wasn't the only one. Mrs. Baynes was a woman who liked to laugh. She was always up to some kind of mischief."

Milt and I exchanged shocked glances. We spoke of Mama all the time, but Pa did not, so his comment jolted us. We had wondered about Pa's silence, wondered if he had taken such a liking for travel because he was trying to ride away from his memory of Mama.

Maybe Pa's remark put Thackery off guard for a moment too. He mused, "Mrs. Thackery was the same. Never seemed to get older. She always seemed like a young girl to me, especially when we were away from others. She pulled no end of tricks on me, loved to upset my dignity, had a special way of laughing when she put something over on me."

Then Thackery seemed to stiffen and his voice went brusque, "One other thing. We already have a cabin built, but it's too small for all of us. Besides, I'd like privacy for the girl. I suggest we do some building first thing when we get back to the claim."

Pa said, "Now that we have an agreement, we can start planning what we want to do and how to do it. What say we start for town tomorrow?"

Thackery agreed, and starting the next morning, we had several days of the most pleasant riding as could be imagined. Milt and Luke did all the scouting, which let me stay alongside Kit the whole time, riding in front of the pack mules, with Thackery and Pa bringing up the rear, leading the bushwhackers' horses.

We made quite a circus when we all rode together. Our outfit now consisted of six of us on horseback, Thackery's four mules, our four mules, a bushwhacker mule, and two extra horses.

It was spring, a pretty time of year no matter where a man finds himself, but there was never a happier time for me. A man enjoys everything twice as much if he can share it with someone of like mind. Kit was like a new creature in the world, finding joy and wonder in every track, every bird, every new view over a hill.

Luke, my brother of few words, said it well one day. I'd showed Kit how to find and dig Indian turnips, and she was wagging a bunch into camp, smiling and singing to herself.

Luke said, "She's crossed over the pass."

I knew what he meant. Gently reared in Virginia, looked after by servants, protected from every possible discomfort, she'd turned into a Western woman. She carried a rifle as casually as a man, made do with what she had with no complaining, and never tired of learning new things. A fancy lady who smiled over finding a few stringy turnips had "crossed over the pass," had found her song in the majesty of the land. Not an empty expanse, as some saw it, but a land graced by rugged beauty wherever the eye fell, an unspoiled country of tall trees and endless plains nourished by mountains yielding clean, sweet, falling water.

We rode in when the sun was straight above us, and every man on the street seemed to forget his own business. The town folks took one look at us and all those mules and started following along. Pa and Thackery rode up beside Kathleen and me.

Pa spoke to me in a low voice, "These people can smell a new strike like a hound on a trail. Luke and I will take the gold inside. I want you and Milt to keep watch till we get it all carried into the bank. No need to expect trouble in the middle of town, but Joe won't be carrying anything. He wants his hands free, and his wounds have stiffened up and started hurting."

Thackery said, "Kathleen, you stay close by Ward while I'm busy, hear me?"

Kit spoke up in her pert way, "I planned to, Papa Joe."

Thackery gave me one of his hard looks and said, "Don't give me that flabbergasted expression. You asked for it. She's going to be a hard saddle to rub off, no matter how much you roll."

A chattering crowd was following, shouldering closer when we drew up in front of the Wells Fargo Bank. A fat, grinning fellow in a red flannel shirt, baggy canvas pants, and hobnailed boots asked me, "What you got on all those mules, kid?"

"Ivory," I answered, scanning the growing crowd.

A bellow of laughter went through the group.

Another question came from the cluster of men. "Been elephant hunting, kid?"

I said, "Yep."

"Did'ja git 'em all?"

I answered, "Yep. I don't think there's a single one left out there."

A roar of approval went up. We were now surrounded by a sea of smiling faces.

"Where'd you find 'em, kid?"

"Here and there. You know how that goes. You have to watch for the rainbow and the Indians at the same time."

Pa and Luke went to two of Thackery's mules, stripped the packs off, and went inside with them. I stayed in the saddle because I could see better. Kit did the same. The crowd of good-natured men was keeping its distance, causing no real concern, but suddenly a man with glassy eyes and unsteady gait stepped out of the group. He put his hand on Kit's knee, looked up into her startled face, and asked, "Where'd you find this pretty thing, kid?" The closest men shifted uneasily and went quiet.

Leaving the reins slack, I shifted my weight just a bit to one side, gave Peepeye a little pressure with the knees, and nudged one heel into his ticklish belly. He spun and kicked, just like he'd been taught, and both his hooves caught the drunk in the small of the back. Anybody who's been kicked in the kidneys by a horse will understand why that fellow screamed and fell writhing in agony to the ground.

I yelled, "Whoops. Hey, look out there. Watch it, men. Don't get too close. You're spooking the horses."

I rode Peepeye for four years from Louisiana to Montana, with side trips to Mexico and California plus lots of circling and backtracking. We had our start together back home seven years ago when I pulled him from his dam. My hands supported him when he reached for his first milk. I named him Peepeye for his habit of hiding behind his mama but poking his head around her rump to watch me. Old friends like us learned many a trick from each other.

I swung Peepeye in a quick circle, and Kit sidled her horse toward me till we sat stirrup to stirrup. Two of the onlookers tried to pull the drunk to his feet, but he screamed even louder and fell again, clutching his back and groaning. I saw Luke strip the pack off the third Thackery mule and walk inside.

A short, dark-faced man wearing a threadbare jacket of Union blue caught my eye, winked, and nodded. I figured there was at least one real horseman in that crowd who knew an accident when he saw one, knew he hadn't seen one, but approved of what he did see. Then I saw the unpolished star on his jacket and the tied-down gun.

I asked the man in the red shirt, "Livery stable?"

He pointed. "Down yonder."

The drunk was on his feet now, more or less, being half dragged, half carried off by his two friends.

"Hotel?"

Red Shirt grinned. "Same direction, kid, but not so far. Best one's on the left, but it's expensive. That's where the dress-up folks go."

"Obliged."

Luke came out of the bank and walked over to stand by my stirrup. "Pa and Joe have business in the bank for a while yet. He says for Milt and me to take care of the stock. You're to take Kathleen and get rooms for us. Joe said to get the best in town. It's on him."

"I hear the livery is yonder." I ducked my head to indicate the direction. "There's supposed to be a hotel on the left side of the street. You should see it on your way to the stable. That's where we'll be."

When I looked her way, Kathleen nodded to show she'd heard everything. She kept her horse close beside mine as we started the short ride down the street. We went only a few steps before she asked in a low voice, "Did you make your horse kick that man? Did you do that on purpose?"

"Yes, ma'am."

"That was awful. I don't think he meant to make trouble. He was offensive, certainly, but he seemed just a harmless drunk. I believe he may be seriously injured."

"He was pinching my peach."

She shook her head. "I'm not your peach yet. Are you really that jealous?"

"Yes, ma'am, but that makes no difference. Your Papa Joe put you in my care. That makes the difference. You want to help me explain to him if I let somebody bother you and did nothing? You want to help me with that?"

She turned slightly in the saddle to put her full blue-eyed gaze on me. "No, absolutely not. That would never do." She straightened and spoke, looking straight ahead. "Thank you."

"*A su servicio, senorita.*"

She glanced back at me, grinning this time. "And another thing. You did it so very neatly. When that man touched my knee, I looked right at you, knowing full well you'd do something. It still looked like an accident. But, knowing you, I thought I'd ask. You're full of tricks, aren't you?"

I gave her my round-eyed innocent expression and put my hand over my heart. "No, ma'am, I'm just sincere. I can't imagine why sincerity makes you so suspicious."

We dismounted in front of the hotel. I stripped off our saddlebags and waited a couple of minutes for my brothers to come past with the horses and mules. I walked out in the street to hand up the reins of our horses to Milt as he came by.

Milt pulled up and spoke quickly, "Pa said for Luke and me to talk to the marshal about how we came by the saddle stock and mules from those bushwhackers. He said to turn those animals over to him since they don't belong to us. The marshal was standing in front of the bank. I spoke to him after you and Kathleen rode off. He said he'd meet us at the livery stable to hear about that shooting."

I asked, "You need me?"

Milt shrugged. "Don't think so. You better see to the girl. Thackery and Pa are going to see a lawyer when they finish at the bank. They want to put the partnership in writing. No sense in Kathleen standing around in the street while all this is going on. If we need you, we'll know where to find you."

He tipped his hat to Kathleen and turned to follow Luke and the string of mules down the street.

Kathleen was smiling when we walked into the hotel. She swept in like she owned the place. The room clerk took a quick look at my clothes and started putting on a snooty expression, but one glance at her seemed to change his mind. Without saying a word, threadbare dress and all, she managed to look like trouble, bad trouble, to anybody who didn't treat her like the Queen of Sheba.

She knew the right words too. Before I could say a thing, she said, "My father and I will require your best suite, and we'll need another large room with four beds for our business associates." With a nod at me, she went on, "My escort, Mr. Baynes, is here to handle the details. Our associates will be along shortly with our baggage. I'll have my key at once, please. I have much to do before my father arrives. How soon can you have heated water brought up?"

The clerk never had a chance. He was bowing and shoving a key across the counter before he could stop himself. He said, "At once, ma'am. We're at your service." He turned and opened a door behind him to shout, "Hot water to Suite 21, Fong. Right now."

She gave him a prim thank you and turned to me. "Look in on me when you finish the arrangements, Mr. Baynes. I may have further use for you."

I bowed. "Of course, Miss Thackery. I shall only be a few moments, I'm sure."

She gave the clerk a straight look and asked, "Well?"

He blinked and asked, "Something wrong, ma'am?"

"Is there no one to escort me to my accommodations?"

"Uh, I'm not supposed to leave the desk, ma'am, and we don't usually . . . Uh . . ." He threw a desperate glance my way.

I said, "I'd be honored, Miss Thackery, if I might postpone signing the register for just a few moments?" I lifted one eyebrow in the clerk's direction.

He looked like he wanted to hug me when he said quickly, "Of course, sir, no rush at all. Please see to Miss Thackery's comfort."

I followed her up the stairs and took a quick look around the suite. There was a tap on the door, and I let a Chinese man come in lugging two buckets of steaming water. I left her grinning in the middle of the luxurious sitting room and clumped back downstairs to sign the register.

The clerk leaned over the counter and asked in a near whisper, "Who is she, Mr. Baynes?"

"Daughter of Joseph Finnigan Thackery, Esquire. He owns Thackery International Mining and Finance. Loans money to the King of England and people like that. Owns most of India and Russia. You've heard of him, haven't you?"

"Uh, sure. Yeah."

"All fangs and claws isn't she? Her father's out here thinking about buying Montana Territory. We had a mishap. She lost her fancy gowns and stuff. Is there a ladies' emporium in this town?"

He looked pained and whispered, "Look, Mr. Baynes, I'm just a prospector getting over a broken leg. I need this job. What's a ladies' emporium?"

"Fancy store. Place where ladies buy dresses and . . . Uh, you know, uh . . ."

His head was bobbing. "Yeah, we got a store with some ladies' dresses and, uh, equipment. Three doors down and across the street. Big place."

I stomped up the stairs again. When I tapped on her door, she opened it about an inch.

I said, "Big store just down the street if you want to go shopping."

She showed me one eye through the barely open door and said, "Later. I'm going to clean up first."

I pointed down the hall to the door of the Baynes' room. "I'll be in that room polishing my armor if you have further use for me, Princess Moneybags." She closed the door quickly, but I could hear her laughing when I walked away.

She laughed with rich, sweet, clear notes when she thought nobody could hear, or when she forgot to be the dignified lady. The sound reminded me of a time back when I was a little boy visiting my cousins in New Orleans. I heard a black man play some kind of instrument on a street corner. Don't know what it was. Flute, I guess. I gave him a penny. That was all I had.

FIVE

NOT KNOWING what else to do with myself, I sat looking out the window, watching people go about their business. About an hour passed before I saw Luke and Milt walking toward the hotel with the dark-faced marshal in the blue jacket. I could hear them coming down the hall before the knock on the door.

"Come on in."

My brothers entered, carrying all the family gear. The marshal followed my brothers into the room. Luke started to open packs and remove our best clothes, laying them out on the beds.

Milt said, "Ward, this is U.S. Marshal Frank Jopson. We told him about the trouble we had, and he wants you to come down to his office to tell it the way you saw it."

Jopson stepped forward and shook hands. He said, "I explained to your brothers, Ward, how I like to hear things from each person in private. Otherwise, people get to arguing or prompting one another, and things can get confused. You aren't under arrest or anything like that. I just want to hear the story from you with nobody else around. Your brothers did the same thing with me down at the stable. Each of them told me the story with the other one staying away while we were talking."

I said, "Fine. Let's go."

The marshal said, "I'd like to talk to Miss Thackery first, if you don't mind waiting for a few minutes."

"I think you better put that off for a while, Marshal. The lady had water brought up. I think she'll be indisposed for a while. Mr. Thackery is not present at the moment. I don't think he'd tolerate your talking to her alone in a hotel room anyway. You want me to bring her to your office later?"

Jopson turned to Luke and Milt. "If you gentlemen will excuse yourselves, I can hear the story from your brother here and now. I don't think this is going to take long. Maybe, by the time we finish, Mr. Thackery will return. In this case, I'll go along with what he thinks is proper. I'll talk to him and his daughter together."

Milt said, "We can get out of the way in about two minutes, marshal. First, though, Luke and I have to gather up some clothes. We need to take our best suits out to have them pressed. Our pa believes in putting in a good appearance."

As soon as my brothers walked out, the marshal looked me in the eye and said, "I like the way you ride."

With my most innocent expression, I answered, "A fine horse can make any man look good. Pa gave me that one when I was thirteen years old."

He nodded, asked a couple of questions to get me started, and listened to my description of the shooting. I had no sooner finished when Pa walked in. It was my turn to get out. I took a walk downstairs and joined Milt and Luke in the dining room while Pa talked to the marshal. Pa came down after a while and said the marshal had finished with him and was talking to the Thackerys. We sat drinking coffee together for another half hour till Jopson joined us.

He shook his head at the waitress when she picked up a cup, pointed at it, and gave him a questioning look.

His tone was indifferent when he spoke to Pa. "I'll keep the personal items you brought in, Mr. Baynes. It's too bad there isn't anything to help identify those men. I think I've seen those horses before, but I can't remember the riders. Maybe somebody here in town will know who they were. In the meantime, I'm satisfied. It's just a good thing you men came along when you did."

Jopson hesitated for a moment as if he was considering his next remarks carefully. Then he looked at me and said, "Being a lawman can be interesting work. Everybody sees things in a different way." He paused again before continuing.

"Thackery was angry and embarrassed to get caught flat-footed. His daughter was amazed at how quickly she felt safe again after meeting up with you men."

Shifting his gaze between Pa and Luke, he said, "You two were concerned about Thackery's wounds, even a little sad about the men who were killed."

With a glance at Milt, he said, "For you, the incident is past, simply water under the bridge."

Then I felt the shock of his pale blue eyes on me. "I found you only concerned about the chance one of those men might have gotten away. You think like a lawman. We like to tie up all the loose ends, clean everything up with no doubts leftover. If you have an interest in becoming a peace officer, come to see me."

Abruptly, Jopson rose, shook hands with each of us, and walked out.

Pa put his elbows on the table and leaned forward. We all drew closer when he spoke in a low tone.

"That's a good man to have on our side. Now let's talk about our own business. Thackery's gold is safely in the bank. Boys, most of that gold is rough little chunks and slivers, not gold dust. Thackery was able to work during the winter because he wasn't getting wet, wasn't panning. He found what he says looks like a small pocket of rotten quartz on dry land near a creek. It must be fantastically rich."

Pa took a quick look around the room to make sure nobody else was listening before he went on. "Anyway, he just broke the quartz with a sledgehammer and picked out the gold with his fingers. The banker says the gold needs to be worked on before the value is exactly known, but it looks like more than fifty thousand dollars. The banker will see to all that and give him an exact figure in a few days."

Nobody said a word. I guess all of us were stunned.

Pa went on, "The banker gave Joe a wad of paper money big enough to start printing a newspaper with it. He said it was a loan, with the gold as collateral. Boys, my partner is a rich man now. He could hire men to work his strike. Seemed to me he didn't need us anymore, and I told him so. Joe said we shook on a deal, and that's that. He wasn't about to back out, so we went to a lawyer and signed an agreement just like we planned."

Milt said, "Pa, he'd be crazy to go out there and work like a field hand when he's got all that money. We may have to fight Indians or tangle with bushwhackers again. I can hardly even imagine fifty thousand dollars."

"Yeah," I agreed. "And Kit won't be cooking and washing for such as us. No girl with a rich father is going to do that kind of work. This has to change everything."

Pa said, "Listen, boys, I told him all that. He did say that he might offer some changes when he's had a chance to think things over. He did say that. But he also said he wouldn't try to make any changes that would hurt a Baynes. Remember, this man is no fool. He knew how much he was worth before we met him. Thackery said he wasn't about to forget what we did for him. I think he got a little mad at me. His voice got pretty sharp when he said that no Thackery ever broke his word."

Milt said, "Maybe we can put down our lantern."

Pa looked blank until I said, "Yeah, maybe we've found an honest man."

Then Pa laughed and said, "Let's go find our honest man and take him down to the land office or whatever they have here. We need to register our claims."

And that's what we did, but there were some surprises. None of us expected to face a crowd of twenty or thirty men, obviously waiting for us. They stood back until we walked into the building. Then they crowded around us like a colony of bees around its queen. There was some fumbling around with maps for a few minutes, but Thackery was clearly an expert at reading them. I suppose he learned that skill when soldiering.

At first, it was almost impossible to get anything done because of all the pushing and shoving, with so many men trying to shoulder into the small office to see where our claims were located. We had advantages, though. Marshal Jopson showed up and backed them off enough to keep us from being crushed, and Thackery's cold eyes persuaded many of the men to back up to avoid being pushed too close to Kathleen.

After leaving the claims office, we walked down to the big store the hotel clerk mentioned. We bought little, spending the time looking around and making up a list of items we planned to buy tomorrow. However, Kit bought every item of clothing in the place that fit her, or so it seemed to me.

Later, we went back to the hotel, cleaned up, put on our freshly pressed suits, and went down to meet the Thackerys in the hotel dining room for dinner.

We were having coffee after the meal when Milt said, "We'll be in the center of a circle of new claims. In fact, we better get out there fast or I'll bet we'll find people sitting on our claims and working them."

Thackery commented, "Milt is surely correct. At least, my claim is marked. We need to mark your claims or arguments are sure to come up. Still, I need to buy a lot of things to make Kathleen more comfortable. We may need to buy more mules to carry it all. It's too bad, but I don't think we can get a wagon in there without going to a lot of trouble and delay to make a road. We'll need all day tomorrow to get ready."

"We were talking about you this afternoon," Pa said. "With all that gold in the bank, do you still intend to go back out there and start swinging a pick and sledgehammer again?"

"I do." Thackery's tone was stubborn. "I'm not a trusting man. Although I'm convinced all the men at this table are honest, I intend to look after my gold by being present when it's taken from the ground."

Thackery tapped his finger sharply on the table for emphasis. "Darnell, we need a better idea of how much gold is left out there. I was working a narrow little wedge of rich quartz, and it didn't look like it went very deep. In fact, the wedge was getting thinner as I went deeper. We have to decide whether there's enough left out there to spend a lot of money developing the mine. In the meantime, I have no intention of having a bunch of hired men filling their pockets with my gold. I feel very strongly about this. I want no man on the property whose name isn't Baynes or Thackery."

"Is Kit coming along too?" My attempt to make the question sound casual was fairly successful, seemed to me.

Kit didn't look up from her coffee when Thackery turned to answer me. He said, "My daughter has endured terrible hardship without complaint since we left Virginia. Unfortunately, I lacked the funds to provide an acceptable domicile for her there while I attempted to repair my fortune out here. Besides, the circumstances of my departure would make it difficult to go back for her. Until I find a proper place for her to stay which meets my standards for propriety and safety, she'll continue to abide with me. I regret the continued discomfort this involves. However, Ward, you'll be interested to know this decision meets with her approval."

Kit looked up to meet my eyes when my next question was obviously directed to her. "You going to wash and cook, just like you were still poor?"

"Yes."

A short silence fell after her blunt response. Sometimes a comment is so absolute and definite, people need a moment to ponder it.

Then she added, "Of course, Papa Joe has assured me I shall have a few more amenities and comforts. For example, I shall have the things I need to provide tea and, perhaps, a small pastry or two if we have guests."

Turning her smile and her eyes directly at me, she said, "Back in Virginia, I was known for my fine cookies."

SIX

THACKERY BOUGHT eight more horses the next morning, since we could find no mules for sale, and we spent most of the day arranging and packing all the new fixings he picked up all over town. He was determined to make Kathleen comfortable, and I suppose he would have purchased a grand piano if he could have found a mule or a horse big enough to carry it.

Loading the packs for eight mules and eight horses can be tiresome. Every load must be packed just right or it won't balance, and an animal with an unbalanced burden can be restless and hard to handle. Even worse, the pack can start slipping around and gall the animal's back. That means a man ends up with a useless horse or mule till the galls heal. The hostler at the livery stable didn't have space in the tack room to put all our gear, so we had to line the filled packs up on the ground in two of the stalls.

After supper, Pa said, "Ward, you're the lightest sleeper. Go down to the stable and sleep with our stuff. I don't want to go down there in the morning and find any of it missing."

I nodded, and Milt said, "I'll go along too."

When Pa raised an eyebrow, Milt shrugged and said, "Somebody picked up those bushwhackers' animals. Seems funny to me. Maybe whoever claimed that stock didn't want us to see who they were. They waited till we went away from the stable."

Pa asked, "You think somebody has hard feelings? You figure they might like to come at us when we're not all together?"

Milt shrugged again and said, "Since they don't know him, Ward would look like the easiest one to get if somebody wanted to take us on one at a time. I figure to let him go down there by himself. I can slip around and join him. If somebody is trying to pick off strays, I'd like to give him a little surprise."

Pa thought that over for a moment before asking, "You think we may be up against kinfolks of those bushwhackers? Maybe we're into a blood feud?"

Milt answered, "I'm not thinking much beyond how easy it is to be careful, Pa, and how bad being surprised can be."

Pa nodded and said, "All right then, do just that—be careful, boys. Don't get trigger happy and shoot some poor drunk."

I walked down to the stable just before dark. The hostler was outside, seated in a straight chair tilted back against the front wall. He nodded in wordless greeting to my wave when I walked past him to go into the stable. After clearing a spot in one of the stalls containing our equipment, I spread some fresh hay and unfolded my blankets on it. Peepeye watched my every move like he always did, proving again he was the most curious horse in the world.

Milt slipped in the back door, grinned at me, and pointed first at himself, then up at the loft. At my nod, he went up the ladder without saying a word.

When I stepped out the front door, the hostler said, "Another chair here, youngster. Make yourself comfortable. We'll just set a spell and watch the sun go down."

I said, "Thank you, sir."

The gray-bearded hostler leaned forward, spat tobacco juice at an unoffending beetle, and said, "You got good manners, young feller, but you don't need to 'sir' me just because I got this here gray hair. I appreciate it, but it ain't necessary. My name's Cooper. Just call me Coop. Everybody does."

I said, "Yes, sir. I'm Ward Baynes."

He grinned when I said 'sir' again, shook his head, and said, "All right. You do like you been taught." He spat again before he went on, "I know who you are. Saw you around here most of the day, just never had a proper chance to say howdy. Probably, most everybody in town knows who you are by now."

We sat there without speaking for a while, watching the shadows grow longer. Coop's voice was low when he spoke again. "The marshal brung two men down here today. They claimed those animals you turned in. That's them same two men coming now."

I said, "Obliged," and casually looked down the street, following the direction given by his glance.

He chuckled and came to his feet. "I'm going inside for my shotgun. Them boys was talkin' mighty rough when they was down here with the marshal. Maybe they got to learn how much I like things peaceful and quiet around this here barn. You got time to get away through the back corral, son."

"Obliged," I said again. "But I'm comfortable, Mr. Cooper." Without raising my voice, I asked, "Milt, you still up there?"

From above me, Milt spoke through the open hayloft door, "Yeah, I'm here. Don't see anyone else coming this way, just those two. They both had their pistols out checking them before they started our way. Mind yourself. I'll take the one on the left."

Cooper stepped back into the dark interior of the stable and spoke with an edge of wonder in his voice, "Fancy that. I didn't know he was up there. Now that I think on it, I believe I'll just stay out of the way and watch."

The two men walking toward us strongly resembled each other. Both were short, heavy men, with dark hair and thick beards. One strode forward with arrogant, hard-shouldered purpose, leading the other by half a step. The other seemed more cautious, looking around nervously as if ready to veer off in another direction.

The first man came to a sudden stop in front of me, causing the other to jerk to a halt so quickly he stumbled. I could hear the second man speak in a low, relieved tone, "Aw, hell, Sam, he sure enough is just a kid. This'll be easy."

The arrogant one, Sam, spoke sharply to me. "You one of that Baynes crowd? You one of those came in here and told a pack of lies to the marshal?"

I ignored the comment about lies and said, "Yes, sir, I'm one of that Baynes crowd. Who're you?"

He said, "I'm Sam Hartlow, kid, and this is my brother Sid. One of those horses belonged to our cousin. You and your family lied. Jim Hartlow, our cousin, never bushwhacked anybody. We think you're the bushwhacker."

"I don't know Jim Hartlow," I said. "Maybe you're right. Maybe somebody stole his horse, and the thief was the one who caused us trouble."

"Don't try to talk around me, kid." The man was practically shouting. "I found Jim's pocketknife and a couple of other things of his in that stuff you brought in. That was a smart trick, taking that stuff in to the marshal and putting on an act. But you don't fool me. You laid for my cousin and killed him. I figure to get even."

His loud voice was attracting attention. I could see several men coming slowly down the street, drawing closer to see what was happening.

I said, "There were three men. They set out to shoot a man who had a woman with him. What kind of a gutless bastard shoots when he might hit a woman?"

Sam Hartlow could see the gathering crowd and was beginning to enjoy himself. He wore a hard grin now, satisfied with my remark. I figured he wanted me to argue back at him so he'd have an excuse for gunning me.

He sounded like a circus barker when he half shouted, "I say every one of you Bayneses is a liar, and that little whore riding with you is probably the biggest liar of all. You got a smart mouth, kid, and I'm just the one to teach you better."

The other, Sid, snickered and said, "Yeah, soon's we cut you down, we'll get the others. When we get around to that little whore, we'll know what to do with her too."

From above me came Milt's chuckle. He asked, "Well, what're you waiting for? You waiting for more of a crowd?"

Truth to tell, I didn't know whether Milt was talking to me or to them. But at the sound of his voice, both Hartlows went rigid. Their eyes jerked up and down, trying to watch Milt up in the loft door and me on the ground at the same time. The expressions on both men went from gloating confidence to shifty-eyed alarm, and they both edged back a couple of steps.

The odds had changed on them. Instead of facing what they took to be a lone, green kid, now they had Milt to deal with too. That turned things around in an instant. Nobody had taken Milt lightly since he was about fifteen.

Sam recovered first and spoke with nearly the same bluster as before. "We just came to give fair warning. We're going to get even. You're just gonna have to worry about us. We'll pick our own time. No telling when we'll decide to teach you a lesson."

He turned as if to walk away but stopped when I came out of that old straight chair. I took a couple of steps forward and said quietly, "You got a gun." Then I shouted, "Pull it."

Sam Hartlow must have been a slow-witted man, and this was an occasion when he had no time. When I shouted, "Pull it," he flinched in surprise and snatched at his gun. I think he'd decided to walk away, and my challenge changed his mind at the last minute. He was still half turned away from me. Maybe he was dumb enough to think I couldn't see him draw, wouldn't know what he was doing before his gun came in sight. Whatever he was thinking, Sam was slow as cold molasses, and a man should never reach for a gun when he's still trying to decide what he's going to do.

When he made his move, I shot him twice before he could clear leather. The first shot knocked him backward a couple of steps, and the second one put him flat on his back. He tried to sit up, looking around for the pistol he'd dropped. I walked up close and shot him in the face, driving him down into the dust. He arched his back and jerked spasmodically a couple of times before his body went limp.

When I turned to Sid, he was standing stiffly with his arms far away from his sides, looking up into the barrel of Milt's rifle.

I said, "Now you."

Sid started backing away, saying, "No. No. I just come with Sam. I don't want no trouble. Not me."

Without looking, I knew there were ten or twelve men along the street who'd heard and seen everything, including both the Hartlows' references to Kathleen.

I said, "When my brother counts to three, Hartlow, I'm going to kill you. Milt, count to three."

Milt blurted, "One, two, three," as fast as a man can count.

Sid's nerves must have been frazzled by the quick count. I think he went for his gun from sheer confusion. He was faster than Sam, and he was harder to kill. He took the last two rounds Jesse had but didn't go down, although the shots turned him clear around so he stood with his back to me. Sid swayed drunkenly, swinging his head back and forth as if bewildered, trying to figure out where I'd gone.

By the time he slowly got himself turned back around and found me again, I had picked up Sam's pistol. I shot him again. His knees gave way suddenly, and he dropped into a sitting position, holding his pistol in his lap as if he'd forgotten it was in his hand. I walked up close and shot him a fourth time, this one in the face. I stood over him, looking down the barrel of Sam's pistol till his twitching body grew still.

I stuck Sam's pistol in my belt and quickly reloaded Jesse. As soon as Jesse was ready to go again and in his holster, I threw Sam's gun contemptuously into the dusty street beside his body.

It was really turning dark now, but even in the failing light I recognized the marshal walking toward the knot of men that was forming around me and the two Hartlows. I eased back to my chair and sat down, finding Coop already seated with his chair tilted back against the wall of the stable. There was no sign of the shotgun he'd mentioned.

Milt strolled out of the stable, a straw stem between his teeth. He smirked at me and said, "I wonder if they got a newspaper in this town. If they do, I was thinking about headlines. How about, 'Baynes Boys Bane of Hartlows'? Or maybe, 'Ward Baynes Gives Hartlows Last Pains'? Naw, I guess that last one's probably too long."

Coop said in a matter-of-fact tone, "That was quick thinkin', picking up that man's pistol. If you're gonna take 'em on in bunches, young feller, you ought'a start wearing two guns."

Marshal Jopson shoved his way through the growing cluster of men. Before he could open his mouth to ask what happened, Coop said sharply, "You're a hell of a marshal. This kid was a-settin' here with me talking real respectful-like when them two outlaws come up. They talked nasty about a lady and tried to kill this here poor boy. What kind of town is this, where old men like me and children like him ain't safe on the street in broad daylight?"

Five or six men surrounded the marshal, all trying to talk at once. He silenced them with one swing of his hard gaze. I had a sudden hunch that Frank Jopson had seen the whole thing. He arrived quickly, within half a minute after the shooting, yet he wasn't hurrying when I caught my first glimpse of him.

He spoke with the same cold indifference I'd heard the day before. "I warned them to stay away from you people. I warned them when they came to me to claim those horses. They were talking tough then, making threats."

The muttering crowd hushed to listen to the marshal's quiet voice. In the sudden silence, his next remark must have carried through the whole group. "I especially cautioned them to stay away from you, Ward. I think they misunderstood me. I believe they thought it was you I was trying to protect."

He shook his head in disgust. "There are some men so dumb their heads must hurt. They must live in constant pain. It's a favor to put them out of their misery."

A hard-eyed man wearing buckskins laughed and said, "That baby-faced kid is faster with his favors than anybody I ever saw, Marshal. And it don't seem to upset him one bit. I'll bet he's done favors for people before."

I asked, "You want me, Marshal Jopson?"

He answered shortly, "I do not."

"I'll turn in then."

I walked back into the stable. Some kinds of admiration a man can do without. But the man in buckskins was right three times in a row. I was fast. And I wasn't upset. And I had been through all this before. I rubbed Peepeye's nose for a couple of minutes, listening.

From Peepeye's stall, I could hear clearly when somebody said, "Marshal, I've never seen a more cold-blooded pair of killings in my life. That young fellow didn't just defend himself. He kept shooting. He blasted those men to doll rags, kept shooting after they were already down. That kid's vicious. He's a public menace."

Jopson's voice was cold as a blue norther when I heard him say, "He is when somebody pulls a gun on him."

Coop said, "I heard everything and saw all of it. Ward Baynes was a-settin' here talkin' to me as mild as warm milk. Them two came all the way down the street to make trouble. They brought it to him. If I'd been his brother here, I'd of shot one of them."

Milt's voice was so low I could barely make out his words when he said, "Pa wouldn't like that. We let Ward do his own work. Pa says it's too easy for a little brother to get spoiled if his big brothers look after him too much."

Milt's comment seemed to stop the conversation. There was a moment of complete silence before mumbling and whispering started again when the marshal picked men to help cart the bodies off.

I rolled into my blankets and went to sleep.

Looking back on it, I guess that was when the words "vicious" and "cold-blooded" began to be linked to my name. The last shots, the ones fired into the faces of the Hartlows, were what bothered people, I think. The smarter way might have been to let them lie out in the street choking on blood and hurting until they died. They might even have taken a couple of days to die if I hadn't fired those last shots. I should have allowed them to suffer. Then, maybe, people wouldn't have thought me to be vicious.

SEVEN

FOLKS DON'T MOVE FAST with a string of pack animals. Yet, the next morning, it only took a couple of hours to put Bannock behind us like it was an odd dream. The town smell and noise faded from memory fast, replaced in the mind by the pine-scented breeze and the quiet of the pristine countryside. We settled into our road habit, Milt and Luke scouting, Kit and I leading the pack animals, Thackery and Pa coming along behind.

Surely, two quieter hours never passed between Kit and me. Every time I tried to start a conversation, she'd nod or answer with a few words, but she seemed evasive. In fact, she never looked straight at me, not once. I had grown used to her direct gaze, had come to take pleasure from it. This morning, though, she acted like she didn't want to see me at all. When she glanced my way, she seemed to look around me or through me.

Finally, I leaned toward her and touched her arm. I said, "Kit, are you all right?"

She stiffened and looked down at my hand in such a way that I drew it back at once.

Looking straight ahead, she said, "A man Papa Joe knew when he was in the Confederate Army came by to greet him at the breakfast table this morning. You, your pa, and your brothers had just walked out. The whole conversation was about you killing two men yesterday."

"Mighty poor subject to talk about at the breakfast table."

She flashed a furious glance at me and snapped, "Don't joke about it. Don't you dare joke about it. That's despicable."

That put me to blinking. Both her words and her tone showed she was sorely upset. I rode awhile trying to figure what I should say next and came up with a blank.

Finally, not knowing what else to do, I said, "I beg your pardon. I just meant to say I didn't think men talked about that kind of thing at meals with ladies present. I didn't mean to make a joke."

Her face was rigid as she rode looking straight ahead. She said, "That man told Papa Joe he was astonished to see a man like you in our company and advised us to be careful around you. He said he never saw two more vicious, merciless murders in his life. He was shocked and horrified when the marshal refused to arrest you."

I said, "Look, Kit, those men were relatives of one of the bushwhackers who nearly killed your pa. They made threats, said they were coming after us to get even. It was better to settle it right then. Otherwise, they'd come at us by ambush or from behind. It was plain they planned to do just that."

"He said you walked up close and shot them both in the head after they were already down. Is that true?"

"Yeah, but . . ."

"Then what he said was correct. Anyone who would do such a thing makes me sick. I don't see the need for further discussion."

We rode for a long time without speaking. I was doing some serious thinking, and she'd made it clear she didn't welcome any more talk from me.

I knew there was plenty I didn't know about Kit, but one thing I just learned hit me hard. My idea that we were of like mind had been dead wrong, plain wishful thinking. From the minute I first saw her, I must have been blind to anything but how pretty she was. I knew myself to be young, too young to feel much confidence about how smart I was. But I was old enough to have seen a few things. I'd seen men make bad mistakes by getting themselves all torn up by women long on looks but short on understanding.

Like most men who spend the majority of their time on horseback, I found the saddle a good place to think. A couple of ideas came to me early and wouldn't go away. One thing was, Kit wouldn't even hear my side of it. The only man and woman I ever had a chance to watch living together were my pa and my mama. They talked things out, always knew where they stood, and always worked together. Their way seemed to work mighty well, it seemed to me, so I just figured that was how I would do it when my time came.

Kit had, in her own way, told me to shut up, that she didn't care to hear what I had to say. Mama never told Pa to shut up, to my knowledge, in her life. I couldn't imagine how a family could get along without talking things out. From the time I was a little boy, I was allowed to speak my piece, and it hurt to be cut dead. I didn't like that, and wanted no part of people who treated each other in such a fashion. A dose of that left a man feeling small, like he was nothing, his opinion of no weight.

Another thing was, Kit didn't seem concerned about the fact that I could have been the one to do the dying yesterday.

It came to me, finally, that she was right. Conversation was useless. She was more concerned about appearances, about what other people thought and said, than she was about me. Once a man knows that, what's left to talk about?

The best thing for me to do would be to ride away. Since I couldn't do that, not wanting to leave my kin when they might have need of me, what was the next best thing?

I could go tell Joe Thackery I'd like to ride with my pa for a while. Joe would just naturally come forward to ride with his daughter. That'd raise questions after a while, though, since I'd let my mouth overload my savvy as a suitor, had stated hasty intentions about Kathleen that couldn't happen now.

My fast mouth made my failure to attract Kathleen's affections a public matter. So I learned something the hard way. Don't reveal any feelings about a woman until you have some notion how she feels about you. Seemed to me I was learning something any damn fool should be born knowing.

Although it was the hard road to take, the best plan was to do nothing. She looked prettier than ever riding along beside me, digging a hurt into me every time I looked her way, but the thing to do was to act normal and gradually back off. I'd best just let things cool and try to avoid trouble.

So if the ride to town had been the most pleasant of my life, the ride back to Thackery's mine and our claims was the longest and hardest. After that first day on the trail, Kit said nary a word to me nor I a single one to her. Spending every day looking at something he wants and can't have, mixed with feeling like a big-mouth fool, can be a trial to a man's soul. Kit was no company at all, and I was down on myself, feeling dumb, hurt, mad, and bitter all at the same time.

I finally gave it up. There comes a time when a man just has a gut full. I asked Luke to trade riding positions with me the morning Thackery said he expected we'd see his cabin before nightfall. Bless Luke's quiet way. He just nodded like it was the most natural thing in the world. Nobody had said anything or given any sign of noticing the silence between Kathleen and me, but Luke had a way of sensing things.

Before I rode out with Milt that morning, Pa called us over and said, "Now, boys, we've all seen men overtake and pass us on horseback. We have reason to think the place may be crowded when we get there. Do I need to tell you boys not to do anything foolish? Other men filed claims close by ours, and some of them are probably already there. Men have a way of claiming what's theirs plus a little extra for good measure. No telling what you may find. Don't be too quick to start trouble."

So I wasn't surprised when Milt and I rode into sight of that little log cabin and saw smoke coming from Thackery's mud brick chimney.

My luck seems to run in spells. I seemed to be in the middle of a string where if something could possibly go wrong, it would.

Milt and I pulled up in the edge of a grove of trees a couple of hundred yards from the cabin. We just sat there and looked around for a minute or two.

Milt said quietly, "Damn."

I said, "I agree. What do you think? Should we go down and raise hell or wait for Pa and Thackery?"

Milt said, "We better wait. After all, it's Thackery's cabin, and it's on partnership land. Pa as much as told us not to do anything but look around."

We could see a goodly stretch of the creek from where we sat. Six or seven men were in sight. All were hard at work. Two rockers were operating and the beginnings of a sluice was already taking shape.

I said, "Looks to me like half the men in sight are working on ground I thought was on our claims."

Milt answered, "Yep."

"That means, if they've hit any pay dirt, it's ours. They're taking our gold, and they must know we're coming. Those men look unconcerned to me. They must have lookouts posted somewhere."

Milt grinned and said, "Right again."

"I don't know exactly where Joe's mine is, but I'll bet they've found it and are busy there too."

"You're figuring it all out by yourself," Milt said with his mocking grin. "It's nice not to have to explain everything to you."

"Yeah, I been feeling pretty dense lately. I guess I deserved that."

Milt gave me a quick look and said, "Whoa, there, little brother. Remember me?" He leaned toward me and poked himself in the chest a couple of times with his thumb. "I'm Milt, your brother. You and I are the jokers in the family. I don't like that worn down and sad tone of voice from you."

I took a deep breath, once again trying to come up with something to say, but ended up just giving Milt a shrug.

He spoke quietly. "Our bunch is still at least a couple of hours away. Why don't we have a little talk while we ride back?"

Peepeye turned away from the cabin and headed back down the trail like he'd been listening to Milt. I said, "Kathleen heard about the killings in town. She sees me as a ruthless killer. That's it. Not much to talk about."

"Oh, it's Kathleen now, not Kit anymore?"

"Yeah, I guess so. Man has no call to use pet names for people who don't like him."

Milt asked, "Does she know who they were? Does she know about the threats they made?"

"I tried to explain. She cut me off. Didn't want to hear it."

"We all took to that girl, especially Pa. Nobody talks about it, but we've all seen that something was wrong." Milt's eyes were scanning the brush, alertness as much a part of him as his right hand. "She's Virginia aristocracy, Ward. I hate to think it, but maybe she's the kind of woman who finds it hard to understand men like us."

"Yeah. It's hard on me, Milt. I'm not doing too good with this. I'd rather ride away. Being around her all the time gives me the miseries."

Milt nodded and said quietly, "Maybe this is one of those things that needs a little time. Sometimes a man can be too impatient. Don't break your eggs. They may still hatch."

"Not my decision. She told me I make her sick. She hasn't said another word to me since."

Milt made a pained face. "She talks plain, doesn't she? I'll speak to Pa. He'll probably try to keep you away from camp, send you out hunting or something. Besides, we aren't tied to this deal forever. Maybe Pa'll catch an itch to ride on pretty soon anyway. We got along before without a gold mine. We can do it again. Thackery can have it."

I flashed a grin at him. "Milt, you're talking wild now. Whoever heard of a man giving up a half-interest in a gold mine because his son got a harebrained mush-up on a girl that turned sour? This may be Pa's last chance to replace what we had to leave behind in Louisiana."

Milt gave a huge shrug, bringing his shoulders almost up to his ears. "Whoever heard of a family like ours, a family that rides across the most beautiful country in the world for four years without ever talking about stopping anywhere? Whoever heard of a man like Pa, a man who rides away from his home, his land, money in the bank, and his wife's grave to keep his sons from going to war? Nobody's like us, Ward, nobody. Me, now, I'd rather trap furs in Canada than hang around Montana Territory breaking rocks. You realize we haven't even seen Canada yet?"

We rode the rest of the way back without talking. It's a marvel how silence could be so comfortable with Milt but such hell with Kathleen. My mind wandered, and I started remembering the times I'd hunted

or fished with my kinsmen without them saying anything for hours. Pa
and my brothers knew how to say nice things all day long without
speaking. Kathleen gave me a lesson on how a person could say harsh
things without words.

Pa and Thackery both took the news about the claim jumpers
calmly, as if they were hearing exactly what they expected. Pa said, "I
think we should stick together but avoid riding too close to each other.
Ward, you stay back here with Kathleen and keep watch over our
stock. I figure the rest of us should ride right in and do whatever we
have to do to keep what's ours."

His eyes narrowed when I spoke quietly, "I figured to go up there,
Pa. It'd work better if Joe stayed with his daughter and let us see to
this. Our family has ridden together a long time. We know each other
better."

Milt spoke quickly, "I think that's a good idea."

Pa's quick glance went from Milt to me, meeting my eyes squarely
for a slow moment before he turned to Thackery and asked, "All right
with you, Joe?"

Thackery drew back slightly, his eyes on me. "What is it? What's
going on all of a sudden?"

I said, "Seems to me, if anything happened to you, Kathleen would
be left out here alone with us. It wouldn't be fitting." Thackery's
questioning gaze didn't waver, so I laid it out in the open. "She's not
comfortable with me, Joe."

Thackery blinked a couple of times and then gave me a smile that
would freeze a grizzly's heart. He said slowly, "You're saying you'd
rather face gunfire, maybe, than stay here with my daughter?"

I knew Kathleen was somewhere nearby, listening, but I'd taken to
the habit lately of not looking at her, so I'd lost track of exactly where
she was. My face heated up, and I knew I must be turning all kinds of
colors. Suddenly, I was sick and tired of the whole thing, worn-out
with being upset because she had no respect for me. My nerves had
grown tender with feeling insulted to the core by Kathleen's attitude. I
wasn't going to put up with anybody trying to make me ashamed of
myself, not for another minute. It was childish to step around the
issue. Dodging never solves problems.

"I'm a damn good gunfighter, Joe, but I'm next to worthless in your
daughter's eyes. I'd prefer to keep my distance."

Kathleen gave a little gasp, but Thackery looked her way with an expression that allowed no comment. He gave me a brief nod and said coldly, "I think we need to discuss this further at a better time, but until then, we'll honor your preference, sir."

Matching his tone, I bowed slightly and said, "Much obliged."

I mounted, turned Peepeye with my knees so my back was to everybody, and gave my attention to checking Nadine and Jesse.

EIGHT

WE HAD JUST LEFT the Thackerys behind with the string of pack animals and were still riding close together when Pa said, "We'll go to the cabin first. With the girl along, we'll need to get that problem solved first so she can make herself comfortable."

Milt asked, "We going to ride straight in? They must expect us, Pa. They probably have a lookout or two."

Pa answered, "I don't figure we're up against a gang of crooks. These are probably just men who'll push till they're stopped. All we need to do is make it plain that we own the place and won't take any foolishness."

"Those men are taking our gold," Luke said quietly. "It's not enough to stop it. We need to take back what they've stolen. It's not righteous to steal, and it's the devil's work to tempt men to do wrong by allowing it."

"What do you think we should do?" Pa asked.

Luke said, "We should take the guns away from every man we find working on our property. We should strip them. They keep coins and paper money. We keep all the raw gold we find on 'em. We keep their guns and send them packing."

"I hate to send unarmed men out into Indian country," Pa said.

"Small punishment for a thief. They'll be angry to lose what they've worked to steal," Luke said. "Taking their guns might keep us from having to kill them. By the time they replace their weapons, maybe their minds will have cooled. We must do our duty without killing if we can, but we must do our duty."

Milt nodded agreement to Pa's questioning glance, and I did the same. Milt said, perfectly serious, "We can stop anywhere along here to let Luke rest. No need to rush into this with him all winded."

Luke made a pistol out of his closed fist, with his index finger extended stiffly and his thumb upraised, aimed his finger at Milt, dropped his thumb, and said, "Bang." Milt grunted, clutched his chest, and reeled in the saddle.

Luke said, "You and Ward been hoggin' all the fun lately. I think today might be my day to have a frolic."

"Here's what I think," Pa said. "Those men probably aren't ready to fight. If they have a lookout, they plan to be warned. They'll expect to walk off our claim with the gold they've taken and look innocent. Some of the men close by are respectable and have honest claims, but they figure the stealing done by others is none of their business. We need to ride in hell-for-leather to catch the ones we want with no upright men mixed in.

"Ward, you stay on my right side but keep a little distance. Milt, you stay to Ward's right and fall back a bit. You fall back and keep to my left, Luke. Ward was up to the claim with Milt today. He'll tell me to go to the gallop as soon as we get close enough to be seen by their lookout. When you see us take off, come with us."

I said, "Pa, you need a bugle and I need a guidon."

We were all laughing while we spread out. When we were only about a half a mile from the cabin, I waved at Pa and we went into a gallop. We came tearing into that little valley at full charge. Peepeye pulled out in front with no effort at all, being the fastest horse with the lightest rider, and I didn't bother to hold him back. We rode along the edge of the water, avoiding the brushy hillsides and tearing across the claims men had downstream from ours. When we passed, eight or ten men dropped tools and straightened to watch us pass, all of them wearing startled expressions.

I turned to see Luke cross the stream to keep to the left as Pa had directed. The water was only about knee-deep, but Luke's mount threw spray high and wide. Then Pa crossed too, vanishing from sight for a moment or two in the spray that seemed to explode from under his horse, erupting into the air like sparkling fans of gems in the bright sunlight. I slowed to cross at a sedate pace, much to Peepeye's disgust, but I wasn't in enough of a hurry to risk breaking one of his legs on a rocky creek bottom. Slowing him down put us back about where Pa wanted us anyway.

Three men were running up the slope from the creek toward the cabin, but they didn't make it. Pa's shout brought them to a halt as I swung wide of him. I was almost to the front of the cabin when two men came rushing out with rifles. One of them raised his toward Milt, who had crossed the creek behind me and was closing in from my right. I snapped a shot and saw the rifle drop. The man grimaced and bent over, dropped to his knees and held his hands together over his stomach. The other rifleman dropped his weapon and raised his hands, looking up into Luke's gun barrel.

Luke towered in the saddle like the giant he was, holding his rifle like a pistol in one of his huge hands and flashing a big white grin through his beard. He roared, "Man was given intelligence, a divine gift you used just in time, little man."

The poor fellow shrank back against the cabin wall while Luke's big plow horse pranced around excitedly, but the empty eye of the gun barrel held rock steady while both rider and heavy animal twisted and danced before the woeful fellow's eyes.

The other man surged back to his feet, shaking both hands and making sucking noises between his teeth. He looked down at his hands and then glanced up at me. "God, that hurts. You do that on purpose?"

Shocked that the man seemed to be unwounded, I said, "I do everything on purpose."

He answered back, "Well, that was the damndest shot I ever saw. When your lead hit my rifle, it felt like you set my hands on fire. Anyhow, kid, thanks for not shootin' me, I guess. Damn, my hands hurt!"

It would've been a shame to tell him it was an accident. My snap shot evidently hit his rifle, which he'd lifted across his body to aim at Luke. He had the right to believe I made a fancy shot if it suited him.

I slid to the ground and jumped through the cabin door, dodging to the side. A quick glance told me that nobody was hiding inside. I walked back outside just as Pa rode up behind his three prisoners. None of them was armed.

Luke was having a great time. He gave a belly laugh when he dismounted and roared, "Strip! Get your clothes off. We'll have every speck of our gold back!"

One of the men said, "Like hell, I ain't strippin' for nobody. Nobody can make me do that."

Luke bellowed, "Build a fire, Ward! This sinning thief took up arms against righteous men. He's possessed by demons. Set up a stake and we'll cleanse him with fire! We'll burn out the devil's demons. Praise the Lord." Luke came out with the wildest cackle a man ever heard this side of hell and started dancing around like an enormous madman.

I rushed to the woodpile and started throwing sticks of firewood toward a cluster of small trees nearby. "Tie 'em to trees, Milt. I'll stack the wood around 'em," I yelled. "Let's burn 'em before the demons get loose and come after us."

Clothing flew every which way. I never saw men get naked with such frantic haste. One of them held out a pouch toward Pa, saying, "Here, take it. We ain't been here but two days. We didn't get much. This is all of it. I swear to God."

Luke pounced on the clothing as it dropped, powerful hands ripping off pockets instead of taking the time to turn them inside out. Pa watched the men without expression. Milt edged off to the side, his eyes roving. Nobody was ever going to creep up and take Milt by surprise.

Pa's voice was stern when he said, "You men get dressed. Get off this property and never come back."

One of the men, jerking trousers on, said, "We got stuff in the cabin."

"Leave it," Pa said flatly and glanced at Luke. "Take 'em to their horses. Get 'em moving. They don't need saddles. They don't need anything except to get moving."

"Wait a minute," one of the men said. "I got a claim right over yonder."

"The next time we see you, we'll hang you."

Without another word, Luke mounted and motioned with his rifle for the men to walk ahead of him. They started trotting up the slope, some of the slower ones still struggling into clothing.

When Pa said, "Ward, go tell the Thackerys to come on in," I gave him a pained look, pulled Jesse, and replaced the cartridge I'd fired. He never blinked, just said, "Never mind. Milt, you go get the Thackerys."

I said, "Pa, I'm going up the hill to look for the mine. I think it's a good idea to look around some anyhow." At his nod, I climbed on Peepeye and moved toward the overhanging ledge at the top of the ridge, quartering back and forth to inspect the land while moving up the slope.

As soon as I crested the ridge, I saw Luke sitting on his horse while he watched the five men ride off bareback. The ridge turned out not to be a ridge at all but an escarpment, dropping from a rolling, lush meadow that was hidden from below. This was the natural place for all the horses and mules we had to care for now. One of us would have to watch the stock constantly. We might be able to replace stolen horses, but mules were obviously hard to come by in this country. We'd seen no Indians, but that meant nothing. Any Indian brave worth his salt could smell poorly guarded stock from miles away. No need to invite trouble by being careless.

When Peepeye cantered over toward Luke, I clapped my hands and hollered, "Encore, encore. Wonderful act, Preacher Baynes."

Luke beamed, laugh lines deepening around his eyes. He gave me a little bow and a big grin but said nothing. He had enjoyed the act but was back to his old, silent self again. Some folks think big, quiet men are solemn or even slow-witted. Those that think so never knew Luke, the gentle giant, always laughing behind a still face, missing nothing, hiding a brain that snared and held ideas like a steel trap.

I said, "Let's find the mine."

Luke shrugged. "Waste of time. Let Joe show it to us. They'll be riding in any minute now with all those animals to be unloaded. There's work to be done."

Peepeye followed Luke's big horse through the trees and down the slope. We saw eight or ten men gathered in front of the cabin, and our string of horses and mules was just starting up from the creek.

"That must be men from the other claims," I said.

Luke nodded with a twinkle in his eyes. "I doubt they're just passing through."

I gave him a grin. "You got me, Luke. I get credit for the day's dumbest comment."

He nodded once more. "Yep. Again."

"Ouch. Hey, I'm already down. No fair stompin' me."

Luke slapped my shoulder. "Good to see you grinnin' again. Don't take yourself too seriously, Ward. Try to relax and let things take their course. That's the end of your big brother's lecture. Now let's pay attention and see what this crowd is up to."

A closer look showed that every man in the crowd was armed, and they didn't look happy. I pulled up and hissed at Luke, "Look out!"

We were only fifty yards or so away, but I didn't see Pa. I gave a wave to Milt, who was riding up the slope with the Thackerys, and saw him jump his horse away from them. He galloped a short way up the slope, and I saw his mount start into a sliding stop just before he vanished among the trees. When my attention came back to the Thackerys, both of their saddles were empty.

When we started scattering, the little crowd of men at the cabin ran inside, obviously running for cover.

Luke vanished somewhere off to my left while Peepeye lunged into a little gully and slid to a stop. I hit the ground and crawled to a cluster of rocks, slapping my hat off so it hung on my back by its rawhide chin loop. When I took a peek from around those rocks, nothing was moving except Luke's horse, which was trotting down the slope toward the other stock. The animal looked confused and awkward, like horses always do when they hold their heads to one side to keep from stepping on loose reins.

Suddenly Pa appeared, clumsy and off balance with his hands behind him. A man waved a gun at Pa and shoved him forward, then jerked him back, keeping him off balance. That fellow yelled, "We ain't fooling around! Come out with your hands up or I'm going to blow this man's head off! Hurry up! We ain't goin' to put up . . ."

That's as far as he got.

Milt's bullet struck him squarely, as I saw later, in the forehead, peeling him loose from Pa and slamming him against the wall of the cabin. By the time he bounced off the wall to fall on what was left of his face, Pa ducked around the corner of the cabin and was running a zigzag course up the slope toward me. I emptied Nadine at the only window on my side as fast as I could work her lever. Bark and splinters flew every which way from that cabin as Luke, Milt, Joe, and Kathleen blasted away like they owned stock in a munitions factory.

Pa vanished while I was busy shooting.

I yelled, "You all right, Pa?"

He answered, "Yeah," in a lower voice from close by, but I couldn't see him.

"You behind something? You hid?"

"Yeah, but my hands are tied, son."

I was cramming ammunition into Nadine as fast as I could while I moved to a new spot, trying to get closer to him.

"What's going on, Pa?"

"Bunch of idiots in this valley formed themselves a vigilance committee just yesterday. An absolutely perfect damned fool got himself elected their leader. He insisted we were claim jumpers. Ward, some of the men down there have good sense. They remembered me from the claims office and tried to talk that birdbrained imbecile into slowing down. He wouldn't listen. Then they saw you coming and either had to go along or shoot that silly bastard who was holding a gun on me. I bet they're ready to talk."

I took a quick look, and sure enough, just like Pa said, there was a piece of white cloth waving from the end of a rifle barrel poked through the window.

Pa shouted, sounding as angry as I ever heard him, "Come out of that cabin without guns, and we can talk. Otherwise, I'll cut my partner and my sons loose to kill every damned one of you. That's the deal. Take it or leave it."

The first three men walked out as soon as Pa stopped talking. They walked about twenty steps away from the front door, sat down, and struck matches to cigars. Then two more came out and joined the first ones. Pa didn't bother to wait for all of them to show. He stood up and asked, "Where are you?"

"Over here, Pa. Just walk toward my voice. I'm in a little gully. That's right, keep coming, walk straight ahead. Good. Come down in the gully, and I'll be a little way to your right."

I cut the rawhide from his wrists, and Pa said, cool as you please, "I'd like to borrow Nadine for a little while if you don't think she'd mind."

Keeping a straight face, I said, "She doesn't mind dancing with an older man once in a while."

I handed her to him and he said gently, "My, my, Nadine, such a hot barrel." He winked at me. "Talking so fast has made her feverish."

He pulled the cocking lever down a little to check for a round in the chamber.

I said, "She's all dressed up and her hair's combed."

He gave me his grin with the corners pulled down, snapped the lever shut, and said, "No offense intended."

NINE

PA TILTED HIS HEAD toward the dead man. "Drag that out of sight."

Four of the men picked up the body and carried it to the nearby grove of trees. Pa stood without speaking, his eyes on the men carrying the dead man until they came back to join the group. I stood beside him, watching the others. Luke walked down the slope to join us, looked inside the cabin, and strolled over to stand beside me.

When the four body carriers returned, Pa spoke again, "As soon as we finish talking, take that man off our property and bury him somewhere. Any of you men know where his family is?"

Two of the men nodded reluctantly.

"I suppose you'll be willing to notify them and send them his personal effects?" Pa asked. Both men nodded again, showing they had good sense. The tone of the question didn't invite a prudent man to refuse.

Pa went on, "We have a lady coming up the hill in a few minutes. Does anybody need to be reminded how to talk when a lady's present?" His glance went from man to man. Each shook his head.

Milt rode up cautiously, snapped his head in the downslope direction, and shot a questioning look at Pa. At Pa's nod, he waved. The Thackerys appeared, swung into their saddles, and started the string of pack animals moving toward us.

When one of the men spoke, Pa cut him off by saying sharply, "We'll wait for my partner to get here before we do any talking. I'm sure he'll want to hear."

Kathleen dismounted at the front door and jerked her store-bought broom off one of the pack animals. She walked into the cabin with broom in one hand and rifle in the other. Her father, rifle casually resting in the crook of his elbow, sauntered up to Pa and stood facing the group.

A clatter drew my attention to the packed ground in front of the cabin door. Kathleen was tossing out the weapons the men had left inside. Several of the men showed pained expressions as the weapons hit the dirt.

She stood framed in the doorway, eyes flashing, just long enough to say, "Unless your name is Baynes or Thackery, don't wear or carry a gun into this house again." She brushed her hands together as if she'd soiled them by handling the weapons and disappeared inside.

"The first thing we need to get settled," Pa said, "is who owns this claim."

Thackery pulled a leather folder from his coat and drew papers from it. "These documents prove that this claim and the one beside it belong to me and my daughter. There are four other claims which belong to the Baynes family."

Pa produced a similar folder.

Thackery went on, "I'm Joe Thackery. Darnell Baynes here and me are partners. Our family members have each filed a claim and thrown it into the partnership. I invite all of you to examine these papers right now. I also expect you men to return the courtesy. I expect to see your proof that you have a legal claim. Step up, one by one, and we'll have no more mistakes."

Not a man protested. Each pulled his own claim receipt and lined up to pass Thackery. None made a move to retrieve a weapon from the scattered pile in front of the cabin door.

A small, dark miner with a wide, waxed mustache said, "We was told you men was jumping this claim. We was told that the Baynes family led a gang of outlaws which robbed and killed all over Louisiana till they got run off by the law."

"Tell me who told you my family is part of a gang of outlaws," Pa said. "Anyone who says we ever took anything not rightly ours is a liar. There's been killings, that's true, but not because of us robbing anybody. Both white men and Indians have come at us. We defended ourselves. We got that right."

The small miner spoke again. "My name is Mack Thomas, Baynes. No telling how such tales get started. It was all over town. Before I left to come out here, I heard that one of your sons killed two men right there in Bannock a few days ago. Is that true?"

I said, "That was me. What you heard was true. Those men were kin to a man who bushwhacked Mr. Thackery and his daughter and wounded him twice. They said they planned to do the same to us, spoke in a slighting way about Miss Thackery, and then pulled iron on me."

Another man spoke. "I'm the one who's been talkin' 'bout that gunfight."

I recognized the man who had been wearing buckskins that day in front of the livery stable in Bannock. Wearing a cotton shirt and pants changed his appearance.

He went on, looking straight at me, "You ought to know, kid, that I been sayin' all along that those men brought the trouble to you. You outdrew and outshot them men fair and square. I also been saying that the marshal was right there and didn't have a thing to say to you. Trouble is, ever since the days of the Plummer Gang, miners been seein' outlaws behind every tree."

"I remember you speaking against that fellow who held a gun on me and tied me up," Pa said. "What's your name?"

"Mike Freere." Mike stepped forward and offered his hand.

Pa shook hands and said, "That man would be alive this minute if he'd listened to you. We don't want trouble, but we intend to keep what's ours."

Freere shrugged. "This here country is hell on damn fools. A man should keep that in mind before he pulls a gun. Just happens I've seen three of 'em fall in the last few days from pullin' a gun on the Baynes family."

Thackery, finished trading and inspecting papers, asked, "You men ready to talk? I'd like to hear about this vigilance committee. I suppose you men have already come up with some rules for keeping order around the diggings?"

"Yeah, we have," Freere answered. He turned to the others and said, "Let's help unload those pack animals, men." He pointed to the weapons lying in the dirt in front of the cabin and raised an eyebrow toward Pa.

When Pa nodded, Freere went on, "Pick up your weapons and be careful about it. We don't want to be burying nobody else. As soon as the animals are unloaded, since we're all here, we might as well get a grave dug and elect a new leader. Then we can explain our camp rules to these new folks."

We moved closer to the front of the cabin with the men when they went to retrieve their weapons. I was standing beside the door when Freere said quietly, "You willin' to take some advice, kid?"

"Name's Ward."

"Fine, Ward, no offense. Call me Mike." He stepped closer, shook hands, and continued in a lowered voice, "It's none of my business, but I've seen some of the good ones. You're the fastest with a handgun I've ever seen, but you wait too long, way too long. The Hartlows were fairly fast, but you got away with it with both of 'em. Maybe you knew the marshal was watching, so you were extra careful to leave no doubt about who drew first. In the future, was I you, I wouldn't give away such an edge, even fast as you are. I damn sure wouldn't."

His eyes shifted and I followed his glance. Kathleen stood in the doorway, holding an oversized, brand-new, steaming coffeepot. Mike Freere jerked off his hat and stepped aside. "Your pardon, ma'am. I guess you heard some man-talk there. Didn't see you. Sorry."

Kathleen ignored him. She looked straight at me for the first time in a couple of days. I had mighty near forgotten how pretty her eyes were, looking straight-on at a man. She said flatly, "The cups are on the table. Bring 'em out . . . kid." She stepped through the doorway and walked past us without waiting for a reply.

I turned from Freere's startled expression and went for the cups. Sometimes it's best for a man to do what he's told.

Turned out Freere was a talker, and from that day forward I was Kid Baynes. Some fellows get to pick the name they're called by. Not me, damn it. Kit Thackery and Mike Freere hung that on me intentionally. Mike thought it was funny, didn't see any harm in it. Kit thought it was funny too, but it was disputatious in her case, pure Virginia high-nose, cantankerous, ornery meanness.

TEN

OUR CLAIMS lay in a line, with the Thackerys' property in the middle. Pa's adjoined theirs on the upstream side, with mine the one beyond. Milt's and Luke's lay downstream. We decided to build our cabin on Pa's claim, as near to the Thackery place as we could, to be close in case of trouble. Only a hundred feet or so of lightly wooded ground separated the two buildings.

Pa and my brothers were out felling trees while I worked on the logs already dragged to the site. They left the notching, most of the trimming, and the fitting to me, since I had a knack for it. On the other hand, each of them could have three trees down to my two. Luke, the fastest, could actually down two to my one, and he never seemed to tire.

A Scot writer named Adam Smith called what we were doing "division of labor" in his book *Wealth of Nations,* only he talked about people dividing up the work in a pin factory to increase production, each worker doing what he did best. Smith wrote that book in 1776, but Pa said nothing in it was out-of-date, and it was one of the books we carried with us in our travels.

We had our cabin about half built when I looked up one morning to find Kit walking toward me. As soon as I felt sure she was headed my way, I leaned my axe against the front wall and shrugged into my shirt. By the time she drew near, I had my shirttail tucked in. The smell of coffee from the pot she carried beat her to me by twenty steps.

"You have cups over here?"

"Yes, ma'am." I grabbed two cups from the flat rocks near our campfire and placed them on the smooth, trimmed surface of the top log of the front wall, which only stood about waist high.

"Have to offer you a seat on the wall, ma'am, since we haven't put together any furniture yet."

"Are you willing to talk to me?"

"I've always been willing to talk to you, but somebody told me you didn't want to hear any more of it. Let me think back. Now who could that have been?" I rubbed my forehead with a finger and squinted as if trying to remember.

She looked at the cups and hesitated. "You want this bug with your coffee, or shall I dump him out?"

I grabbed my cup and flipped a tiny green beetle from it. She poured a little coffee into the cup, swished it around, and pitched it aside, smirking at me. "I guess bugs don't bother hermits."

"No, ma'am, I suppose not. Little fellow meant no harm, just snooping around to get to know his new neighbors. That's his nature. But I'm no hermit."

She perched on the wall and took a sip of her coffee. "Why don't you ever come to our cabin to eat with everyone else?"

I looked down at the cup in my hand for a moment to escape her direct gaze. She sure came right to the point. I answered her the same way I'd answered Pa. "Just a preference."

"You prefer not to eat with us?"

"I prefer not to go where I'm not welcome."

"Who said you weren't welcome?"

I said nothing, but I looked up from my cup and met her stare. The silence dragged while we studied each other. Finally, she looked away. "Maybe I did, not meaning to."

"No 'maybe.' No 'not meaning to.' I found your meaning clear and no doubt about it. You said I made you sick. I shall not be unkind enough, little lady, to ruin your meals."

"I didn't mean it like that. I meant the idea of you killing those two men like you did made me . . ."

"Sick?"

"It surprised me. You don't act like you could do such a thing. I didn't think you . . . I never knew anyone who . . ."

"I see. You never knew any killers before."

"You're twisting everything around."

"If I am, maybe we can get it untwisted if we talk about it. You wouldn't allow me to explain. You like your thinking done by somebody else over a breakfast table when I'm not even present."

"That's not fair."

"Then you tell me what really happened. All I got to go on is what you said. Was it different from what you said?"

"See how you twist things. Now you're trying to make me say I lied about something. I was shocked and confused. I didn't know what to think."

"For mighty near three days in the saddle on the way out here, you were so shocked and confused you couldn't talk to me? Not a word?"

Kit put her cup down beside her and glanced my way with a wry smile. "I felt stubborn. I wanted you to speak first."

"I was forbidden."

She tittered mockingly. "You take orders from a woman?"

"If I appreciate her feelings, or if I want her to be fond of me, or if she's paying my wages, or if . . ."

"All right, all right. You sound like Papa Joe. He hasn't been happy with me, been fussing at me ever since we got here."

"Well, we can't have that. I'll just run right over there and kill him."

"Oh, Ward, that isn't funny." She held her hand over her mouth, but I could tell from her eyes she was trying not to laugh. "Suppose I told him you said that."

"Joe knows he has nothing to fear from me because he knows I'm not afraid of him."

"Not afraid of him? What does that mean?"

"Why do you think I killed those men?"

"Because . . . I'm not sure. Papa Joe talked to that man, Freere. Freere told Papa Joe those men made threats, and, uh, said some things about me." Her face pinked up and she looked away again.

"Kit, those men scared me so bad I had to kill them or get all of us to ride clear out of the country. They scared me practically into the blind staggers."

She gave me a derisive glance, and her lip curled. "That's not the way Freere told it. He said you were practically yawning. He talked on and on to Papa Joe about how calm you were. Papa Joe just nodded and said, 'He'd do it like that. Yep, sounds just like him.' "

"Put yourself in my place. Imagine men shooting your pa and your brothers from ambush. Then they shoot Papa Joe. Then think about them being mean and nasty to the lady you're taken with. Does that make you feel scared? Made the bottom fall out of my stomach, I don't mind telling you."

Kit stared off into space for quite a while before she looked back at me. "You still taken with me? Did you say that?"

"No, ma'am, but I was taken with you at the time. That was before you wouldn't let me tell my side, before you listened to somebody else but wouldn't listen to me. Didn't seem fair. You got to be fair, Kit."

"I promise not to do that again."

"What? Be fair?"

She giggled. "No, don't be silly. I meant I won't tell you not to talk to me."

"Obliged. I'll hold you to that. It's important to me, Kit. I'd like to ask another promise if you don't mind."

She stiffened. "What?"

"Even if you're mad at me, don't refuse to talk to me and don't look through me like I'm not there. I'd be obliged."

"I promise, but I still feel sick at the idea of you shooting people."
She sat there staring at me with her jaw set.

"I try to avoid shooting people as much as I can."

"That's just another flippant remark, another bad joke."

"In this country, it's not a joking matter. I don't make a habit of
shooting at folks unless they come at me or my family. When they do
that, Kit, they may get me, but it won't be because my eyes are full of
tears about having to use a gun. I'm duty bound to defend myself and
my kin. Montana Territory is a long way from Virginia."

"I suppose I must tell the rest of it. If I don't, he'll probably tell you
himself."

"What?"

"I'm hatefully stubborn. Papa Joe made me come talk to you. He
was very stern, said if I didn't he was going to come over here and eat
with you from now on, said he was tired of watching me pout."

"Then I'm obliged to him. I'd be pleased to thank him if you don't
mind."

"I wish you wouldn't. I think he'd be embarrassed, but you must do
what you think is right. Papa Joe says you will anyway, and I might as
well resign myself to it." Her grin was just a bit sour.

We sat for a while without speaking. I was feeling more and more
awkward. Seemed to be a time I should be saying something, but
nothing came to mind. Somehow I feared anything I'd say would be
wrong and ruin everything. Finally, I picked up the pot and put it on
the coals to reheat the coffee.

When I turned back to her, she showed me a devilish grin. "Might
as well keep the coffee hot. I'm going to sit for a while yet and listen to
you talk."

"Oh?"

"Papa Joe said he wouldn't worry as long as I was with you. Since I
had to crawl all the way over here, I might as well stay a while."

"Crawl? Aw, I bet he didn't say that. On a mission of mercy?"

"What mission of mercy?"

"Well, you have magic ways, you see. You had me under a spell so I
couldn't say a word to you. It was a mercy to release me. That didn't
take crawling, just a mite of sweetness."

She sat smiling at me for so long I began to feel uneasy. My hands
started growing and turning into clumps of bananas. She laughed and
said, "No wonder it hurts you to be told to keep still. You can talk in

circles and make everything into what you want it to be. Another two minutes and you'll have me believing I really came over here on a mission of mercy. I like that. It lets me forget how bad I felt before I came. I wanted to come, but I was embarrassed. I was afraid you'd snub me."

"I sure feel better, Kit. The sun came back out for me."

Kit hit me with the full power of her blue eyes again. She stared at me for the longest time without blinking before she spoke quietly. "That's the paradox about you. You seem so gentle, so forgiving, almost weak. Your brothers treat you like you're half-grown, poking fun and teasing you. But I remember an odd thing, or at least it seemed odd at the time. I recall when you met Papa Joe and spoke up, bold as brass, about courting me. Your pa stepped back when he thought there might be trouble, didn't he? He stepped back to let you handle it."

I shrugged, wondering where this was headed. "Seemed to me I noticed your rifle moving around. Wandering rifle barrels make Pa jumpy. He always hates it when he has to shoot a woman. Makes him gloomy for a couple of days."

"You are trying my patience, sir," she snapped, pointing an accusing finger at me and making a tight mouth like a strict, if undersized, schoolmarm. "I'm going to have to do something about your awful sense of humor. Can't you stay serious for even one minute?"

I looked down and put on my sad face. "I try, but I don't have a watch, ma'am."

That drew a suspicion of a grin to her lips, but she sat there making her face stern, obviously waiting for an apology, so I said, "Pardon me. I'll be serious as a drunk Indian if you want me to."

"Are Indians serious when they're drunk?"

"Yes, ma'am, they can get terrible serious. One time we saw a drunk Indian bite his wife's nose off. He suspicioned she'd been looking calf-eyed at another brave. If you want me to get serious, I don't figure to do a half-hearted job."

I leaned forward and pretended to inspect her nose. There was no way to avoid snickering when she covered it with her hand. She jerked her hand away real quick and gave me a disgusted look.

"As I was about to say before you changed the subject to lecture me on drunk Indians," she said with a sharp edge in her voice, "I've seen other things that were more important than I realized. Another sign I hardly noticed at the time was when you stopped those men who ambushed Papa Joe and me. Your pa sent your brothers on errands, but he kept you on guard until he was sure the trouble had passed."

Shaking my head, I said, "Nothing to it. Just happened that way. Maybe Pa didn't want to worry about me wandering around and getting lost, so he made me hold still."

With her voice turned thoughtful, she went on as if speaking to herself as much as to me, "Then, when your pa broke away from that man who was holding him, the one Milt shot, he ran straight toward you as soon as he got loose. He couldn't have had time to think about it. Your pa just ran toward the best help he could find . . . you."

She leaned toward me with her eyes narrowed, her expression dead serious. "Everyone knew about you but me. Papa Joe knew almost the minute he saw you. You're the toughest one from a hard family, aren't you, Ward?"

I started to laugh, but her expression told me she wouldn't appreciate it. She never moved, just sat there eyeing me. Holding my breath to keep from chuckling, I walked slowly over to the coffeepot and loafed back to fill our cups.

"Kit, did you ever take a close look at my brothers?" I stopped to take a couple of quick breaths before going on.

"Luke can pick me up, turn me upside down, and stick my head in a bucket anytime the notion strikes him. Last time Milt and I had a scuffle, he punched me up so bad nobody could recognize me for a week. He's got arms like an ape, about a mile long. Truth to tell, I'd rather fight Luke. He just lays me down and sits on me, squeezes all the air out of me. Luke weighs two tons, and it's terrible to be crushed nearly to death, but at least he doesn't bust me up like Milt does."

She asked, "When did you have your last fight with either of your brothers?"

"Oh, me, a long time ago. We haven't had a dustup since way before we left Louisiana, thank goodness. My mama may have reared a runt, but I'm not an idiot."

For some reason, my answer started her head bobbing up and down like I'd said something important. She asked with a trace of a smile, "You sure?"

"Aw, Kit . . ."

"Seems to me you're still looking at your brothers through the eyes of a fourteen-year-old. They were full-grown men back then and you were still a boy."

I nodded solemnly and said, "You may be right. I'll pick a fight with both of 'em next time we're in town. Might be wise to have a doctor close by when I put your idea to the test. My conscience would hurt me if my brothers had to lie around without somebody to set their broken bones, stop the bleeding, stitch up the cuts, and . . ."

She came off the wall as slick and smooth as a mountain cat and started back to her cabin. Without even a glance at me as she walked away, she said, "Got to fix lunch. You coming to eat?"

"Be honored, ma'am."

"Bring the coffeepot with you."

"Yes, ma'am."

I watched her all the way out of sight through her cabin door before I moved. Many's the time I've seen a man hurt himself when he's distracted, falling over a sharp axe or stepping in the middle of a bed of hot coals.

ELEVEN

PA ALWAYS BELIEVED in observing the Sabbath, so the Baynes brothers came to it by habit from our earliest memory. However, we observed the day of rest in a different way from most folks. We spent our time, after the Bible reading, doing restful and interesting projects some people look upon as work. Mama, I remember, took pleasure from sewing, loved to create pretty things with her needle, and found no work in the doing of it.

Nothing in the world grinds on a Baynes worse than forced idleness. Doing nothing isn't restful to our kind of people. Doing things that are worthwhile but give pleasure at the same time, now that's restful.

Back home in Louisiana, one of our neighbors complained to Pa one time about me "training" my horse on Sunday. I didn't hear the complaint until Pa told me about it later, but I did ride up in time to hear Pa's response to it. He said, "Ward has no toys but that horse and his guns. You want me to tell the boy to play with his guns on Sundays?"

Anyway, I liked to spend a few hours up on the high meadow above the mine playing with Peepeye. Bigger than most of his kind, standing at sixteen hands, Peepeye was by an Arabian stallion from Our Fair Winds, Pa's best mare. That Morgan mare was Pa's prettiest and proudest possession at the time. Actually, Peepeye's real name, Arabian Fair Winds, I never spoke where he could hear, not wanting to encourage him to take on airs. He was a bay, bright as a polished copper penny, with mane, tail, and legs turned dark.

We played all kinds of games. I'd sneak around the edge of the pasture until he caught sight of me. Then I'd run like the devil and he'd chase me, going into a big act, snorting, squealing, and plunging. Scared the fire out of people when they saw it for the first time. Everybody said he looked like a killer horse running me down.

When he'd decide to catch me, he'd canter past real close so I could grab him around the neck and swing one heel up on his back. I'd ride along hanging beside him, hollering, "Pow, pow, pow," while I pretended to shoot under his neck at imaginary enemies. Then I'd drop both feet to the ground, use our speed to bounce me to his back, slide across, and hang from the off side, shooting at enemies from the new position. Sounds crazy, but it seemed as much fun for Peepeye as for me. He galloped smooth as a rocking chair, so it wasn't much of a trick for me to stay on.

Then, often as not, I'd swing up and ride bareback for a while, draping myself all over him in different ways, not even needing a hackamore to guide him. He'd whoa and back on command and change direction when I simply put a little signal to him with my knees. He was a "thin-skinned" horse, meaning that he had a thin and tender hide, quick to feel and respond to his rider's signals. In later times, that expression came to be used about people who were sensitive, easy to hurt or anger.

I never needed a rope to catch Peepeye. He'd come if I called his name or whistled like a quail in the daytime or even gave an owl hoot at night. Another thing, I never owned a set of spurs in my life. I carried a whip on my saddle from the time I was six, and I used it for all manner of things, but never to hit a horse.

This Sunday I didn't know anyone was watching while I sneaked along the edge of the woods till Peepeye caught sight of me. I busted loose, running so fast the wind whistled in my ears, hearing the thumps and squeals as Peepeye tore up the pasture behind me. For a second, I thought I heard other screams, but I paid no attention.

We went through some of our little routines before settling down to a nice smooth lope and swinging back toward the mine. After we came about, I saw a little cluster of people at the edge of the meadow behind the Thackery cabin, so I headed Peepeye in that direction, letting him put on a burst of speed, just to show off a little bit.

Mike Freere, Kit, and Milt stood watching while Peepeye came to a stop. I slid off his back to stand leaning against him.

Kit said breathlessly, "Ward, you scare sane people to death. What in the world were you doing?"

Milt butted in with a falsetto voice, "Yes, yes, you just scared us all to death, simply to day-yuth."

"Oh, hush, Milt!" Kit stamped her foot and glared at him. "Don't you dare mock me."

Darting behind a little tree about an inch wide, Milt crouched and peeked around the skinny trunk as if he was hidden. He yelled in a terrified voice, "Don't let her find me, Ward. She's mad at me again. She'll hurt me. Tell me when she goes away."

She looked up at me, held her hand to her forehead as if feeling for fever, and said, "For heaven's sake, Ward. Mr. Freere drew his pistol. Milt had to stop him. He almost shot at Peepeye to save you. What were you doing? It looked like Peepeye went wild and tried to stomp you to death. Then you jumped up and rode off at breakneck speed without a saddle. If you fell going that fast, you could have been killed."

"Make her go away, Ward," Milt hollered in his terror stricken voice.

"Oh, hush!" Kit screamed at him. I noticed her hands were clasped together so tightly they were turning white, and her face seemed pale. She turned to Mike and said harshly, "I think both of them are insane, both of them."

"Come on out," I said to Milt, beckoning with my head. "I won't let her get you."

"I don't know. She's awful fast. You better hold her till I can get away, Ward."

"Come on, Milt," I said, giving Peepeye a pat on the shoulder as I stepped forward. "Quit teasing her. I think she's about to get really and truly mad."

"I am indeed, Milton Baynes. You come back over here and pretend you have good sense," Kit snapped.

Milt crept around the little tree and tiptoed toward us, looking like he was ready to run at the slightest move from Kit.

Freere said, "I can see why Miss Thackery got upset. Scared me too. Never saw such wild riding, and that horse covered ground fast as a flash of lightning. If he'd of stumbled, you'd have a broke neck right now. You ever race that animal?"

I nodded. "Sure, mighty near everyplace between here and Mexico City, and he's never been beat. He even walks faster'n other horses, don't you, Peepeye?" I turned toward him as I asked the question, so that I could hide the signal with my body. He nodded with huge up-and-down swings of his head.

Kit clapped her hands and cried, "Oh, look. How'd you get him to do that?" Her color was coming back.

"I asked him a question," I answered with a straight face. "He's got good manners. He wouldn't just stand there and ignore me."

She turned to Mike and spoke in a voice gone quiet and calm, "Mr. Freere, may I borrow your pistol? I've decided to shoot half the Baynes family."

Mike laughed and said, "Don't blame you much, ma'am. Little show like we just seen's enough to give a person heart flutters. Did you mean it, Baynes? Is that horse a real racer?"

"Never been beat," I said again. "Nearly every town from here to Mexico City has its favorite horse or two or three. Amazing how folks like to gather up their money and contribute to the Baynes Traveling Fund, just to see Peepeye outrun the local plow horses."

I began running my hands down Peepeye's legs, feeling for excess heat which might mean injury, watching him for any reaction if I touched a sore spot, and lifting each hoof for a careful inspection. He never passed a day in his life without me doing this at least once. I liked to check him right after a run and again after he cooled.

"He does love to be petted, doesn't he?" Kit asked. "Look at him. If he were a kitten, he'd be purring."

"They have races in Bannock every month, you know that?" Mike asked. "Hundred dollar entry fee, winner take all, and devil take the hindmost. No trouble for a bettin' man to find takers neither, none at all. The races is all on the first Saturday of the month when the miners have full pockets. They may run three or four races if there's enough entries."

"Didn't see a racetrack," I said.

"Naw, they don't have one of them round ones. They just got a measured half-mile. Some races is for just a half-mile, running in a straight line from pole to pole. Other times, the horses round the pole and come back to make it a mile run. Folks come from all around. Ever'body has a good time."

Milt spoke with contempt around the stem of grass he'd been nibbling. "Most of what I've seen in Montana Territory is scrub stock, mustangs, ten-dollar horses under forty-dollar saddles. Since we left Louisiana, I don't think I've seen more than three or four men who have any idea how to look after a horse."

He took the sprig from his mouth and threw it away with a sharp, angry swing. "They ride them hard and mean till they're ruined, then catch another mustang or buy one cheap, mistreat it something awful to break it, and start the whole thing over again."

I dropped a hoof and started on another leg. "Maybe they learned that from the Indians. You've heard about why the U.S. Cavalry can't catch the Apaches, haven't you, Mike?"

"Naw, why not?" Mike stepped forward to pat Peepeye on the shoulder, standing by his head. I noticed he had enough horse sense to stand beside rather than in front of my horse. A man directly in front of a horse is subject to getting knocked around if something startles the animal into lunging forward.

My back was to everyone while I bent to check Peepeye's off rear hoof. "They have a better method than the Cavalry, the Apache method of riding. It's a tribal secret. You mean you never heard about that?" I glanced over my shoulder at him.

Mike's dark face was lively with interest. "You ain't funning me are you, Kid?"

"No, no, gospel truth. Hey, Peepeye." When my horse swung his head to look at me, I said, "I'm going to walk behind you to check that other hind leg. You wouldn't kick at me, would you?" I gave him the signal covered by his body so Kit couldn't see. Peepeye swung his head back and forth. Mike ducked just in time, but the sleek, swinging head knocked his hat to the ground as I stepped around behind Peepeye.

Kit asked, "How do you get him to do that?"

"Smart horse. Most all Louisiana horses and women are smart like that. Good-natured too."

Kit answered, "Ha, ha, big funny."

Milt spoke sincerely, "That's true, ma'am. That's no joke."

"You're no help," Kit said sharply. "Just another case of one brother telling a lie and the other swearing it's the truth. You have my permission to keep quiet, Milton Baynes."

I went on, "Anyhow, Mike, we found out the secret when Milt was married to an Apache woman."

Peepeye shifted his weight and waited for me to lift the hoof. I glanced back in time to see Kit direct a surprised look at Milt. She asked, "Really, were you married to an Apache woman, Milt?"

When Milt smirked and lifted four fingers, Kit's mouth went into a straight line, and she swung around to give me a murderous glance.

I ducked my head real quick to look at the last hoof. "Anyway, Mike, the American soldier is taught that his horse is government property to be carefully looked after. The Apache has a different notion about stock. When chased, he rides his horse to death, tortures it till it gets back on its feet, and rides it another ten miles. When the horse finally falls down dead plus ten miles, the Apache squats beside it and eats it raw. Then he just runs off. You know they can run as good as a horse anyhow. That's the Apache method of riding."

I dropped Peepeye's hoof and straightened to find Mike grinning at Kit while she shook her head in disgust.

"Mr. Freere, anytime Ward mentions Indians, anytime at all, he's going to tell some kind of windy story. I guess he's made up a hundred infantile falsehoods. No telling how much time his idle mind takes to invent such poppycock." Kit turned and started toward her cabin.

"Oh!" She stopped and spoke over her shoulder, "I forgot what I came up here for because you scared me to death riding around like a madman. I have some little things to put in the oven, and I'm going to brew tea. You're invited in an hour, and don't come in the house smelling like horse."

Milt swept off his hat and said, "Be honored, ma'am."

"Not you. She's talking to me," I said quickly.

He slumped and stood dragging the toe of his moccasin in the dirt.

"You may come, Milt, and you're also invited, Mr. Freere," she said sweetly.

"Milt's got a headache," I said, giving him a hard look.

"And three's a crowd," Mike said. He caught on quick, thank goodness. "Another time for me, ma'am, but thanks."

Milt said, "I got no headache."

"You will in just a minute," I said. "I'm going to shoot you right between the eyes."

Smirking, he said, "I am feeling a little peaked. I better go lie down. You might get Ward to bring me a sample when you send him home, ma'am. You wouldn't forget a sick man, would you?"

Kit looked at me and said, "One hour then, and don't make excuses because you don't have a watch. Be late and I'll pull in the latchstring." She walked off without waiting for my response.

I made one anyway. "I'll count the seconds, ma'am. One, two, three, four . . ." I kept counting till she walked out of earshot.

Milt grinned at Mike Freere and said, "You flung a craving on Ward, my friend. He purely loves to race that pet horse of his. Start saving your money, borrow all you can, and keep quiet. I think you may make yourself a big profit betting on a horse race along about the first Saturday of next month."

"Mike, betting on Peepeye is like having a license to steal," I said. "Milt, we need to get Pa to start looking for somebody to guard the mine for a few days. I think the Baynes and Thackery crowd need to spend a few days in town."

Milt nodded. "We'll figure something out. Meanwhile, you better get busy. You really do smell like a horse. Seems to me your lady told you to go jump in the creek."

TWELVE

Luke found the nugget the very next evening. Pa, Milt, and Joe had already quit, had left the mine to wash up for supper. Luke, as usual, fresh and untired after a day swinging a pick, stayed behind a few minutes to hit an extra lick or two. I ran the stock down the slope from the meadow into the makeshift corral near the cabin for the night, washed up, and headed for the Thackery cabin.

I should have known Luke had something up his sleeve when he came walking up last, because he most always arrived early for meals. He could eat faster than anyone else I ever saw and still use proper table manners. Considering that he ate about as much as three ordinary men, he had to put it away fast, else he'd spend most of every day at the table. Of course, Luke spent his time at meals eating instead of talking, so he had an advantage.

Unless rain changed the routine, we ate outdoors beside the Thackery cabin, off a long split-log table with benches on each side. Kit learned quickly to put out the evening meal while there was still plenty of light. Milt simply wouldn't eat exposed in a circle of lantern light at an outside table. Without comment, he'd just pick up his plate and move into the shadows. Kit tried to tease Milt about that habit only once. Joe Thackery gave her a straight look and shook his head. She stopped her teasing in mid-sentence and had meals ready in daylight from then on.

We stood around talking the way men do while waiting for grub to be served. The table was set in the pretty way Kit always laid things out, clean and neat, everything ready except for the hot food and the plates. Without a word, Luke walked up, put the nugget in the center of the white tablecloth, and stepped away.

Most people think of gold nuggets being little and round, like a ball for an old-fashioned pistol or smaller. This one appeared more like a rough, splintered chunk of volcanic rock, except for the color.

Conversation stopped. Nobody asked what it was. To see it was to know. The silence brought Kit to the door of the cabin, then out to join us when she saw the nugget.

Joe picked it up, hefted it, and handed it to Pa. Pa did the same before handing it to Milt.

Milt asked quietly, "Fifteen or twenty pounds?" before passing it to me.

Pa shrugged, and Joe answered, "I'd guess about the same. Never saw anything like that before. I heard about nuggets that size and bigger, but I never really believed it."

I handed the nugget to Kit, and she replaced it carefully on the table.

Joe said quietly, "That chunk is worth more than an ordinary hard-working man can earn in years. No telling how long it would take to save that much money. Pretty nice day's work, even for a man strong as you, Luke."

Luke put his hand to his stomach and directed a pained look at Kit. She laughed and said, "You can help me bring everything outside if you're so hungry, poor thing."

With the quickness which always seemed to astonish those who weren't accustomed to speed from a man so large, Luke vanished through the door of the cabin. Kit walked after him, smiling and shaking her head. Glancing at Pa, she asked, "Aren't any of your sons ever going to grow up?"

Pa, without cracking a smile, answered, "Heaven help me if that one grows any more."

"Where do you want this while we eat?" I asked, lifting the nugget from Kit's tablecloth.

"Just put it out of the way somewhere for now," Pa said.

I pitched it to the side.

"Hey, Ward! Don't do that." Joe threw up his hands in exasperation. "That's no way to treat a fortune in gold. Let's put it inside the cabin. We don't want it to grow legs and walk away."

I shrugged and glanced at Luke walking out of the cabin with a stack of plates. "We could leave it on the table as a tip for that cute waitress."

Luke started mincing along, swinging his hips, looking like a trained bear trying to imitate a woman's walk.

Kit, walking behind him with a venison roast, spoke quickly, "Don't you dare drop my plates, Luke Baynes."

Milt said, "Ward, what got you interested in a girl with such a sharp tongue? Besides, she seems kind of smallish to me. Seems to me a little guy like you would have gone for a nice big girl."

I picked up the nugget and headed for the cabin, but I moved slowly so I could watch Kit's reaction. "Aw, I don't know. She's got good teeth, and she's got nice big hands and feet to grow to. She'll probably fill out some after I put her to plowing."

Kit put the roast down for carving in front of her father's place at the table, put her hands on her hips, and turned to face my retreating grin. "Little man, big talk."

I flinched in fake pain and changed my walk to a limp to indicate she'd scored. "Beats being a big man and being all talk," I shot back, just so she wouldn't think she'd spiked all my guns.

"Don't go in the cabin, Ward. She'll have you trapped," Milt cried in mock alarm when she started after me.

Inside the cabin, she said, "Plowing, huh, that's what you plan for me?"

I dropped the nugget beside the fireplace, grabbed a pot of hot stew, and paused to grin at her. She was rescuing bread she'd put on top of the coals to warm in a big iron skillet. The display of the nugget had distracted her, and the bread had overbrowned on the bottom.

"Naw, I was just joking, Kit. I figure you'll be too busy burning my food."

She dropped the bread in a basket and covered it with a clean cloth, every move quick and graceful. *"Touché."* She copied my flinch and imitated my limp as she headed outside again. "Bring the stew *tout de suite.*"

"Oui, tout ensemble," I answered, blinking, as we came out the door. Kit had never mentioned knowing a word of French.

"What'd that mean?" Thackery asked, looking at me with his eyebrows raised.

"All together, Papa Joe, all together."

"My, my," he said mildly, with one of his rare smiles. "Maybe I need to send you two into the cabin alone for fifteen seconds more often if it makes things so peaceful afterward."

I returned his smile. "Just takes a couple of licks with one of her big wooden spoons, Papa Joe, and she goes reasonable. Works every time."

He nodded solemnly, "So that's how it's done. I'll remember that."

Kit said, "Don't listen to him, Papa Joe. He can't pass a hornet's nest without poking at it or say a single word without making it into some kind of a fib."

"Good liars are scarce." I shoved Milt aside when he went through his habitual pretense of trying to sit in my place beside Kit. He staggered around to the other side of the table and collapsed.

"Milton Baynes, get up and sit at the table like a big boy. I'm never again going to fall for one of your dying-from-hunger acts." She ignored him when he rose, wearing a twisted, tearful expression, and sat down across from her.

I waited till we were about halfway through the meal before saying, "Pa, Mike Freere mentioned that they have some good horse races in Bannock the first Saturday of each month."

Pa raised his eyebrows to show interest.

"I figured we could time our gold shipment so we could be in town to watch."

"Watch?" His brows went a notch higher.

"Yes, sir. I'd like to know what kind of competition they have around here before running Peepeye. Then, next month I thought I might make a few bets. By then, if they have spoilers, I should know who they are."

Pa shook his head. "Running for prize money is honest competition, but you know I don't approve of betting."

"Pardon me, I hate to butt in, but what are spoilers?" Joe asked, directing the question at me.

"Western races aren't like the ones you're probably used to in Virginia, Joe, or like we had in Louisiana. Racing isn't a sport limited to gentlemen out here. I've ridden Peepeye in races where about the only thing riders couldn't get away with was shooting each other. A spoiler is an entry whose only purpose is to hinder others to make sure a particular rider wins. They can be mean as snakes, swerving to cause collisions, trying to quirt a horse across the eyes, or even trying to knock a rider off his mount."

"Kit told me you said Peepeye had never been bested." Joe didn't put it like a question, but I knew that was how he meant it.

"Yes, sir. She caught me in an unguarded moment, and I told the truth before I had time to think." Ignoring Kit's grin, I continued, "Mike Freere's the only man around here who knows about Peepeye, unless some traveling man happens to remember him from down south. Milt told Mike to keep quiet, and I think he will. He's a betting man and wouldn't want to mess up a good thing."

Joe nodded. "You plan to limit yourself to watching? Seems to me there'll be different horses nearly every month anyway."

"That's probably true. Still, I can see what kind of time the best ones run, and I can take Peepeye over the course. That's a smart horse, Joe. If he knows where he's going and how far, he pretty much runs the race on his own. Another thing, if it's a rocky track like some I've seen, the deal is off. He's too valuable to take that kind of risk."

"Sounds like you're trying to make a sure thing out of a horse race." Joe sounded interested.

"Yes, sir, as much a sure thing as a horse race can ever be. I also like to get a good look at the riders. Not just to find spoilers, but to see how many real jockeys are in the crowd. I weigh about 140 pounds. If

I'm up against a true jockey who saddles up at about 110, Peepeye has a big disadvantage. They don't usually weigh riders out here, but we can spot a real jockey a mile away through a dust storm."

"On the other hand," Milt said, "most of these horses race under a big old Western saddle which may weigh forty pounds. Even more important than that, we think the Western work saddle puts the rider's weight too far back on the horse for speed and good balance. Ward has a special racing saddle we had custom-made for Peepeye by an English craftsman in New Orleans." Milt grinned. "It's about this big." He spread one hand on the table.

I leaned forward to meet Joe's eyes. "Winning races means taking every advantage you can get away with. I'll need to put Peepeye's racing shoes on him and give him a couple of days to get used to them."

Joe leaned his elbows on the table and asked, "Racing shoes? Are you joking again?"

I shook my head emphatically. "There's nothing funny about taking care of a racehorse, Joe. Racing plates are lighter than work shoes, thinner, made of steel instead of iron, and they have lugs on them to keep the horse from slipping, especially on a grass track."

"And I suppose you carry these around with that fancy saddle?" Joe was beginning to smile.

I answered him with a nod and went on. "You've probably noticed me grain feeding Peepeye, even though the pasturage out here is good. I can buy more when I'm in town and maybe some hay if the quality is good enough. When I'm getting him ready, I watch everything Peepeye eats for at least a month ahead if I can. I'll also train him on a course as much like the one in town as I can lay out. I've already started building a shed. I don't like to see him standing in the rain if I can help it."

I straightened and took a deep breath. "Training racehorses is a serious business, Joe."

"And betting on horse races is gambling," Pa said flatly.

"Then I guess you reared a gambler, Pa." My voice could be just as flat as his.

"Two." Milt added his vote in the same tone.

Pa glanced at Luke and received a head shake and a sad expression. Luke sided with Pa, being against gambling just as much, but he didn't look happy about it.

"Just what do you intend to gamble with?" Pa asked.

"I figure to use my portion from the Baynes' share of the gold we've dug so far."

Milt nodded agreement when Pa's glance went to him.

"Planning to bet it all, boys?" Pa's voice always dropped when he was holding his temper.

This time Milt spoke first. "We haven't talked about that, Pa. How could we? We never had anything to bet before, and we don't know how much we've got coming now. Besides, just because a man might be interested in a bet or two doesn't mean he wants to risk everything he has."

Pa answered so softly we could barely hear him. "That's the way gambling men start out talking. Seems to me, sooner or later, they forget to hold back anything . . . sooner or later."

THIRTEEN

OUR SIX CLAIMS were now surrounded by fifty-seven others, all placer mines, but most of them were hardly paying enough to justify the work needed to bring out the gold. Joe Thackery's concern about the ledge of jewelry rock playing out on his claim was beginning to look like a sad prophecy. The vein of brittle quartz, heavily laced with ribbons and wires of pure gold, grew narrower and thinner by the inch as we dug into it.

We put in so much time and labor breaking solid rock to reach the diminishing vein Joe suggested we hire a powder man. Pa agreed, but nothing had been done about that yet.

Meanwhile, no others had found anything similar to Joe's ledge, only discovering meager patches of gold dust and nuggets by digging through the thin topsoil down to bedrock. If there existed a true mother lode, nobody found it. We located nothing interesting on the Baynes' claims or on Kit's. Our efforts other than on Joe's claim weren't a complete waste of time, but the small pockets we found didn't amount to much.

June was wearing thin. I spent my days working with Peepeye and guarding our other animals. Milt used up most of his time hunting to keep us in fresh meat. He sold some of the meat to other miners at a price high enough to stop an honest man's heart, but the men paid gladly. In fact, arguments started, and the miners voted for Milt to keep a list so they could buy his meat in a fair rotation. Otherwise, bidding contests flared up and hard feelings resulted.

Joe and Pa came out to the pasture one day to watch me work with Peepeye. Nobody can tell another man exactly how to train his horse, and there's a good reason for that. Horses aren't alike. First and foremost, a man has to listen to his horse. Horses can talk just fine if a man cares enough to pay proper attention.

But then, he has to know how much to believe of what the horse tells him. Some horses lie just like people. Some are more lazy, more inclined to sulk, more likely to get mad, more upset by a change in their routine, more easily frightened. Others just don't give a damn.

I never knew a horse I'd call smart, but most were willing to do most anything if a man took the time and used the patience to show the way. Most men, it seemed to me, were too quick to punish if the horse didn't do like they wanted right away. That kind of a man ended up complaining about nervous, sometimes mean horses. That same sort of man never gave a thought to rewarding a horse who did good work. I'd be nervous and mean if I was under the saddle of such a man.

Peepeye liked to warm up by lollygagging along beside me while I trotted a couple of miles. He'd follow along like a big dog, just having fun, and I didn't even need to put him on a lead, although I'd do it once in a while if I needed to make him get serious and quit fooling around.

I'd throw on his saddle after we finished that little game, and we'd keep moving around slow for another half hour, mostly at a trot. Neither of us liked the trot much. Peepeye was a fast walker, our normal trail speed, but we both liked to vary from a walk to a slow canter and back again if we were in a hurry with a long way to go. Besides, I'd stand in the stirrups almost the whole time he was at a trot, which can get tiresome. Peepeye knew when I put him to a trot we were either getting ready to race or to have a serious workout.

I was saddling Peepeye, tending to my own business, when I heard Joe ask Pa, "Why does Ward do all that running? Seems to me he could warm up the horse while sitting in the saddle like everybody else."

Pa answered, "You're right. He does it that way sometimes, but he likes to run too." I could hear amusement in his voice when he went on, "Ward thinks his horse gets bored if he does the same thing the same way every time. Another thing, Ward's running off weight. He can run off ten pounds in a month, sometimes more. He'll stop drinking water and he'll stop eating the night before a race. By the next afternoon, when he hits the saddle, he'll have dropped another six or seven pounds. Sometimes he gets down to one-twenty."

Joe asked, "Doesn't that make him weak?"

"Nope, not him. But it makes him mean as a snake with sore feet. He goes inside himself, stops talking, sleeps with his horse. It's best to walk around him before a race, Joe, and the horse too. We stay close, but even his brothers don't talk to him. Don't even try to wish him luck. He'll either ignore you or just give you a snotty look and turn away. Peepeye acts even worse. Gentlest animal you'd ever want to see, ordinarily. But before a race that fool horse will bite and kick and nearly go plumb wild if anybody but Ward comes near him."

I could feel my ears warming up. Both of them knew damned good and well I could hear every word. Pa was having fun teasing me again, making me feel like a pinhead. True enough, I liked to be left alone when I was getting ready to do something important. Some people like company to chatter at them in times like that. Not me.

Joe sounded surprised when he asked, "Does racing scare him?"

Pa chuckled. "Ward? Scared? No, he's just a prima donna, and his fool horse copies him."

The stirrups for the racing saddle were beyond my reach. I was backing off to get a running jump, had already clapped my hands to get Peepeye to look at me so he wouldn't be caught by surprise, when Pa called, "Wait. I'll give you a boost."

He walked over, cupped his hands for my boot, and hoisted me into the saddle. I was ready for him, but he didn't try one of his favorite jokes he pulled when feeling frisky. Pa dearly loved to hoist me clear over the horse. He and my brothers never failed to enjoy a real knee-slapping laugh when I bellyflopped to the ground on the off side like a dead duck.

We trotted back and forth till I was sure Peepeye was moving nice and loose, ready to run hard with almost no chance of injuring himself.

Now all play stopped. Peepeye, at seven, was a mature stallion in his prime. He'd never be faster or stronger. Probably, barring injury, this and the next one or two years would be the peak time of his life. Furthermore, nothing bothered him, a benefit that comes from experience. Straight, round, or oval tracks, running on sand, clay, or grass, long or short runs—nothing was new to him. He'd started races from behind rising tapes, at signals from flags, and at the firing of a gun. Mike Freere said they used a gun in town, so that's how we practiced.

Pa said, "When you're ready, I'll start you."

Peepeye went to the post I'd set in the ground for a starting line. No dancing or nervous jerking around. I could feel the calm purpose radiate from him, a trained, experienced horse setting himself in preparation for his work. Power came throbbing into me through my hands and legs. A child on his first ride would have felt the signals coming through the light racing saddle; I could feel the massing of muscle as he drew his hocks up under himself, bunching like a huge spring for the starting lunge.

My own body began to tense. When this horse got the signal, he would bolt as if chased by a grizzly. He would unleash a surge of power and speed that would leave me behind on my backside unless I was perfectly poised and ready. A horse can't win races by himself; his rider has to be in the saddle, not sitting on a busted butt in the dust and manure, giving folks something to laugh at.

Pa's pistol cracked, and we slammed to full speed in about five jumps. Perfect balance. Grass and weeds smoothed into a carpet of green under hooves moving too fast to be seen except as a blur of motion.

Choppy, high-pitched, my "Hi! Hi! Hi!" told Peepeye we were off to a clean start, told him we were doing good, told him I loved him, told him to keep it up.

A twist of a slicked ear answered, "Hang on! Isn't this fun? What a great day!"

The half-mile post sprang at us with impossible, frightening speed. Now my biggest challenge as a rider raced toward us. Peepeye eased his speed just a notch, getting ready. He knew exactly how to come around that pole at the greatest twisting, pounding speed. My job, on a postage-stamp saddle, was to stay with the horse.

Shortening stride and stiffening forelegs cut our speed for the sharp, lunging, digging spin. Flying, spinning bits of sod seemed to hang aloft in a wheeling world. Erect again from the lean, an explosion of power from thrusting hindquarters, and we were off again—a great turn!

"Hi! Hi! Hi! Peepeye!" Three tiny figures came at me, growing with each reach of mighty hooves. A skirt billowed in the wind and molded against one of them. Kit was watching!

The post flickered by, a thin, still shadow among flashing, swift, elusive glimpses of a world sweeping past. A subtle shift of weight eased back in the saddle drew Peepeye's instant answer—slackened speed. No need for me to pull on the reins; he knew what to do without insulting him with unnecessary instructions. The digging, frantic speed fell to a smooth flow, to a rocking, slowing, relaxed beat.

Now just the least pressure of the knees brought him around in a gentle curve, heading him back toward the watchers. Next, he came down to a rocking-chair lope with a jaunty, happy motion.

Every step sent a cocky "Want to do it again, boss?" up to me. Peepeye had a good, clear horse voice, with a laugh behind it. Easy, rhythmic breathing between my legs said, "Lots of miles to go before I'm tired." His breath would hardly flutter a candle flame.

I slapped him on the shoulder and ran a hand down the smooth neck. "Feeling good, you show-off studhorse?"

One erect ear twitched back my direction, saying, "Feeling great. You?"

When I spun off the saddle and slid to the ground, the landing was soft and springy. Peepeye wasn't the only one who was fit and feeling good. Keeping my stride at a swinging trot to match Peepeye's fast walk, I yelled to Kit as we passed, "Come walk with us, and I'll let you help rub the sweat off my horse."

She grabbed a fistful of skirt to lift the hem above the grass and ran after us. Flashing a big smile, she said, "What girl could turn down an invitation like that?"

I answered with a smug voice, "None. Gets 'em all, every one of 'em, every time." Laughing, I said over my shoulder, "You better come on. Nobody wins by falling behind."

I slowed to a fast walk and Peepeye matched his gait to mine. She trotted the last few steps to catch up, grabbed my belt to make me pull her along, and gave me a grin. "You love to ride more than anything, don't you?"

"W-e-e-ll, better than almost anything."

"What do you like better."

"W-e-e-ll . . ."

"Well, what?"

"Never mind. Let it pass."

"You want me to get Papa Joe to explain what you mean?" Our pace was slowing, so she released my belt and moved up to walk beside me, eyes wide with fake innocence.

"Oh, no, don't do that, Kit. Uh-uh, just forget it. For heaven's sake, if you tell Joe everything I say you'll get me shot, sooner or later. How about you, Peepeye? You want to be around ladies who tell their daddies everything?" I was walking too far back, and he didn't see my signal.

"Ha. He didn't answer you this time."

"Of course not. I shouldn't ask him questions like that. Embarrasses him. Besides, he doesn't like to take sides."

"Papa Joe told me several of the miners volunteered to watch the mine. He said they were good men, so there's no difficulty about all of us going to town together."

"Yep. We leave day after tomorrow."

"Your plan is just to watch the races?"

"We'll do a little more than that this time."

"Like what?"

"This will be the first time we plan to bet. Before, all we did was race for the prize money."

"What's the difference?"

"This time we make people mad. We're going to smirk and imply all the local horses are hopeless nags, stacks of flaws and blemishes piled fourteen or fifteen hands high, slow and ugly."

"Why do that?"

"Makes people mad. They'll feel like we're really saying that they're a bunch of rubes who don't know a real horse when they see one. We'll show Peepeye around. He's slick as a watermelon seed, and I'll have him all shined up."

"Isn't that warning them? Won't that make them afraid to bet against him?"

"No, no, and again, no. They'll ask if he's raced much, and I'll say he has. They'll ask where, and I'll say vaguely that he's been lots of places. When I don't answer with details, they figure I'm just a bragging kid with a pretty horse. They'll bet against me because I insulted the local horses. Nothing makes men so mad as a smart-talking kid. They all love to teach a cheeky kid a lesson, especially one they can teach and take money from at the same time."

"How interesting." She didn't sound like she believed a word of it.

"The most fun is after the race. They all stand around with their pockets turned inside out, and I tell them in a sad voice, 'I told you he was great, didn't I? Didn't I tell you he'd raced all around the country? Why didn't you listen? I tried to warn you.' "

"That's terrible, Ward. You just make people furious."

"Yeah, they get mad, but they don't feel like they've been tricked or cheated. They have to admit they were warned. We've never had to run from a town yet, like crooked gamblers have to do. The losers get mad at themselves because they mistook the truth for empty bragging. Know what it reminds me of?"

"No. What?"

"When I told Joe I intended to court you. Most men would have put that down to empty talk. Not Joe. Your dad's too smart. He knew about me in one minute. He took me serious. That doesn't happen often."

"Why do you think he knew?"

"Because your pa sees everything about a man. He has a special kind of an eye."

She grinned at me. "And what do you think he saw when he looked at you?"

I didn't smile back. "He didn't just see I was smaller than most men and stop looking—he looked at my horse and my guns too. Your pa judges a man, not by his size but by what he can do. Always look at a man's tools. If you want good work done, which would you hire, a man with fine tools or a man who's tall?"

"I'd hire the tall one," she said, with devilment twinkling in her eyes. "Meanwhile, you're shrinking. You're getting skinny as a wormy cat."

"Please, ma'am, you don't need to do like all those other girls. You don't need to be flattering me all the time."

"What other girls?"

"Ha. Girls are everywhere. The better question would be, what flattery?"

"What flattery then?"

"Polished manners, intelligence, looks, and . . . uh, let's see. Well, never mind. They talk about how much they admire a man as near perfect as I am."

"You're lying again."

"You got me. I confess. Fact is, most girls keep losing me. They keep forgetting to look down far enough to find me. That's the main thing I like about you. You're down here on my level."

"I told you, Kid, I don't like your short-man jokes."

"I told you I don't like being called Kid, but you do it anyway."

"It fits you. Everybody calls you Kid. It has nothing to do with me."

I gave her a hard look, but she just grinned and looked innocent again. We walked along without talking for a while before she turned my own words back on me.

"Your horse and your guns, those are your tools? You plan to make your living with horses and guns?"

I didn't answer. My family had lived a good life on a farm. I'd just lately realized that most of the crop we'd raised had been fed to the horses. Pa hired most of the plowing and such, while our work centered around the stables. It dawned on me that I knew an awful lot about horses, but not all that much about farming. In fact, now that I thought back on it, I didn't like farming.

I remembered a life of hard work around horses, but there had been plenty of time for us to travel frequently to New Orleans to see Mama's family, and we'd always had enough money. In fact, I didn't remember money ever being a problem, but maybe I'd been too young to notice.

We'd had no trouble making a living since leaving Louisiana, racing now and then, working here and there, and just moving on, mostly living off the land. When I'd set my sights on Kit, I knew the traveling would have to stop. If I took a wife, I'd have to settle somewhere, but that seemed far into the future. Now she'd thrown a rock into my quiet pool.

I was going to have to figure something out, and I had better do it quick. Our mining venture didn't look like it was going to last much longer.

"What would you think about living on a horse ranch, Kit?"

"A successful one? I might consider it. I told Papa Joe I've decided to marry a rich man, a man who knows enough and works hard enough to be a success. He said that was a sensible idea."

I gave her a good long look and she stared right back. She was smiling like it would never rain. Why did I have the feeling I'd just said what she wanted me to say?

FOURTEEN

PA AND LUKE sat on one side of the table with Milt and me on the other. Suppertime was still about an hour away, but work had stopped early today. Thackery and Pa had agreed to start for town tomorrow morning, carrying the gold we'd dug out of rock for the past month. Half the miners from the claims surrounding ours were going along, eager for safety in numbers when taking out their own gold.

Pa's voice was slow and quiet when he asked, "Well, boys, what's your plan?"

"We'll be looking at the competition and the track," I answered, knowing horse racing and betting was the subject of his question. Showdown time had come.

"Why don't you want to go ahead and race? We never hung around for a month before?" Pa's eyes were on me. Milt didn't move a muscle, so I figured he planned to let me shoulder most of Pa's disapproval by myself.

"We never stayed in one place long enough to do it before, and this race is going to be more important than any of those others. Don't you think it's a good idea, Pa?"

He eased his elbows down onto the table and said, "Let's stop shadowboxing and talk business. I don't like gambling. Not only do I not like it, but it doesn't make sense to me. Let's think about the numbers. Freere says they race no more than ten horses at a time. Right?"

Luke, Milt, and I nodded like judges.

"The entry fee is a hundred dollars, winner take all, with distances being a half and a mile, take your choice. I figure Peepeye is as close to a sure thing as a horse can get running a go-and-come-back mile. Some horses can challenge him over a half, or over a straight mile, but he comes around the pole better than any other horse I've ever seen. From the way you're training, I think you agree and plan to run Peepeye in the mile?"

I nodded again.

"Good. The way I figure it, we put up a hundred dollars to win a thousand. Actually, a hundred of the thousand we win is our own money. I work that out to be us putting up one to win nine. That's good odds. Nobody's going to offer those odds in a bet. If you boys bet on the side, you're risking your money for less return."

"Maybe we could compromise," I said. "I don't like to go against you, Pa, but I don't see the difference you find between winning the entry fees and regular betting. In a poker game, people put money in a pot and the man with the best cards wins. That's gambling. In a horse race, people put up entry money and the man with the best horse wins. I don't see the difference."

He lifted a hand to stop me. "A man plows, plants the best seed he can get, cultivates, and harvests, each in its proper season, putting in long, hard days when he'd rather be sitting in the shade. He expects to come up with a better crop than the man who plows shallow, plants cheap seed, doesn't bother to chop weeds, and so on. A horse is like a crop, bringing forth a reward from hard work, patience, and good judgment, not from luck. A poker player draws cards by pure chance . . . if the game's honest."

Milt and Luke sat like spectators, watching Pa and me throw hot rocks back and forth across the table, waiting to see which of us got burned.

I couldn't help but grin. "I hear that knowing when to hold 'em and when to fold 'em has something to do with winning at poker. That's a thing a man has to work hard to learn."

"Fiddling with pasteboards all day doesn't seem like productive work to me, son. You want to debate the definition of work?"

Now Pa was grinning back at me, waiting for my response. I vowed I'd try to be as good at working with my sons, if I ever had any. He wouldn't tolerate a shouting contest, but he was always ready to talk things out. He also knew none of his boys wanted to go against his wishes, which gave him an advantage he took care not to abuse.

"Suppose I make use of a special talent. Anything wrong with that?"
I asked.

Pa hesitated and narrowed his eyes. "Not if it's honest. You're wearing an innocent look, so I'd better be careful. What are you up to now?
I smell a trap."

While Pa was speaking, both Milt and Luke shifted weight forward,
showing interest. Maybe Pa was about to get caught in an awkward
position, have to hang on to the hot rock too long.

"My special talent is irritating people. Suppose I talk about their
nickel-and-dime racing, talk them into raising the entry fee when I
race, make it a serious main event for real horses rather than the usual
collection of mules, donkeys, and big dogs. Suppose I make them want
to raise the entry fee to a thousand instead of a hundred. Seems to me
I'll get better odds for my thousand dollar bet than I could otherwise.
At the same time, you don't get mad at me, because you don't see it as
a bet, just an entry fee."

Pa sat staring at me for a good long time before his glance shifted to
Luke. Milt was busy rubbing a grin off his face, trying to look bland.

Luke went to the heart of it with few words, like always. "You never
cared about money before. Why now? Kit?"

"What else?"

"You want to start a home with winnings from gambling?" Luke
made it sound the same as stolen money.

"Seems to me gambling money will put curtains on Kit's kitchen
window same as any other."

Luke pursued. "What kitchen window?"

"The one on the horse ranch I'm going to have."

"Where?"

"California."

"Why California?"

"Lots of men there, both Mexican and Anglo, with money and an
appreciation for good horseflesh. If I raise horses to sell, somebody has
to buy them. *Yo hablo Español.* I'm comfortable with people who speak
Spanish. Plenty of good land there, not too expensive. Good climate."

Pa asked, "You put the question to Kit?"

"Not yet."

"Another gamble?" Pa looked me straight in the eye. "Suppose she
says no. Suppose she doesn't want to go to California and live on a
horse ranch."

"I think I'm learning how she feels about things, Pa. I don't expect her to say no. The truth of it is, I'm not sure it wasn't her idea anyhow. But she can't say anything if I can't ask her, can she?"

Nobody spoke for a little while. Milt looked away. Luke stared at the table in front of him. I could hear strain in my own voice when I went on. "It costs money to start the kind of a place I have in mind. If she says no, then I might try thinking up something else. Her daddy's a rich man now. I got to have something to offer, don't I?"

Pa drew a deep breath and relaxed. Both hands came up to rub his face. When the hands came down, he was laughing. "The world turns, time passes, and nothing new ever happens."

Lightning glances passed among my brothers and me, each of us raising shoulders a bit to show puzzlement.

"Boys, many years ago, I took a couple of my horses to New Orleans. I had my eye on a pretty little rich girl. I figured she was going to be expensive and her family troublesome. Turned out she was expensive, just like I expected, but the best seldom comes cheap. Her family was troublesome at first too, but that changed later. I also figured my horses would win all the prize money I'd need without me having to make bets, and they did."

Pa came to his feet and walked around the table to stand behind me with his hands on my shoulders. Still laughing, he said, "Must be something in the blood, boys. We like rich girls. Looks like the Baynes line will die out if our horses start losing. We just won't be able to afford our women."

Luke's voice reflected shock. "Mama? Expensive?"

"Son, your mama was no country girl. A man doesn't fill a house with books for nothing. I recall one time I called her hand on the cost. She'd paid dear prices at a lean time for me. She said, 'The father is a cultured gentleman. The sons must not grow up to be less. It would shame the father.'"

Pa chuckled and rubbed a hand across his face again. "I chewed on that for a couple of days. Never did come up with an answer."

Luke nodded solemnly, the laugh wrinkles around his eyes deepening. "Lucky she didn't have daughters to buy pretty things for, Pa. It would've been awful."

Pa broke into our laughter, his tone half-irritated, half-wondering, "Think about all those funny-looking little fancy silver forks and

spoons she had me buy 'so the children learn proper table manners.' I
could've bought a good saddle with a handful of those dinky spoons."

Milt finally found his voice. "Speaking of table manners, let's go sit
around the Thackery cabin and do some howling and scratching.
Maybe somebody'll throw scraps of food out the door."

FIFTEEN

JOE THACKERY RODE UP from his usual trail position beside Pa to tell
Kit and me, "I already booked and paid for the same rooms in the
hotel and the same stall space in the livery stable."

Surprised, I asked, "When did you do that?"

He lifted one shoulder, just a twitch, an almost invisible gesture.
"Well, when your pa and I heard about the big horse races, he said
we'd be coming back. I made arrangements before we left town to go
to the mine."

"You mean you and Pa knew about the races before Freere told
me?"

Joe repeated his meager shrug. "Darnell said you would find out in
good time, no need for him to be telling you everything."

He pulled aside and reined up to wait for Pa. Kit rode along without
looking the least bit surprised. I asked, "Did you know about the races
before we left town?"

"Sure. Papa Joe said to keep quiet. He said if your Pa didn't think he
needed to be telling you every little thing, no reason for me to show
off how much I knew. Said it wouldn't make you feel better to find out
I was smarter than you."

"Pa got me again, made me look like a pinhead. Right this minute I
admit to feeling dumb as I ever felt."

"No need. I find all the Baynes men to be wonderfully clever, and
you're the smartest of the lot."

"Why, thank you, ma'am. Thank you very much. What else has
your Papa Joe had to say about things?"

"Oh, this and that. He told me Darnell said Luke was just like him, that he took pride in seeing so much of himself in his oldest son. Darnell said you're the picture of your mother, that she was the smartest one in the family till you came along, that more than half of his ideas that worked out good came from her."

That rocked me back in my saddle. Pa and Joe Thackery didn't have much to say when the rest of us were around. Luke left the talking to Milt and me, but we spent most of our chatter teasing Kit and having a good time. Now it was obvious that Pa had found himself a real partner. Quietly, without me noticing, the two older men had become close friends, else there would have been no such talk as Kit was repeating.

Pa had high standards. I had figured Joe to be quite a man from the first sight I'd had of him, but this jacked up my opinion of him even higher. Lots of men liked and respected Pa, but he kept his distance from all but very few. In fact, outside of Mama and my uncles, her two brothers, I couldn't remember Pa being particularly close to anybody.

Kit must have known the effect her words had on me. She waited till I looked her way again before she spoke. "Darnell told Papa Joe that Milton and you think a lot alike, just like he and Luke do, so family votes likely come out two against two. But Milt is the wild card in the family. Your Pa said Milt is like nobody else. He's suspicious, a loner, most happy when he's miles away from other people. Milt is just Milt, take it or leave it."

"Well, that's about it. I guess you know us pretty well, Kit."

"Milt doesn't seem all that suspicious. Sure, he always seems as cautious as a wild Indian, but he has fun around me."

"We read a lot, but we're really simple country people. He sees you as belonging to me. You're already family in his eyes. There's no suspicion inside our kind of family."

When I looked at her, she met my gaze squarely. Although her face took on a little extra color, her voice was calm and firm when she answered. "Milton is correct. I shall not disappoint him."

Women have a way of talking about one thing but casting meaning in another direction. She wasn't talking about not disappointing Milt. That was me she was talking about, and she didn't dodge being considered part of the family. The time was coming for me to say more, but I wasn't going to say it while in a saddle on a dusty trail under a blazing sun.

For now, I just looked away and said, "He knows that." Women aren't the only ones who can say one thing while meaning another. Maybe both of us felt enough had been said, but the silence between us was a far different thing from the awful, grinding, painful affliction it had been when we left town.

When it came into view, Bannock was a different place from the one we'd seen before, but it held no surprises for us. The Baynes gang had seen this sort of thing happen over and over again. Western men wouldn't think twice before riding fifty miles to see a good fight, or to watch a horse race, or to dance with a pretty girl. Come to think about it, the girl didn't need to be pretty.

The town had swelled like a herd spreading to graze, tents springing up in every patch of shade for a mile around. Miners came to town packed twenty to the ore wagon, hitting the dusty streets already singing and swaggering with a rolling step akin to sailors newly ashore. Small whiskey barrels rode on the seats beside the enterprising teamsters, who could handle half-broken teams on a rough road and fill tin cups with whiskey at the same time, hardly spilling more than half of what they poured.

We went through the same routine to deliver our gold to the bank, but no one seemed to pay us any mind. We didn't represent a new strike this time. Milt and Luke took the stock to the livery, and Kit dragged Thackery off to the big general store.

Pa and I went up to the hotel room. The place seemed quiet after the clamor and clatter of the busy street, but the rumble of wagons and the hum of excited voices crept in like dust to hang in the air. Pa stripped off his shirt and poured water into the big washbasin while I stood shifting from one foot to the other.

Bending over the basin to dip his hands into the water, he looked up at me and asked, "You look mighty uncomfortable. Got a problem?" Then he lowered his head to splash water on his face.

"I need some money. I'd like some of my share."

"What for?"

"Well, uh, I got something I'd like to buy. It might be a little expensive."

"That so? How much you need?"

"I'm not sure. Maybe two or three hundred dollars."

"My, my! You better be sure you need it before you buy something with a price so dear."

"I think I need it."

"You think? You aren't sure."

"Some things aren't ever sure, exactly, uh, but you need to be ready."

He groped for the towel and dried his face. "Son, dig in my saddle-bag over yonder and get a little brown wooden box for me, will you?"

"Sure."

"It isn't very big, just a little brown box about as big as your fist."

I found it and handed it to him. "You have money in there? Nuggets or something?"

Poker-faced, he answered, "I think I have what you need." He loosened two small hooks on one side, flipped back the top, and pulled out a square of folded silk. He unfolded the cloth, leaving it draped across his hand, and turned to me.

Extending the cloth-covered hand toward me, Pa asked, "Would these do?"

Like a man turned to stone, I stood looking down at the two small objects on the silk.

His voice was soft and shook a little when he said, "You may not want them. They're old and a mite worn, and they never were much, I guess, but they were the best I could get at the time."

"Mama's rings?" I reached forward and touched them with a tentative finger. "But . . ."

He shook his head and, knowing my thought, said, "No, son. She told me not to bury them with her, no need to bury pretty things with lifeless clay." With a slow grin, he went on, "She said it'd be nice if I needed them again. Your mama was a practical, knowing wife." He stopped to clear his throat. "But I couldn't give them to another woman. You could, though. Your mama would be pleased. She had a sentimental streak like most females."

"But Luke and Milt . . ."

"They know. We're all taken with your Kathleen and would be proud for her to wear these. One more thing, she might not like the idea. Women are skittish and nervy, have their own notions. Maybe she might want something new, something all her own. She's the one who deserves to be pleased in matters like this."

With his free hand, he pulled a heavy leather poke from his belt and dropped it on the bed. "Take that gold with you. You ask her straight out and watch her close. If she looks doubtful, go buy her something she likes, bring these back to me, and let there be no trouble between you about it." He folded the silk carefully around the rings and handed them to me.

"Thanks, Pa."

"When do you plan to put the question?"

"Tonight, after supper."

"You going to talk to Joe first?"

"Oh, yeah. I better do that."

"I'll send Luke and Milt down to supper early. Then I'll get Joe to come to our room, and I'll go on downstairs to leave you alone."

"Thanks again, Pa."

He shrugged, put his arm around my shoulders, and said solemnly, "It's worth it to me. If she went off with somebody else, we'd have to hire a cook."

We went downstairs to meet the others and ate a meal in the hotel dining room. The races weren't going to start till mid afternoon, but I was getting restless. I spoke across the table to Pa, "I'm going down to the stable. Got a man I want to see."

When I walked out, I saw Milt come to his feet. He would follow along behind, watching. Milt had a near-superstitious attitude about going back to places where we'd found trouble. He believed lightning could and often did strike again in the same place.

Coop sat in his back-tilted chair as if he hadn't moved a step in the weeks since I'd seen him. He stood up and walked to meet me, extending his hand. "Good to see you still alive, Kid."

"Good to see you again, Mr. Cooper. Why shouldn't I still be alive?"

"Can't never tell about gunmen, Kid. Can't never tell. When they're fast as you, somebody comes at 'em from behind. Gunmen don't last long, and that's a fact."

Grinning, I said, "I'm not a gunman, sir. I haven't shot anybody since I saw you last."

Grinning right back, he turned his head to spit tobacco juice at what looked like the same beetle as before. "You ain't been back to town neither. Somebody hunting a reputation ain't coming after you out in the country. Mostly, they want a crowd."

"I have no reputation."

"Do tell. Ain't you Kid Baynes? A young feller with that name, little feller from Louisiana, killed two men right on this very spot here awhile back. Since then, it's all over town that he's gunned down men from New Orleans to Tucson to Los Angeles to Denver. Funny, you and him being the same size and having the same name, ain't it?"

I decided to let that pass. "I came to ask about the horse races. You ever go out to watch?"

"Damn right. Wouldn't miss it for nuthin'. I figure horses is my business, and I know every one of 'em what can run a decent race."

"Yeah, that's the way I figured it might be. I'm going out this afternoon to watch. Wondered if I could tag along with you and learn a few things. I plan to race my horse next month."

Shrewd eyes set deep in a spiderweb of sun wrinkles lingered on me for a long moment before he looked away. "Figured to learn a few things, you say?"

"Yes, sir."

"Smart boy. Not no know-it-all. Got some manners, some respect. You just foller along, son. I'll give you the story about every horse out yonder if he's ever raced here before. And I'll tell you about the riders too. How about that?"

"I'd be obliged."

"Your brother up in the loft again?"

"Yes, sir, I'm here." Milt's quiet voice came from above.

Cooper laughed and slapped his knee. "You two are a caution, a pure caution. One you see, the other you don't. You up there, you're Milt ain't you? Ain't that your name?"

"Yes, sir."

"And you won't be with us when we watch the races, will you, Milt?" the old man asked.

"I'll be nearby, sir."

Cooper sat looking absently across the street, chuckling. Finally, he turned his leathery face toward me and said, "Stepbrother, is he, or maybe a half brother?"

"No, sir. He's a natural brother with the same blood."

"Hm. Took him for an Indian last time I seen him, or at least a breed. I've changed my mind about you, Kid. I don't think they can get you from behind. You might live to a right tol'able old age. Yes, sir. You just might."

SIXTEEN

"THIS HERE PLACE is both the starting line and the finish line for the mile races. The crowd mostly gathers up behind both sides along here," Coop commented as we walked toward the edge of town. "We string ropes between wagons to keep a lane clear past the finish line. The half-milers start out at the far end, o'course, so's they finish in front of the congregation. The milers start at this end, race around the post down yonder, and get back thisaway as quick as they can."

"Who watches out for rough stuff?"

"The U.S. Marshal, that there Frank Jopson, he's usually around. Our sheriff, feller called Chip Dodd, he always comes out too. Nobody fools around with either of them fellers."

"You mean they actually judge if somebody fouls another rider? The law does that?"

"Naw, Kid, I thought you meant trouble with the crowd. Some of these ol' boys get pretty drunk, and some of 'em don't see nothin' funny about losing a bet. The town men formed a racing committee to watch the riders and announce winners. I guess you could call that committee the judges. They scatter out and try their best. Ain't no easy job. The grass is mostly wore off the track. It gets dusty and hard to see good."

Coop didn't glance my direction when he added, "Mostly it's ever' man for hisself. No shootin' or using a bullwhip. Otherwise, it's devil take the hindmost, I reckon."

A crowd was already gathering, although the races wouldn't start for another hour, according to Coop.

He went on, "Watch for them Indian horses, blanket horses, some calls 'em. Others call 'em Appaloosas. You can't miss 'em. They got a spotted gray patch spread like a blanket across the rump. They're plenty fast, some of 'em. Mostly, they do best in the half, but they ain't bad over the mile neither."

I nodded, determined to say as little as possible. If I talked and showed how much I knew, he might find it disrespectful and clam up. We walked through the gathering crowd while he described the horses to look for, animals which won in the last couple of months.

"There's a couple or three riders you got to watch for, Kid, and there's one of 'em. Look yonder at that cotton-haired skinny boy."

I followed the direction of Coop's gaze and located a tall, painfully thin individual with hair sun-bleached almost white over a darkly tanned face. Easily picked out of the roughly dressed crowd, he wore no hat and appeared immaculate in English boots, dark riding breeches, and a fancy white shirt.

Coop lowered his voice almost to a whisper. "Watch for him and another one looks almost like him. The Crager brothers, they are, Lonnie and Ronnie, and both work for Amos Chintry." The old man casually looked around to be sure no one else was close enough to hear, hitched up his pants, and continued.

"Amos has a big, tall, black horse there ain't nobody beat yet. Ain't nobody caught them two Cragers doing nothin', not exactly, but many's the time they go into a cloud of dust with another rider and come out all by theirselves. Ever' time that big Chintry black runs, he jumps out in front. Them two always rides in the same race with the black, and something always happens to anybody who looks like he might catch up."

My face must have been a study because Coop chuckled, so I turned away from Crager so as not to be caught staring.

"He don't look much like the other miners who work for Chintry, does he?" Coop asked quietly, and when I didn't answer, said, "Him and his brother do about the same thing as a hired gun would, I reckon, 'cept they do it a-horseback."

"How do they manage it? Anybody complain?"

"Not no more. Them what complained got beat to a pulp. Seems them Crager boys carry quirts with leaded handles, and most riders just lay out in the dust real quiet after being hit upside the head. With a sore noggin already, them riders'd just as soon pass the chance to meet up with friends of the Cragers."

I cocked an eye at the neatly dressed, almost fragile figure. "He's tall, but he looks like he has to turn sideways to make a shadow. That fellow doesn't look like he'd be any better than me in a fight, looks like a stork with the wings clipped off."

Coop made a sour face. "The Crager brothers don't roughhouse

around none their own selves. You never did see such innocent lookin'
sickly angels. Butter wouldn't melt in their mouths when their feet is
on the ground, but they're demons in the saddle. Chintry has other
men for knuckle and skull jobs."

"I'll be saying some things from time to time today, Mr. Cooper.
Maybe I might stir up interest in the races next month when I'll be
running. I'd consider it a favor if you paid it no mind. In fact, you
might not want to be seen with me too much."

Coop grinned sourly and looked away. "Worried about me, are you,
Kid?"

"No, sir, but I wouldn't want to bring trouble to you. I been meaning to ask you, how do you get your boss to let you loose to come to the
races? Seems this is a busy time at the stable."

Coop nodded. "Ain't never had no trouble with my boss. I own that
stable, Kid, and a few ore wagons, and a couple or three dozen good
horses. I even bought myself two extra pairs of pants last week. Business is good."

"Oops. No offense intended, sir. I thought you were just a hostler.
Uh, nothing wrong with that, but . . ."

"But you pick your friends not carin' 'bout what they got? That it?"

"Well, I didn't figure you to be a big businessman."

"Let it pass, Kid. When I first saw you, I didn't figure you to be a
fast gun, nor a gold miner, nor the owner of a racehorse. You just
looked and acted like a nice young feller, so I took to you."

"Thank you, sir."

"No need to thank me. Thank your Pa for teachin' you how to act
proper." He unloaded the bulge from his cheek and started carving its
replacement from a black, lint-covered plug pulled from dusty, stained
trousers.

"One more thing, since we're leveling with each other. Don't you be
surprised that I'm one of the town men on the racing committee and
one of Chip Dodd's special deputies during the races."

"Oh? What's next, Mr. Cooper? You planning to be the next territo-
rial governor?"

He nodded without showing a trace of a smile. "Yeah. I just might
consider it if the pay's good 'nuff. Meantime, I'd be happy if you don't
get tempted to take any of the towels from that hotel of mine you're
stayin' in. I'll be moving on now, Kid. Got some work to do. Just you
remember one last thing. No matter what happens, the horse that

crosses first is the winner. Elsewise, we might have a riot out here. You got that?"

"Yes, sir."

"It's just like that war we done had. Ever'body remembers the dirty tricks from one side or t'other, but none of that changes who won. Come to think on it, why don't you come on along with me to meet some of the local big chiefs?" Coop walked toward a row of tables in the shade of a gnarled old tree.

"This here's Kid Baynes, gents," he announced to the group of men dressed in town clothes. I shook hands and heard too many names at the same time to remember more than one or two. This was where men signed up and paid entry fees. Big slate chalkboards were propped up to display the races by number and distance, and the names of the horses, the owners, and the riders.

Several horses trotted back and forth on the racecourse, warming up. A hard look at them, their riders, and their equipment told me that Peepeye had nothing to worry about among this bunch, but maybe the best ones had yet to show.

A man shouldn't get the idea he can always tell how fast a horse can go just by taking a quick look. But the conformation of a horse and his way of moving can tell a knowing man a lot. Judging horseflesh only gets chancy after the horse passes a few crude tests. The simple balance between length of leg and depth of chest, matched by length of body, can tell much of the story.

Fine horses have a certain way of moving, a spring in the step, with muscles working nicely under the skin, plainly visible to a casual eye, not hidden by a thin layer of fat. The skilled horseman can tell the difference at a glance between most real flaws and harmless blemishes.

I watched a couple of men pay entry fees before I spoke. "The entry fee's a hundred dollars?" I kept my tone one of innocent curiosity, with a flavor of wonder.

One of the town men, Sparks, winked and asked, "Too much for you, Kid? We keep the entry fee high to keep out the jokers."

"High?" I managed to sound dumbfounded. "But doesn't that mean the winner only gets a thousand dollars?"

Eight or ten men stopped what they were doing and turned toward me. I snickered as if I couldn't help it. "Really? Is that all there is to all this huffing and puffing."

Sparks reddened a bit around the ears and asked, "What's so funny?"

I acted like I was fighting to keep a straight face. "Nothing, sir. Pardon me. Out at the mine, some of the men were talking like you had some real horse races here in Bannock. They must have been pulling a joke."

I held my features stiff like I'd finally choked down my laughing but was having a hard time holding my face under control. Seriously, like I was trying my best not to give offense, I went on, "Those scoundrels, always poking fun, they knew we were new around here and wouldn't know the difference. We thought these were real horse races. I see it all now, you just race harness stock and plow horses. Hell, I bet you have a good time anyhow." I tried to make it sound like I'd caught grown men playing with themselves in the bathtub.

Coop stepped closer and spoke in a voice that carried, "You think the entry fee's too low, Kid?"

"Oh, no, sir. This way everybody gets to play. This is a nice way to let all the boys and girls race their little ponies." I chortled and looked around like I expected everybody to laugh with me and agree. They didn't.

I pretended to sober at once. "No offense intended, gentlemen, but I thought everybody knew you can't expect men who own fine horses to race for small change like that. Now, a thousand dollar entry fee would give you a modest prize, but respectable. Owners of good stock might pay attention."

I looked suggestively over my shoulder. "You'd see some fast horses instead of those, those, uh . . ." I stopped and shrugged as if nothing more need be said.

Coop asked, "You willing to run a horse if we set up a race with a thousand dollar entry fee?"

"Certainly, sir. I'll put up my entry fee today if you'd like, but I won't be ready till next month." I looked around with a grin. "I'll have to take off the plow harness and get my horse used to a saddle again." I laughed, glanced around, and pretended again to be surprised when nobody looked amused.

Coop asked, "Anybody got any complaints with the idea?" The men shook their heads.

I nodded. "It's agreed then, ten horses to run a measured mile, if you men can find nine other racehorses around here." I cast another glance at the horses on the track. "Maybe some real horse people will hear about it and come. I doubt the owners of the stock here today will be interested."

"I'm interested," said a voice behind me.

When I turned, Kit and Thackery stood there with a smiling man. On sight, I knew him to be a natural enemy.

SEVENTEEN

THACKERY SAID, "Ward Baynes, meet Amos Chintry."

When I stuck out my hand, Chintry ignored it and said, "I've heard of you, Baynes. I think you are the man I saw shoot two others in a gunfight in the street a few weeks ago. I was amazed that you weren't arrested on the spot."

When he acted like he didn't see my hand, I dropped it and shrugged. Chintry sounded like he'd appointed himself to be the conscience of the community. Something about his kind always set my teeth on edge, and I swear I could pick such men out of a crowd, on sight. Besides, I remembered his voice the minute he opened his mouth. This man had spoken to Marshal Jopson when I'd walked into the stable that evening after the shooting, had called me a public menace.

"That's one of the benefits of travel, Mr. Chinless," I answered with a friendly smile, staring straight into his eyes. "A man sees and hears many an amazing thing."

"The name is Chintry," he said coldly. "And you should be in jail." A colorless man of medium height, his spotless clothing was perfectly tailored. He carried his head with his chin lifted arrogantly, wearing an expression that made him look like he smelled something mildly offensive.

With my smile still in place, I said, "Just shows you haven't learned the ways of the people in this part of the country yet, Mr. Chinfree."

"Once again, my name is Chintry. I am a gentleman, but that's something you could hardly be expected to understand. I shall never learn your kind of conduct, sir."

"Well now, it's interesting to meet a man who's against learning. That reminds me of a story about one of Napoleon's mules, Mr. Chinwag." I was determined to grin this arrogant bastard to death. "He didn't benefit from travel either, that mule didn't. Went through every battle of every campaign with old Napoleon, traveled all over the Continent, and even went to Russia. But when it was all over, he hadn't learned anything new either. He was still just a damn mule."

"I find the comparison insulting, sir. Watch yourself. Also, I resent this childish playing with my name. For the last time, my name is spelled C-h-i-n-t-r-y." His long, pale face grew rigid, and I saw the signal I was watching for. He pressed his right arm briefly against his body, the unconscious gesture of a man wearing a sleeve gun, assuring himself it was in proper position.

Things were coming together now. I was ready to bet this dandy, with his flawless, expensive clothes, was the same man who poisoned a few days of my life. What Kit had heard about the shooting sounded just like this man's way of talking.

"Watch myself?" I dropped my smile and put on a horrified expression. I mimicked his pompous manner of speech. "Are you threatening me, sir? Perhaps you intend to shoot me with that nasty little lady's gun you have up your sleeve?"

I told my pa he'd reared a gambler, and maybe my next move proved it. Jesse came into my hand, and I had the muzzle against Chintry's stomach before Kit could gasp. Sometimes a man simply has to bet on his own judgment, and I decided to take the risk. Chintry, caught flat-footed, stood frozen in surprise.

"If you move your right arm, I'll shoot you, Mr. Chinbag," I said in a soothing voice as if speaking to a child. "Yes, sir, I'll shoot you right in your little tummy-tum."

Coop's voice came from close behind me. "What's goin' on, Kid?"

I grabbed Chintry's arm, keeping Jesse's muzzle firmly against his shirtfront, jerked up his sleeve, and removed the hideout gun that was held in place by a spring clip. If that little gun hadn't been there for the taking, I'd have been the most foolish-looking jackass in Montana Territory.

"Mr. Chinwave just decided to give Kit this little ladyfied hideout gun, didn't you, Mr. Chinflap?"

Chintry was beginning to recover. At least, his mouth wasn't still hanging open, but a downward glance at Jesse's eared-back hammer kept him standing motionless as a post. My gaze never left his eyes while I held his gun out to Kit and felt a quick touch of her fingers when she lifted it from my hand.

I wanted to laugh and dance when I heard her speak in a prim, pleased voice. "Why, thank you, Mr. Chinrun. Look, Papa Joe, isn't that pretty? It's got a pearl handle."

With one move, I stepped back away from Chintry, lowered Jesse's hammer, and dropped him into my holster. Now that Chintry didn't take all my attention, I realized a silent crowd had formed and was moving closer now that Jesse was tucked back in bed.

Chintry trembled, either from released tension when Jesse left his shirtfront or with rage, maybe both. His voice came out tight and low from almost unmoving, thin, bloodless lips when he said, "I'll kill you for this."

In a loud voice, I asked, "Hear that, men. This hero threatens to kill me because I took his little coward's hideout gun away from him." An angry murmur rose. Miners seldom wore guns but understood why men in other lines of work did so. Hideout guns, however, were a hated thing, associated with men who were up to no good.

I glanced around. "Who wants money bad enough to do a killing for it? He's not up to it, so he'll be wanting to hire it done."

Chintry wheeled and started away, shoving onlookers aside. A burly miner shoved back, sending him headlong into another man, who shoved him away too, dropping him to his knees in the dusty street. He sprang to his feet, brushing angrily at his soiled clothing while he continued his retreat.

Again, in a loud voice, I called out to the crowd, "Wave goodbye to the fake gentleman, boys."

Thackery spoke urgently, "Ease up, Ward. You left the man nothing. You've made an enemy for life."

Still watching Chintry's retreating back, I answered, "No, sir, I didn't. I simply exposed one. That man was born to be my enemy."

Kit opened her parasol awkwardly, still holding Chintry's gun. "What should I do with this thing?" she asked.

"Here, let me help you." I squeezed the clip down real small and clamped it on her arm over a lacy sleeve. "There now, you'll start a new fad, the latest thing for the stylish lady."

A couple of the men nearby grinned and elbowed their friends, pointing to Kit.

She snapped, "Ward, take that off at once. You embarrass me to death."

I slipped it off her arm, tucked the tiny, double-barreled pistol under my gunbelt and the spring-clip holster into my shirt. "You don't seem as enthused about Chintry's gifts as you were about his opinions."

After a startled, wide-eyed look at me, she nodded. "You're right. I don't know how you guessed, but he's the one who made everything sound so shocking and terrible that morning before we rode out of town. I had almost forgotten about that. It seems such a long time ago. Why do you associate with such a horrid man, Papa Joe?"

Thackery shrugged. "I don't. He invited himself to join us for coffee one morning, and he invited himself to walk down to the races with us today. You were the one who paid attention to his big mouth, not me. You didn't even discuss it with me till after you'd already tied poor Ward here to a stake and lit a fire under him. Just because I don't drive a man away with a whip doesn't mean I like him."

I nodded like a judge. "See there, you're better off around a good-hearted liar like me than a nasty old gossip like Chintry."

Thackery shook his head and looked away, but I got a little crooked grin from Kit. She reached up and perched a shy hand on my arm, and we walked toward an open spot to watch the races, with me feeling big as a plantation piano and twice as grand. Clever girl, she walked on my left side. I'd make a bet she did that on purpose, so as not to be holding my gun arm.

We found a teamster selling seats. He'd found some rickety chairs somewhere and lined up a couple of rows on his high wagon bed. I bought three seats, and a pleasant man moved so we could sit together.

This time, they had enough entries to run three half-mile races and three more at a full mile. Thackery let me borrow his watch. The winners of all three half-mile races came in a solid four or five seconds behind Peepeye's regular time. That was a mighty big gap over a short distance, even though the competition hadn't impressed me much. I made a mental note to check carefully for a sandy spot or two; surely, soft going somewhere along the line must be slowing the whole field.

After the third race, the crowd relaxed and wandered around, mostly gathering around makeshift bars made up of rough boards laid across empty barrels. Coop sauntered past and told us they always had at least a half-hour break before the mile races. A thrown-together band of miners and town men played their way into a small fortune as the crowd milled around the naked plank bandstand, dropping coins or pinches of gold dust into a bucket.

Two men squared off and started swinging wildly at each other. Kit gave me a questioning glance when I laughed. She had no way of knowing that, after watching Milt, most men looked so awkward and ungainly as to be funny. Milt had a smooth, sliding way of moving, keeping his feet under him with perfect balance and coordination. He punched with a power, speed, and accuracy most men couldn't imagine, let alone achieve.

Milt pounded people into submission so easily it never seemed like a fair fight. I probably knew more about that than anybody. He'd practiced on me often enough. I loved to watch Milt fight anybody thick-headed enough to challenge him. Mostly, it just made me feel good to see somebody else get the whacking instead of me.

A tall, stooped man strolled slowly toward the fighters, walking as if favoring sore feet. I saw a flash of gray hair when he lifted his hat and ran a long-fingered hand across his brow. The scuffle was too far away to know for sure, but it looked like he didn't even need to say anything when he came close. Both fighters froze in mid-swing when he came into view.

He looked at one and pointed the way for him to drift. Then he looked at the other and raised an arm in the opposite direction. The men exchanged glares briefly and stalked away from each other stiff-legged, a couple of roosters telling themselves how lucky the other guy was to get off so light.

I said, "Coop mentioned a man named Chip Dodd is sheriff here. Maybe that's him, Joe."

The answer came without interest, "Don't know him. Whoever that fellow yonder is, Dodd or somebody else, I'd say he doesn't take any backchat." He leaned forward to rest his elbows on his knees and lifted a thumb toward Kit, seated between us. "Her friend, Amos Chintry, has an entry in the next race. Chintry told us he has a black horse running from number-four position."

Kit said with a tired voice, "Oh, dear, I can see I'm going to be teased to death about that horrid man."

Thackery's bored, offhand tone continued. "Good man to ask if you want to know anything about Ward Baynes. Yes, sir, that fellow sure has Ward's number."

Kit sighed. Thackery winked at me and leaned back in his chair.

The black was easily sighted. Coat shining in the sun, he was a beautiful creature, a picture of power, and he had a real jockey aboard. I leaned forward, watching every move, wishing to be closer. Not a kind horse, he showed an ugly temper, letting us see too much white of the eye and too much kicking and snapping. Nice length of leg, a little delicate for my taste but showing potential for speed.

The jockey, hard-pressed to keep his seat, didn't look happy being thrown about. Lather streaks showed plainly in front of the saddle.

"Kit's friend tell you his horse's name?" I asked.

Kit groaned.

"Wicked," Thackery said.

"That all?"

"Just Wicked."

"Yeah," I said softly. "Fits him well enough. Bundle of nerves. Already foaming up too much, way too much. Horse like that needs to be handled just right else he'll burn up and go flat at the finish. That shouldn't be a big problem. I'd . . . Never mind, not my horse."

"What would you do?" Kit asked.

I grinned at her. "I'd explain things to him, talk to him about good manners and winning races without making himself so tired. I'd reason with him."

"Ward Baynes, you tell lies with the most wonderful straight face."

"No, no, not lies, gospel truth."

"Be serious."

"I'm serious as a drunk Indian, ma'am."

"What's that?" asked Thackery. "What'd you say, Ward?"

Kit laughed. "Don't ask, Papa Joe. He's got a horrible story about a drunk Indian he likes to tell. Don't encourage him."

The starter's pistol cracked and the line of horses sprang forward. I didn't know I came to my feet till a couple of men behind me spoke sharply. I apologized and sat back down. Coop's description told it all. A dust cloud rose and covered the action. Anything could be happening out there without the crowd at the finish line knowing a thing about it. Obviously, the time for spoilers was in the first half. Once they rounded the pole, at least the leaders would be in full view.

No, they wouldn't! Not unless the race took place on a much windier day than today. The dust cloud hung like a great, deep curtain of smoke, and the racing horses rounded the pole to head right back into it. The crowd wouldn't be able to make out much of anything in detail until the leaders were closing on the finish line. Unless the race took place after a rain or in a spanking wind, spoilers could have a field day. Riders could do what they damned pleased out there.

The black won, but he was laboring, running stodgy, worn-out when he crossed the finish line under a jockey who used the whip too much. The white-haired Crager brothers finished second and fourth. They were either amateurs or had lost all sense of caution about their work. Both rode with necks twisted, watching the horses behind them for any last-minute challenge to the big black. Two riderless horses came trotting in behind.

The next two races were the same, except the winners took more time than Chintry's big black, and only one riderless horse came home in each of them.

I relaxed against the back of my seat and glanced toward Thackery. He leaned forward with raised brows to look across Kit at me. I returned his watch.

Thackery spoke in a low voice. "You were right, Ward. I never saw horse races anything like these. They got no rules at all."

"Combat rules," I said quietly. "The Roman Coliseum has moved to Montana, gladiators and all."

EIGHTEEN

KIT AND THACKERY went back to the hotel after the races while I took an afternoon stroll along the racecourse. The grass along the route had vanished, and the bare earth was churned to powder. Still, I found no rocks on the nearly level track. I'd raced on worse. If it rained, the horses would be plowing through a sea of muck. Peepeye and I both would be wearing a mud suit unless we led the way through the whole distance. Monthly races wouldn't destroy the grass like this. Evidently, the local riders used the same track to train their horses and practice.

Although I expected to find a stretch of deep sand, I didn't. I found nothing to slow the field, to explain what seemed to be slow times. The more I thought about what I had seen, the more I began to think that most of these men raced simply for the fun of it. The riders were too heavy, the gear regular working tack, and most of the horses showed little or no sign of the care and training routinely given to racing mounts back home in Louisiana.

Chintry's big black and three or four others showed signs of careful breeding, but I hadn't been impressed with what I'd seen of either the jockeys or the horses. The way I figured it, if I beat the spoilers, Peepeye could beat these horses on the worst day he ever had. Unless new and better competition entered next month, I'd earn some easy money.

The late afternoon shadows stretched longer as I walked slowly back to town, enjoying the soft, dry southern breeze with its hint of dust.

When I walked into our room, silence fell. My pa and my brothers sat on beds, watching me. My best suit of clothes, freshly brushed, hung from a peg on the wall, and somebody had spread a new white shirt on my bed. Pa pointed to a vanity table, where a bowl of clean water, soap, and my razor were laid out.

"I shaved this morning."

Pa shrugged. "Do what you think best."

Milt pulled a small bottle from his pocket and pitched it to me. "Rub lots of that on you, here and there. She'll appreciate the change from *eau de caballo* to bay rum."

I pulled off my shirt and rinsed my face. Luke grabbed the shirt as soon as I dropped it on my bed, folded it neatly, and put it away in my saddlebag. He snapped his fingers and pointed at my feet. When I pulled off my boots, he brushed the dust from them. Then my family sat watching me without making a sound till I felt like a circus freak.

"You got nothing else to do but stare at me? I'm not going to cut my throat."

Milt shook his head sadly. "You might as well."

"Milt." Pa's tone disapproved.

"Just jokin', Pa. Yuk, yuk."

Pa walked to the door. "I'm going down the hall to have a few words with Joe. We'll be coming back here shortly."

I toweled my face and changed into the clean trousers they'd prepared for me. Luke grabbed me and gave me one of his gentle hugs, nearly cracking three or four ribs, before he turned and walked toward the door. He shrugged without looking back when I said, "Thanks for doing my boots, Luke."

Milt grabbed my hand, looked me in the eye, and flashed a strained expression, looking like a pallbearer who'd just dropped the casket. "Good luck, Ward. Don't look so scared. Maybe Joe will forbid you to ask her. He's a decent man. He might do that for you." He left, chuckling.

I was smoothing the lapels of my coat and admiring myself in the mirror when there came a tap on the door, and Joe stepped into the room.

When Pa didn't come in with him, I asked, "Where's Pa? I thought he was coming with you."

"You need him for something?"

"No, uh, drag up a bed and have a seat, Joe."

He sat on Pa's bed, just sat and looked at me, his back ramrod straight.

"You know I'm fond of Kit."

"Noticed."

"Well, uh, I been sort of making plans. I never saw any prettier country for horses than in California. When we rode through there, I saw a couple of places seemed to me would be top choices for a place to live. People out there, lots of 'em, have the money to buy what they want, and they like good horses. Fact is, there's one special place I have in mind. I think I could raise horses out there and make a good living."

He nodded. "Never been there, but I hear it's pretty country."

"Joe, I think my share from the partnership will be nearly enough to give me a start in business. Matter of fact, if I win the race next month, that alone will be enough."

"Darnell tells me you know more about horses than he knew at your age. Aside from what you know, he says you have a gift for it. So?"

"I want to take Kit with me when I go."

"What's she say?"

"I figured I'd better check with you first, before I asked her."

Joe came to his feet, shifted his gunbelt, straightened his coat, and started for the door.

"You just going to walk away? You got nothing to say?"

He swung around to face me and said flatly, "When you have daughters, you'll understand better. If I didn't like you, Ward, I'd have run you off or shot you long ago. Now, I got nothing to say. You got her to please, not me."

"That's it?"

Joe rubbed the corner of his eye with a finger, as if reflecting on the question before answering, "I might as well try to be helpful. I wouldn't spend time talking to her about grass, water, horses, how much money you have, or any of that. You got enough sense to know what I'm talking about?"

I stood rubbing my hands together while trying to think fast. Fact was, he'd said not to mention about everything I'd planned to talk about. Finally, seeing him waiting for an answer, I said, "No, sir."

He stood quietly for a moment, eyeing me. Finally, he said, "You ponder on it. Maybe something will come to you. Let's go eat. They're all downstairs waiting." He jerked open the door and walked out, with me trailing along behind.

I don't recall what was said or what we ate, but when everybody was finished and about to go upstairs, I asked Kit, "Want to sit on the porch and talk awhile?"

"No thanks, Kid." She took Thackery's arm and headed for the stairs. I didn't even realize she'd said no for a moment, being too busy feeling my vest pocket for the tenth time to be sure I had the ring. Then I must have looked like somebody slipped a chunk of ice down my back.

Luckily, Milt gave me a coy grin and imitated Kit's walk as he followed behind her. His clowning shook me out of standing in the middle of the floor, muddled like a village idiot. Then Kit turned and caught Milt in the middle of his prissy walk, gave him a look that would singe bristles off a hog, and walked back to me. "On second thought, I'd like to sit on the porch for a while. Maybe it'll be cooler outside."

When Milt said casually, "On second thought, I might come along too," his trousers suddenly went skintight, and he rose till only the tips of his moccasins touched the floor.

From hard experience, I knew what was happening to poor Milt.

Luke, standing behind him, had a handful of the seat of Milt's pants and was lifting with about the same power as a shipyard crane. My eldest brother could make a man nigh onto perfectly helpless by grabbing his britches from behind, lifting, and thus shrinking the space available for tender parts.

With Milt quivering rigidly at tiptoe in front of him, Luke said formally, "Good night, Miss Thackery. Good night, Ward." He turned and headed toward the stairs, with Milt suspended in front of him as if by magic and taking tiny, frantic steps.

Kit took my arm, but before we could get to the door, Milt's strained, hissing whisper drifted to us. "Ow! Ow! Ease up, Luke, for God's sake. Ow!"

We made it outside to one of the benches on the front porch before Kit collapsed, hands covering her face, nearly choking with the effort to conceal her laughter.

Truth was, I was having a spell of giggles myself. Not meaning to sound unfeeling or unkind, but Milt's round-eyed look of alarm and discomfort was hilarious when his back pockets started rising.

We wore out our funny bones laughing, one getting under control until the other snickered, then both of us busting loose again. We sat on that old wooden bench together, and I was feeling loose and good. Neither of us said anything for a while. A big moon was already up, softening the crude lines of the rough town buildings with its dim light. The saloons were going full blast, but the street was nearly deserted, the dust settling. Nobody came out to sit on the other bench, so we had the whole porch to ourselves. Pa told me later how Thackery explained things to folks and talked everybody in the hotel dining room into leaving by the back door.

I had pondered on what Thackery's advice meant. Probably, he didn't want me sitting out here too long with Kit, figured it might not look fitting. That's why he didn't like my idea of telling Kit all my plans. Or maybe he was trying to tell me I should get right down to business. Thinking he probably knew best, I went right at it.

"Will you marry me, Kit?"

"Why?"

"What?"

"Why?"

"I heard you ask why, girl, but what kind of a question is that?"

A man asks a woman to marry him, he expects her to say yes. If she says no, maybe she doesn't mean it. He can wait awhile, maybe, and ask again. A man is braced for a yes or a no. A yes or a no make sense. "It's too soon" makes sense. "It's too late" makes sense. "Let's wait a while" makes sense. What can a man do with a why? Why isn't an answer. Why is a dumb question.

She sat staring right at me. "Seems a simple matter to me. Why should I marry you?"

My mind was running around every which way. At first, I could feel myself getting mad. A man deserved a respectful answer, not a dumb riddle to solve. Next, I started to sink down, began to feel smaller and smaller. I couldn't think of a single damn reason to save my life. Then I thought maybe I'd taken some bad advice.

"Look, Kit, I've got some plans." I told her all about the kind of places I'd seen in California, the grass, the water, the soft weather, my prospects for having ample money for a good start, my confidence in myself when it came to working with horses. I told her all of it.

She never looked away while I talked and talked. When I finally ran down, she sat quietly as if waiting to hear something more. The silence ran on for a while. I started feeling the supreme fool. "You don't like the idea of living on a horse ranch?"

"Sounds nice."

"Does that mean yes?"

"No."

"It means no?"

"No, it doesn't mean no."

This hadn't gone anything like I'd figured. It was coming on me pretty hard that I'd been fooling myself all along. I'd been dead sure she was fond of me, but she'd surprised me once before. Still, how could I have been so wrong? She'd fooled everybody. Thackery would have warned me off. He wouldn't put me through this if he knew it was hopeless. He was too square for that kind of lowdown meanness.

My eyes started to sting when I thought of returning Mama's rings to Pa. What could I say to him? I'd been ready to give something to this girl that was impossible to replace. Mama's rings shouldn't be cheapened by being associated with frustrated, misplaced affection, poor judgment, stupidity. I wanted to get mad, but I had no cause. The fault was mine, nobody else's. Mama's rings must go to Milt or Luke. My judgment was too flawed to be trusted with them. That's what I'd have to tell Pa.

I knew the silence had stretched out for a long time while I tried to think my way through it all. When I came to my feet, I couldn't look at Kit. "It's a hard thing for a young woman, having a man mooning around when she's not interested. Your patience must have been tried most every day. I apologize. You've had enough of this. I'll take you to your door now, if you don't mind."

She said, "I love you, Ward Silvana Baynes."

I didn't want to attempt a smile. The soft moonglow and the reflected lantern light from the windows cut through the shadows of the porch roof enough for her to see my face. I'd look like grinning death. No call to blame her. She still wanted to be friends, I supposed. "Yeah, sure, I love you too, Kit."

"Then my answer is yes."

"Of course, it's getting late. Come along." I reached for her elbow.

"What're you doing?"

"I offered to take you inside if you were ready. You said yes, didn't you?"

"No, Ward. I said yes, I'd marry you."

Before I could stop my mouth, I asked, "You did? Why?"

"You finally gave me the reason I most value."

"I did? When?"

"When you told me you love me."

"What the hell! You knew that. You sat there and made me feel terrible, toying with me. That was cruel. How could you act like that?"

"I'm not about to marry you if you don't love me, no matter how much I love you."

"Oh, for heaven's sake."

"Well, you never told me straight out. Not once. Do it again."

"Hell, no."

"Do it."

"I love you."

"I love you too. Isn't that fun?"

"Oh!" My hands started patting around my pockets, searching for the ring. With all the checking and rechecking, I'd forgotten where I'd put it.

"Did a bug go down your neck?"

"No, sweet girl. I have something for you, if I can find it." When the silk unfolded, she caught her breath. "It was Mama's. Now, Kit, you don't have to take it. I'll be most eager to buy you a new one . . ."

She had her left hand extended, pointing to her ring finger with the other hand. "It's so beautiful it hurts my heart to look at it. It goes right there." After I put the ring on her finger, we had a little quiet time together before we walked back into the hotel.

As soon as we came through the door, we found Thackery and the Baynes gang sitting in the lobby waiting for us. I bowed and turned to Kit. "Gentlemen, may I introduce the future Mrs. Ward Baynes." They stood and applauded.

Milt pushed his nose flat with a finger and said in a whining voice, "That dang window was so dirty I could hardly see what was happening out there on the porch." Kit wrinkled her nose at him.

When they gathered around us, I saw Thackery slip a small box to Kit. She said, "Ward, I have something for you," and handed the box to me.

The gold watch seemed to brighten the room as soon as it was revealed. Kit took it from me, pressed the latch, and showed me her picture inside the cover. Then she flipped the timepiece over. The engraved, flowing script read:

To My Betrothed
Ward Silvana Baynes
from Kathleen Iris Thackery
July 25, 1867

I blurted, "How'd you know to have it engraved with today's date?"

Kit blushed but lifted her chin to direct her blue eyes straight at mine. "Had you not asked me today, I would have asked you."

So that's another date which comes to my mind easily. That day I acquired the only watch I ever owned and betrothal to the only woman I ever wanted. The gods can hardly do better in one passage of the sun.

NINETEEN

THE NEXT MORNING, the sound of hurried footsteps coming down the hall popped my eyes open in the near-total darkness. By the time a tap came on our door, the sounds of unguarded breathing from sleeping men could no longer be heard in our room, a sure sign that the whole Baynes gang lay awake.

"Kid . . . Kid Baynes!" The whisper came low but urgent. "Wake up."

I slid out of bed, snagged Jesse from his holster, and leaned against the wall beside the door. "That you, Coop?"

"Yeah, come quick, Kid. Somebody done messed up your horse. He's cut bad and he's down. I'm goin' for the sheriff. You better come to the stable quick as you can."

The bottom fell out of my stomach as I stomped my feet into boots and grabbed my gunbelt. Peepeye? Somebody had cut him and he was down? My left boot stubbornly refused to slip on, so I was half hopping toward the door. "Coming. I'm coming." My voice sounded like I'd been hit in the belly.

"Wait a minute, Ward. I'm coming too." No sound of movement came from Milt's part of the room, but that didn't fool me. He could fell trees without making noise if he put his mind to it. I knew he was up and moving, even though I couldn't see or hear a thing.

"Come on then," I said, jerked open the door, and ran down the hall.

"Hell, wait a minute." Milt's frantic whisper reached me as I hit the stairs, but I didn't slow down.

The front door of the hotel hung when I tried to open it. When I reared back and kicked it with all my might, the glass in the top half cracked in about four places. The damn door sprang open, but it bounced off the front wall and met me again as I charged through. When I shoved it away, it crashed against the wall again. This time the pane shattered, sending splinters of broken glass skittering and tinkling all over the porch.

I ran down the middle of the street as fast as I could, but both boots refused to settle right on my feet. When I dashed through the front door of the stable, I saw Peepeye's stall door standing open, a lighted lantern sitting in the aisle nearby. The dim light revealed a shadowy outline of a downed horse's head lying across the threshold of the stall.

My eyes filled with tears, and I had to hold my ragged breath for a moment to force myself to stop making broken groaning noises. No horseman worth his salt approaches a hurt animal when he's half hysterical himself. I took a deep, shuddering breath, dashed the back of my hand across my watery eyes, and used the morning greeting Peepeye heard every day of his life. "He-e-e-y Ho-o-oh, Peepeye."

His answer, a smug snuckering noise like he was chuckling deep inside, came from behind me! I swung around, almost upsetting the lantern, and he spoke again from across the aisle. On the darkest night, I'd know that beautiful head with glowing eyes watching me from over the stall gate. That head came up, just a bit startled, when I sprang across the aisle and slammed open the stall gate. He snuffled curiously at me while I ran my hands all over him to be sure he was sound.

When I closed the gate on Peepeye to go take a closer look at the downed horse, my legs trembled so much I leaned against the wall for a moment. My stomach was a knot pulled too tight, and I began to feel sour enough to retch.

Milt appeared and asked, "You check around the place yet? Anybody else here?"

I shook my head and he moved away, saying, "Get the hell away from that light."

After moving into the shadows, I ended up looking down at the ground, expecting to empty my nervous stomach any moment. I looked up again just in time to watch the star on his vest flash in the half-darkness of early morning light as the sheriff walked in beside Coop. The tall, stooped figure put each foot down carefully, as if each step down the wide aisle of the livery stable caused torment. When he joined me in front of Peepeye's stall, he stuck out a big hand and said, "Sheriff Chip Dodd."

I nodded and shook hands. "Ward Baynes."

He took a quick, hard look at the suffering bay horse and asked, "Why didn't you go ahead and shoot him?"

I followed his glance to the animal's bloody off-hind leg, where someone had hamstrung him with a single cold-blooded slash. "Not my horse."

Coop snatched up the lantern to take a close look and said, "Well, I'll just be damned. That's one of my horses."

Dodd's expression didn't change when he turned his head slightly toward Coop. "Any ideas who'd do this or why?"

Coop stood for a moment, looking at the horse's pain-glazed eyes before answering, "We can talk later. I don't like standing here watching the animal suffer. Shoot him, Kid."

I stepped back. "No, not me. Sorry, sir. I can't shoot a horse, just can't do it. Can't even watch."

"You're the same Ward Baynes who shot down the Hartlows a few weeks back, aren't you?"

"Yes, sir."

"And you can't shoot a horse?"

"No, sir. If I even watch somebody do that, I have bad dreams about it. Tears me up. Makes me feel awful."

"You have bad dreams about the Hartlows?"

I shrugged and shook my head. "No, sir." His question seemed pointless to me. I started to say that it didn't trouble me to shoot snakes or stomp scorpions either, but I decided to let it pass.

The sheriff looked me up and down, and it suddenly dawned on me that I was quite a sight, dressed in gunbelt, long johns, and boots. Then, when I looked down at myself, I realized my boots were on the wrong feet.

Dodd drew his pistol. "You better look away, Kid."

I walked quickly to the front door of the stable, forcing myself not to look back. I tried to concentrate on getting my boots off and back on the proper feet. A man can brace himself for an unpleasant thing when he knows it's coming, but I still flinched when the shot boomed behind me.

The other horses, startled by the blast and already skittish from the smell of blood, filled the stable with the sound of their frightened plunging and squealing. Dodd and Coop appeared beside me, the sheriff reloading. Switching his gaze from Coop to me and back again, he asked, "Now, what the hell's going on around here?"

Coop said, "Somebody made a mistake. Looks to me like they was after the Kid's horse."

Dodd dropped his weapon into its holster and waited, saying nothing.

Coop went on, "My hired man cleans stalls at night. He moves the horses around so's to get 'em out of the way where he's workin'. I've done told him a hundred times to put the animals back where they came from, but he sees ever'thing through the bottom of a bottle, so he forgets sometimes. Anyhow, the Kid's horse had that stall before my man moved him. That poor bay of mine must have looked just like Peepeye in the dark."

"Why would anybody want to do a thing like this?" Dodd kept his eyes on Coop. "And why do you think they were after the Kid's horse?"

Coop stalked over to his favorite chair, pulled a pocketknife, carved a chunk from his plug of tobacco, and worked it around into his cheek before he responded. "Did you and Marshal Frank Jopson trade chin music on the Thackery bushwhackin'?"

Dodd nodded. "We talk."

"I heard the Kid's brothers tell Frank that one of them bushwhackers called Thackery by name. Chintry's the only one I know of around here who knew Thackery before him and the Baynes men brung a fortune in gold to town. Then Chintry tried to shine up to the Thackery girl, but the Kid showed him up, made him look like a jackass in front of half the town. He's been ridin' high around here, and the Kid cut him down to size."

Coop cocked an eye at me. "You're lucky as sin. Chintry usually has a couple of his men follering him around. He must have waved 'em off before he went over to show your girl what a big man he was." His gaze shifted back to Dodd. "You heard about how the Kid braced him and pulled his fangs?"

Dodd grinned and flicked a quick glance at me. "Yeah, me and everybody else in town. Even Chintry's own hired men are smirking and laughing about it." He looked back at Coop to ask, "Why do you think Chintry knew Thackery before?"

"Friend of mine told me about them havin' a little talk at the breakfast table of my hotel. This was the morning before Thackery left to go back to his mine. My friend said they didn't need no introduction."

Coop sent an amused look in my direction. "I heard Chintry gave you his blessing, Kid. Maybe your little girlfriend told you about it."

When I stood silent, remembering Kit's response to Chintry's holier-than-thou "blessing," Coop added, "This here is a small town, and I figure it good business to keep up with things."

"Any man who carries a hideout gun is vicious, Sheriff Dodd, a public menace," I said in a righteous voice.

Coop snickered. When Dodd lifted an eyebrow in his direction, he explained, "I told you about this boy's sense of humor, didn't I? Chintry used some of them same words and the same bigshot manner of talking to describe the Kid. He tried to talk Frank into arrestin' the Kid after he shot them two Hartlows."

"Way I heard it, you talked Chintry into giving that little gun to Miss Thackery." Dodd's expression was that of a seasoned gambler, but a glint of humor in his eyes betrayed him.

I kept a straight face. "I don't think she took kindly to it, not being partial to guns. I figured to hand it back."

"You run her errands, do you?" Dodd asked bluntly.

"I do," I replied, making the answer as curt as the question.

"Staked a claim, have you?"

"I have."

The sheriff's face seemed to relax. He thought that over for a few seconds before he said, "Fair enough." Then he made a sour mouth. "But if you gave that peashooter back, that'd just rub his hair backwards some more. You give it to me, and I'll give it to him. Then he can't claim he was robbed and make a fuss." He turned back to Coop. "You think Chintry sneaked in here last night to ruin the Kid's horse?"

"Hell, no." Coop spat at another unsuspecting beetle. "He don't do nothin' his own self. He's bought a dozen claims and don't lift a hand on none of 'em. Owns a winnin' racehorse and don't ride it. Hires ever'thing done. Hires somebody to chew his grub before he swallers it, for all I know. But I notice that none of them fellers he bought claims from was ever seen or heard from again. And I notice that anybody on a fast horse who takes a run at his fancy black nag ends up on his butt in the dirt, nursin' a sore head. A man doin' business with Chintry needs to be careful. He likes a sure thing."

Dodd shrugged. "So?"

"The Kid here's different. Anybody who pulls something on him knows damn well he'll answer for it. Of a morning, them Baynes fellers strap on guns before puttin' on their hats. Next month, if they knock the Kid out'a the saddle, it ain't gonna be a matter of beatin' him over the head to shut him up like they done with them others. It's gonna be a gunpowder showdown with the whole family. The way I see it, if they can take out the horse, they don't have to worry about the Kid."

Dodd asked placidly, "You got any proof?"

Coop sat quietly in his tilted-back chair so long I thought he wasn't going to answer. When he spoke after the long pause, his voice was barely audible. "Makes a man mad to see a horse treated like that. Makes a man madder if it's his own horse. Makes a man madder yet if it happens in his own stable. Bad for business."

The sheriff answered mildly, "You know better'n that, Coop. That kind of talk isn't proof."

"That's why it's only talk. I'm just givin' you a chance to do your job, Mr. Sheriff, and you better git after it. Whoever cut up a horse of mine made a big mistake. The day I'm sure about who done it is the day I pick up my shotgun. If there's proof around, you better find it before I do."

"I think I know my job, Coop."

"Just tryin' to be helpful, Mr. Sheriff. One more thing, since you're supposed to keep the peace. The men around town are sick and tired of the rough stuff in our horse races. We know who's doin' most of it, and there's about to be a riot. That's bad enough. But if they pull their dirty tricks on this kid, we'll have worse than a riot. We'll have a bunch of killin's."

"You making threats, Coop?"

"I'm making a prediction, that's what I'm doin'. Darnell Baynes and Joe Thackery rode into town from that little valley of theirs with thirty miners behind 'em, all of 'em looking like friendly neighbors. If Kid Baynes gets knocked off his horse, you're either gonna have to leave town or call the U.S. Army for help, Mr. Sheriff. I'm tellin' you, the top's gonna blow off."

Pa walked out on the hotel porch and looked my way, so I stepped out in the street and motioned for him to come to the stable. "Sheriff Dodd, Mr. Cooper, I'd like to ask a favor. It might be easier to keep Peepeye safe if we spread it around that we just shot my horse." I felt for a pocket before remembering my pants were still in the hotel. "I'll pay ten dollars for that dead horse."

"What?" Coop asked, while he and Dodd both looked at me as if I'd gone foolish.

"Can't have an officer of the law spreading lies," I said. "That's my horse you shot, Sheriff Dodd, 'cause I just bought him. I'll give you the money as soon as I get into my pants, Mr. Cooper."

Coop shrugged and flipped a hand. "At your pleasure, Mr. Baynes," he said, sarcastically copying my formal speech.

"Now you can tell the truth about it, Sheriff, even tell people I couldn't stand to do the shooting myself. It won't be your fault if everybody thinks the horse of mine you shot was Peepeye. We'll take that animal out of town under a tarp in a wagon, pile brush over him and burn it, and then bury what's left. Even if somebody has the guts to check, with the hide burned off there isn't a man alive can tell it's not Peepeye."

When Pa walked up to us, Milt sauntered around the corner of the stable to join the group. I told Pa what had happened and my plan. He agreed and asked Coop and Sheriff Dodd, "You men willing to help? This won't work unless you keep quiet."

Dodd nodded and Coop said, "Hiding that Peepeye horse is like covering the moon on a clear night. There must be a hundred men in town who know that animal by sight. I'll do my best to keep folks out of here today. The kid can try to sneak his horse out tonight."

"I got breakfast to eat and work to do," Dodd said. "I'll be asking around to see what turns up. If any of you men find out anything, don't try to handle this yourselves. I'm the law in this town. Any man who forgets that is asking for grief." He walked away with his distinctive footsore gait.

Pa went to arrange at the hotel for us to stay in town another night. I tugged at Milt's sleeve when he started to follow Pa. "Hey, Milt, bring me some clothes, will you?"

He shrugged and trotted off to catch up with Pa. Coop hitched a team to a wagon and pulled it inside the stable. When Milt and Luke came to help load the dead horse, I asked, "You bring me some britches, Milt?"

He snapped his fingers and grimaced. "Slipped right out of my mind, Ward. I'll ask Pa to bring them down to you."

When everything was ready, I said, "I hate to go down the middle of the street in broad daylight in my underwear. Besides, I'm scared to leave Peepeye by himself."

Coop said, "Hell, I'm gonna be here."

Milt swung up to the wagon seat beside Luke and said, "You stay here too, Ward. We won't need you. Kit would be more handy with a shovel than you are anyhow, but she isn't coming with us either. She said she'd bring you and Coop something to eat at noon. We plan to be back before dark."

As soon as the wagon pulled out into the street, Coop and I closed the front and back doors to the stable. I went over to sit and talk to my horse for a while. Finding that crippled bay in Peepeye's stall had scared me so bad I still had an uneasy stomach.

Coop sat in his chair outside. Six or eight times he brought horses in or came to take them out. Each time Coop stopped his customers at the door. He'd come inside by himself, shut the door, and I'd help him saddle or unsaddle horses.

He told those who tried to insist on coming inside that I was in there grieving over my horse, that I needed time for my mind to cool, that I wasn't acting right, that I wouldn't bother him, but he was afraid I might shoot anybody else who went in. Coop had a hell of a good time giving me the reputation of a crazy man, a wizard with a gun who was lurking around, brokenhearted and angry, waiting for a chance to shoot somebody.

I was half asleep when I heard voices raised in protest at the front door. Curious, I walked closer just in time to hear somebody say, "You can't let that girl go in, Coop. Not with him in there."

Kit, serious as a skinny parson, said, "Oh, don't worry, sir. He hates to shoot a woman. It always makes him gloomy for a couple of days. Besides, he's never shot a woman who brought him food." She paused for a moment, then added thoughtfully, "Unless she brought something he didn't like."

The sound of the front door latch moving sent me scrambling to Peepeye's stall. I turned him a bit so I could stand with him in front of me, between me and the aisle.

Coop opened the door only a narrow crack to let Kit slip through before he slammed it shut again. Carrying a covered tray, she came prissing in like a little girl wearing her mama's new hat. She stopped in the middle of the place and looked around for me. "Where are you?"

"I'm right here." She started toward the stall, and I said quickly, "Uh, don't come over here, Kit. Why don't you put the tray on that old wheelbarrow over there? That'll be just fine. Then you can run along back to the hotel, and I thank you for bringing me a bite to eat."

She paused by the wheelbarrow and said, "Ward, they use this to clean up behind the horses. It's covered with flies. I don't want to put your lunch on this dirty old thing."

"That's fine. That's fine. Don't concern yourself, Kit. Just put it down. That'll be just fine, and thank you very much. Bye now. I'll see you later."

"Ward? Are you all right? You sound funny."

"Fine, fine, fine, just put it down and run along, Kit. You don't want to hang around this dirty old stable."

"Fine, fine, fine, yourself. You sound like a dog barking." She moved her head back and forth, peering into the shadows of Peepeye's stall.

"Look, Kit, I ran down here while it was still dark this morning, and I was in a big hurry. I, uh, didn't get dressed as carefully as usual."

She turned so I could see a flat package wrapped in newspaper tucked under her arm. "Oh, maybe that's why Milt asked Darnell to give this to you. I told Darnell I'd take care of it. No use both of us walking all the way down here."

She stood real still and wore a thoughtful look for a moment before she said, "Come to think about it, I never noticed you looking carefully dressed. If you think you're carefully dressed when I usually see you, you must look a sight now." She took a few steps closer to Peepeye's stall, moving her head from side to side as she searched for me.

"Stop right there. Don't come any closer. Why don't you just put down my tray, sail that package over Peepeye to me, and go away? Could you do that? That doesn't seem hard to me. First, put down the tray. Second, throw me my package. Third, go away. Can you remember all of that, or you want me to remind you after each one?"

"I see a little shelf by the front door. I'll put your tray on that." She walked out of sight. A moment later she came back into view. "How do you want me to throw this package?"

"Throw it, sail it, pitch it, fling it, toss it, chunk it, flip it, do anything you like with it, Kit. Just get it over here to me, will you, for heaven's sake?"

The package came flying over Peepeye's back, and I grabbed it out of the air, ripped off the string and newspaper cover, and gave a sigh of relief to find a fresh shirt and pair of pants. Quickly, I kicked off my boots and unbuckled my gunbelt. With no place to hang the belt, and not wanting to drop it in the stable litter, I started jerking my pants on with my free hand. That's about as awkward as anything a man can try, especially if he's in a hurry.

I was just pulling the second leg of my pants on when Peepeye decided to shift his feet and nudge me with his rump. Bumped off balance, my head cracked against the wall and down I went.

Tangled in my pants, holding my gunbelt up high with one hand so Jesse wouldn't drag in the stable litter, and caught between Peepeye and the wall, I couldn't get up, was left no choice but to squirm around till my pants were high enough to free my ankles and knees. When I glanced up, I found Kit hanging on the stall gate. All I could see of her was a laughing face and the tips of her fingers clinging to the top of the gate. Giggling like a half-wit, she chortled, "Big, bad man."

I grabbed a handful of powdery manure and hay and threw it at her, but she backed away from the gate too quick and that damn stuff just drifted right back all over Peepeye and me. By the time I got myself put together and struggled out into the aisle after her, she yelled, "Don't forget to bring the tray back to the hotel." The front door slammed, and she was gone.

Damn that Milt for not bringing my britches to me himself like a regular human being would have done. And why did he have to go and make that nasty remark? I wasn't such a bad hand with a shovel; a man has to be if he hangs around horses much.

I have never to this day figured it out. All my life, strangers treated me with respect or ignored me. Then later, maybe, they'd hear about my reputation and become cautious, even fearful. No stranger ever laughed at me. But those closest to me, my pa and my brothers, never seemed to tire of making me feel like a clown, a simple little pinhead not quite ready to wear long trousers.

Now, my own woman was picking up the habit. She had to do it. She, absolutely, had to look in the stall and see me fumbling around like I needed help to put my britches on. Things like that simply had to happen to me, always to me, nobody else. Just thinking about it made my face get hot as a Death Valley sunburn.

After washing in a bucket of fresh water, I waved my hands around until they dried. She'd brought me a couple of thick steak sandwiches and a little crockery pot that held three or four cups of hot coffee.

Good grub. My stomach decided to turn agreeable again for some reason.

Coop stuck his head in the door and said, "Well, looks like she got you all polished up and presentable again, little man."

Now Coop was catching it, talking to me like I was about six years old. *"Et tu Brute?"* I asked sadly.

"Huh? Oh, naw, she didn't bring me no brewtay. I et two sandwiches."

TWENTY

MY NEW WATCH told me it was after ten o'clock that night when Mike Freere and I rode out, with me on Peepeye but leading another horse, a leggy sorrel. I planned to ride the sorrel back to town before dawn. Freere was obviously pleased when Milt brought him to the stables earlier in the evening and I asked him to help. He agreed to hide in the woods with Peepeye a couple of hours' ride from town and meet us when we rode out the next morning. That way, everybody in Bannock would see my whole family ride out together, with me on a strange horse.

Coop sold me the sorrel, but he refused to take the ten dollars I offered for the dead bay. He gave me a glance that would have soured milk and said, "I ain't never sold no dead horse to a man in my life. Things like that git around. Bad for business."

Coop blew out the lantern, and we sat in front of the dark stable for an hour before we left. Freere had agreed so quickly when I asked him to help, I wondered if he knew what he might be getting into.

I commented as we were saddling, "Mike, whoever is low enough to cripple a horse might be the kind to shoot at a man in the dark. If somebody's watching this stable, we might ride out of here into trouble."

Mike said with a chuckle, "Thanks, Kid, but you don't need to mother me. I ain't as fast with a shortgun as you are, but I figure to ride with my rifle in my hand."

"Mike done some ridin' in that war we had, Kid." Coop's voice was almost a whisper in the shadows. "He rode with a feller called Nathan Bedford Forrest."

Freere chuckled again. "Besides, Milt already told me what to do if there's trouble."

That brought my head up in surprise. "What? What'd he say?"

"He told me three times, like he thought I was a mite deaf, 'If trouble comes close, get behind Ward or off a bit to one side. All you'll have to worry about is the leavings. The main thing is not to get in his way.' "

"Oh," I said.

"You surprised, Kid?" Mike's voice sounded like he was about to burst out laughing.

"Yeah. Well, you know Milt. He's always joking. No telling what he's likely to say." I grabbed the lead reins of my second horse and swung into Peepeye's saddle.

Leather creaked as Mike mounted. The click when he eared back the hammer of his rifle came plainly through the silence. "Stay here a minute while I ride out, Kid. I know the streets better'n you do. I'll lead the way till we get out of town. You stay behind far enough for me to turn back if I figure there's too much light."

I agreed by saying, "You sound like you've done this kind of thing before."

Coop swung the big livery door open, and Mike walked his horse into the doorway, stopping just short of the line of moonlight on the ground. He leaned forward in the saddle to scan the street before answering. "Yeah, 'bout a thousand times, I reckon."

Then he sat back in the saddle, dropped his reins to his horse's neck, lifted his rifle, and heeled the animal gently into a quiet walk. Guiding his mount with his knees, he crossed into the shadows of the buildings on the far side before turning down the street.

I followed him when he cut down a narrow alley to avoid lighted saloon fronts, made a couple of detours to get around meager glow from windows of late-to-bed townspeople, and reached the edge of town confident we'd passed unseen.

When Peepeye walked up beside his horse on the road outside town, Mike commented dryly, "If anybody was watchin' for us, we either got past 'em without bein' seen or they decided we weren't worth shootin'."

"Yeah, now all we have to do is put a couple of hours of quiet riding behind us."

"Right. The sound of a trottin' horse will wake folks. Best we just ease along for a while."

Shortly after midnight, I pointed to a grove of trees standing black and dense in the moonlight. The thicket lay well back from the road. Wordlessly, Mike swung off the trail in the opposite direction and rode about a hundred yards before wheeling in a wide loop back toward the road. I found myself nodding and grinning.

The man was smart. Anybody trying to track us would probably pull off the road and away from the woods at that exact point, a sure tip-off he was trailing us. That would give Mike a choice of moving on, knowing he had somebody on his trail, or shooting at his pursuer's exposed back. I amused myself for a while wondering if somebody had taught him such tricks or if he laid traps like Milt, just because it was his nature.

Before we crossed the road to get to the woods, I said, "Let's stop here for me to switch my saddle. I'll ride back a good distance before hitting the road again, and I'll ride on from this side."

When I had the saddle on the other horse, Mike and I shook hands. He said, "I'll be somewhere over yonder. See you about two hours after sunup."

"Thanks, Mike." I swung up, leaned over to rub Peepeye's nose to quiet his jealous dancing, and rode off feeling his disgusted eyes boring into my back. I rode other horses lots of times, but Peepeye never took to the idea. He never took it out on me, but he'd been known to bite and kick the other horses to make his opinion plain. It was always easier to have him in a stall and out of sight when I was working with another horse.

Stallions can make trouble, naturally taking a bossy manner around mares and, usually, showing strong dislike for geldings. Most men don't care to ride stallions, finding them to be too hard to handle. Maybe, because of his natural duty to look after a herd in the wild, a stallion is more alert, more curious, more easily excited.

A common sight during my younger days, on buying trips with Pa, was a herd of horses in a pasture with the mares and foals quietly grazing. The stallion, however, always had his head up, watching us and testing the wind, knowing at once that strange horses and men were approaching. Later, I saw the same thing over and over again when watching wild horses. In my case, I always found Peepeye's alertness an advantage.

Not worrying anymore about waking curious people who might be camped close to the road, I made good time back to the outskirts of town. The moon had slid behind clouds, so I doubted if anyone could identify me anyway. Once in town, I rode straight to the stable, since the saloons were quiet and dark at two o'clock on a Monday morning. Even carousing miners have to sleep sometime. The sorrel wasn't tired by the slow night ride and seemed to appreciate a bonus dipper of corn. Without seeing any sign of Coop, I walked through the shadows toward the hotel.

I jumped about six feet straight up and came down with Jesse in my hand when a voice came from the deep shadows almost at my elbow. "You did a good job."

"Damn you, Milt! You made me jump clear out of my boots. I nearly shot your fool head off." I eased the hammer down, holstered Jesse, and stood there swallowing, trying to get my heart to slide back down into my chest.

"We need to get you married off before you die of nervous fidgets."

"Why didn't you scream and pounce on me? Afraid I'd stick Jesse in your ear and make you wash my drawers?"

"Let's go to bed. You're fussy when you stay up late."

"Wait a minute. My knees are all wobbly. What're you doing sneaking around in the dark anyhow?" I leaned forward to put my hands on my knees and took a couple of deep breaths. "Damn you, Milt. My children will be born with their hair standing straight up."

"Just thought I'd look after you, just in case somebody tried to follow you in or out of town."

"Thanks. I stopped two or three times on the way out and pointed Peepeye back down the road. They'd have to stay mighty far back or he'd tell me about them. I stopped a couple of times on the way back in for a good listen and never heard a thing."

"I figured you'd be jumpy and snappish, so I planned to talk them into staying in town if anybody tried to start after you. It seemed like a civic duty. As a public-spirited man, I feel called on to save lives if I can. Besides, it upsets Kathleen the way you keep shooting people."

"Let's go to bed."

We sneaked into the hotel and up to our room. I spent most of the little time I had in bed pop-eyed as an owl. Every time I'd drift off to sleep, I'd dream about monsters jumping out at me from dark alleys and vicious men with knives creeping up on Peepeye.

TWENTY-ONE

THE NEXT MORNING, all four men of the Baynes family walked out the front door of the hotel and right into trouble. Even Milt, with all his cautious ways, got caught as flat-footed as the rest of us, right in the middle of town.

We had barely stepped off the porch into the dusty street when two men walked out of the alley beside the hotel and pointed rifles at us. One said, "Stop right there." I saw two more rifles come level and point our way from across the street. A glance behind me picked up two more. Quicker'n it takes to tell it, we were covered by three pairs of rifles from three different directions. The same man said, "Drop your guns real slow."

We had no choice. As best I could figure, they had us cold. Still, that was about the hardest thing I ever did, dropping Nadine and Jesse into that dusty street. When I looked up, Amos Chintry walked into sight, dressed in a tight, thin, sleeveless undershirt, snug trousers, and what looked like soft dancing shoes. He looked bigger than he did in his fancy clothes. In fact, I didn't even recognize him at first. His neck looked thicker, and ridges of muscle rippled along heavy shoulders and powerful arms. I guessed he must outweigh me by forty or fifty pounds.

Chintry signaled two of his men forward and said, "Be sure to keep the Thackerys inside." The two men walked quickly into the hotel. Pointing to Pa and my brothers, he said, "Move aside." As soon as they took a few steps away, he walked up to me, took a pose with his left arm stuck way out and both hands fisted up, and said, "Let's see what you can do without that gun." The left flicked at my face.

I don't know exactly what Chintry was thinking, but he was too clever by half and too slow by any clock. Maybe he thought I'd be frozen by fear, afraid to move, or possibly he figured I'd be so surprised I'd just stand there to be hit. Anyhow, he was dead wrong on both counts if that's what he was counting on. Or perhaps he was sure of himself for other reasons. His pose and his clothing reminded me of the bare-knuckle prize-fighters I'd seen in New Orleans.

His left I slapped aside with my open hand, and his right went overhead, knocking my hat off when I ducked. My heel crunched down on the instep of his leading foot with my whole weight on it, bringing a sharp gasp from him. "Up and down," Milt used to laugh while he was punching me around. "Always hit a man high and low."

Chintry blinked suddenly watering eyes from the shock of it when, a split second later, his nose flattened in a splatter of blood from the hardest right cross I ever threw. My left jab made a heartwarming spat when it followed my right to his nose. Milt always did that to me. He said the follow-up left was good for a man's balance, set him up so he could step away or punch again, whichever he wanted to do.

When Chintry's fists came up too late to protect his face, his elbows drew in tight, tucked close to defend his body. He'd learned good habits from somebody, covered himself nicely, but he stepped back instead of circling like Milt would have done. That let me follow him easy, so I went right along and kicked him twice on both shins before he caught on that he needed to watch my feet. Up and down, that's what Milt said was best.

Chintry flinched when he caught the last two shots to the shins, and I couldn't help but grin. By this time, I guess a crowd was forming, because I heard men laughing all around me, but I didn't dare take my eyes off Chintry.

Kicking had always been my best shot against Milt. The last time Milt beat me up he'd limped around for two or three days calling me a shin-kicking little bastard. Then Pa heard him and soaped his mouth. Seeing Milt get soaped had almost been worth getting beat up until I started feeling sorry for him. Pa was thorough about everything he did. Milt blew bubbles for a couple of hours.

I stopped grinning when Chintry tried a double jab followed by a right cross. The two jabs I slapped away, but the right cross came in too quick. All I had time to do was duck to catch his fist on the top of my head instead of in the face. It felt like he'd hit me with a hammer, and I felt my knees go limber, but he hesitated and grimaced for an instant, long enough to open and close his right fist.

I hoped he'd hurt his hand. Hitting a man on the top of his head feels the same as hitting a hitching post. Anyhow, that little hesitation earned him another kick, but I was a little high this time, caught him on the knee.

I heard men laugh again, but Chintry didn't find anything funny about it. I could tell he shifted his weight to his right foot and put weight on the left leg uneasily. So I made like I was going to kick that knee again to draw his attention and stabbed a finger into his eye. He sucked air between his teeth and caught me with that fast right. Again, I only had time to drop my chin and catch the blow on the top of my head.

This time I nearly went down, and everything went out of kilter. Maybe my eyes crossed. I don't know for sure if that's what happened, but everything went blurred and out of focus. I kicked him again, and he groaned when I caught him on that tender left knee. Once more he tried to step back instead of circling, but he favored his left leg, so it wasn't much of a trick to catch him on the other shin.

Chintry grabbed my shirt and pulled me up close, trying to keep me from kicking him, I guess. Anyhow, I bit his arm with all my might while I stomped him again as hard as I could on the instep of one of his feet and brought a knee into his groin.

When he groaned and tried to double up, I straightened my knees sharply, catching his lowering face solidly with the top of my head. My feet would probably have left the ground if my battered noggin had missed his face. Both his hands came up to his nose, and he started to turn away. But I slapped his hands aside, gripped the back of his neck, and smashed my head into his face three more times before he could fall away and drop to his hands and knees.

All I could hear was a high buzzing noise, and the top of my head hurt so bad I could hardly keep from dropping to the ground and moaning. I suppose I'd knocked myself half silly butting Chintry in the face, else I'd not have tried the next stunt. At a moment like that, a man has no time to stop and think. He has to move too fast. Besides, my head hurt so bad I was past thinking.

Ballet dancers call a leaping turn off the floor a *tour en l'air*. Show-horse trainers call it a capriole when a horse jumps in the air, tucks its forelegs, and lashes out with its hind legs, then drops to the same spot on the ground. Anyhow, I did both at the same time, except I lashed out with only one hind leg when I jumped and turned in midair. My boot heel caught Chintry in the head so hard it jarred me clear up to the small of my back. It hurt me, and I was the one doing the kicking. My heel felt so numb I feared it was broken.

Vaguely, I remembered talking to a Frenchman at a *savate* match in New Orleans. That contest made bare-knuckle boxing look gentle. The man had told me, "The legs are stronger than the arms, oui? So, what you think, monsieur? You think a kick with the foot come harder than a hit with the fist? Eh? What you think?"

The idea came into my fuzzy head that I'd broken Chintry's neck for sure, and the notion started me to laughing. I wanted to kick Chintry some more, just to make sure he didn't get up again, but my legs were shaking so bad I knew I'd just fall down. My eyes were still crossed, and my feeble-minded cackling died when I turned on wobbly legs to see a blurred Sheriff Dodd standing beside me.

"I done told you stop once, Kid. I don't tell a man to stop twice." His voice sounded funny, like he was talking in a barrel.

"Uh, sorry, sir." I stood there blinking and rubbing my aching head. Hard knots had started swelling already. "I didn't hear you. What do you want me to stop?" People laughed and I wondered what was so damned funny.

"Mr. Baynes?" Dodd asked real loud.

"Yes, Sheriff." Pa's broad shape appeared beside Dodd.

"I believe you were planning to leave town this morning?"

"That's where we were headed."

"Then I suggest you keep moving. Just be sure this kid goes with you."

Pa nodded to Dodd, glanced at me, and jerked his head toward the stable.

I walked over to where Jesse and Nadine lay in the dust. When I bent to pick them up, the knots on the top of my head swelled up another inch and my eyes tried to pop out. My hat went on very carefully, but it went on, which surprised me, since my head felt big and sloshy as a half empty keg.

Six men stood quietly, shoulder to shoulder, beside a row of rifles lying on the front porch of the hotel. After I stood for a moment, blinking stupidly at them, one said in a jittery voice, "No hard feelin's, Kid. We work for the man. Like we told the sheriff, Chintry said he had a bone to pick with you, and all we had to do was keep you from shootin' him."

After I turned and walked a couple of slow steps toward the stable, trying to put my feet down without limping or jarring my head, one of the men muttered, "I think I'll draw my time. I ain't gettin' paid enough."

Another said, "Me too. That kid wanted to remember us, looked like he was ready to shoot us one and all. I'm gonna look for a job somewheres else. To hell with this."

I went on down the street, wondering about people who thought I'd just haul off and shoot them. It was enough to make a man mad, having people talk like that. But I didn't care much right then. If I stumbled or made the smallest misstep, I knew I'd fall flat. I was even more worried about being sick in the middle of the street.

Somebody came past and slapped me on the shoulder. "Nice going, Kid. I done heard of shin-kickin' contests, but I never thought I'd ever see one." He walked away laughing. I kept walking, wearing an empty grin simply because I hadn't fallen down when that fellow touched me.

Pa walked up beside me and asked, "You all right, son?"

"No, sir. I think I hurt myself. My head hurts real bad, and I'm going to be sick in a little while."

"Can you ride out of town all right?"

"Yes, sir, but I don't feel right. Seems like I forgot something."

We walked all the way to the stable before I remembered. "Kit! Where's Kit? Where's my Kit, Pa?"

"We'll take the horses by the hotel. She and Joe are waiting for us there. Don't you remember? You didn't want her walking all the way down here in the dusty street."

I stood there trying to think about it, but thinking seemed to make me feel sicker, so I put it aside. Nothing to bother about. Everybody has things slip his mind once in a while. I went to get Peepeye, but another horse stared over the stall door at me. I went down the line, looking.

Pa asked, "Where you going, Ward?"

"I thought Peepeye was in that stall right there, Pa, but somebody must've moved him. Now I can't find him."

He came to me and gripped my arm. His voice was gentle when he said, "Peepeye's down the trail a little ways with Mike Freere, remember? You took him out of town last night. Peepeye's all right. You come

over here and sit down. We'll get the horses saddled. You just sit quiet
for a while."

"Thanks, Pa. I'll make it up to everybody later, but my head hurts
right now. It hurts something awful." I sat on a bale of hay and started
cleaning the dust off Jesse. Seeing double can sure do queer things to a
man's stomach, but I knew Jesse so well I could look after him with my
eyes closed. In fact, that's what I ended up doing. It seemed like my
insides didn't feel so queasy if I kept my eyes shut.

When I opened my eyes again, I found Kit kneeling in front of me,
her face pale and scared looking in the flickering light of a campfire.
She held my coffee cup in one hand and a wet towel in the other. My
back was braced against a big log and my face felt damp. I asked, "You
been wiping my face?"

She nodded.

"How long I been out?"

She asked, "Are you back?"

"I asked first."

Kit turned her head and called, "Darnell, I think he's coming out of
it. He's talking sense."

Pa came to his feet on the other side of the campfire and started
toward me.

"Have I been saying dumb things, Kit?"

"No, you've been talking real sweet to everybody, so we were all
worried to death."

Pa leaned over me and asked, "You remember having a fight?"

"Yes, sir. I remember going to the stable afterward. Did I fall over?
Did you have to carry me?"

"No, son. You rode out on your own, but your eyes were glassy and
you didn't make much sense. We stopped and camped where Freere
was waiting with Peepeye. I was afraid you'd fall off your horse if we
tried to go any farther. How do you feel now?"

"I think my head'll fall off if I move." I lifted my hand carefully
toward my coffee cup, and Kit gave it to me.

Pa asked, "You sure you feel up to drinking that?"

A sour odor came to me, mixing with the good smell of wood smoke
and fresh coffee. The front of my shirt and one leg of my trousers felt
stiff and flaky. I lifted an eyebrow at Pa.

"Yeah, you been sick all day, all over the place. Kit tried to keep you
cleaned up as best she could."

When I looked her way, Kit grinned and said, "You shouldn't eat so much breakfast if you're going to run right out and pick a fight."

Luke appeared over me, leaned down, and rubbed my cheek. He didn't say anything, didn't need to. His face spoke for him better than words.

Milt laughed from somewhere in the nearby darkness and said, "You broke two bones in his hand, two bones in his foot, his kneecap, his jaw, and his nose."

"How'd you find out all that stuff?" I asked.

He drifted into sight, snatched my cup, took a quick mouthful, spat on the ground, and wrinkled his nose at Kit. He handed the cup to her and asked sternly, "Squaw give cold coffee to wounded brave?"

Then he smirked at me and said, "I stayed behind and bought the doctor a drink before I left town. I told him it was a good thing you didn't get mad. Somebody told him how you laughed through the whole fight. That doctor was mighty upset. He said big brutes like you should be stopped before you beat up people so bad. He didn't believe me when I told him you were just a sickly little runt."

"A sickly little scared runt," I said, carefully feeling the bumps on my swollen head.

"Your feet all right?" Milt asked. He grinned and reached for the fresh cup of coffee Kit was carrying from the fire. She gave him a bright smile, spilled some on his outstretched hand, ignored him when he jerked back and crumpled up his face like he was in agony, and handed the coffee to me.

I wiggled my toes and answered, "Yeah, I think my feet are all right. Why?"

He looked at Pa and said, "I'm going out to take watch. I'll send Mike Freere in for some rest." He swung his gaze back to me. "The way Chintry kept hitting you on top of the head, I felt sure he'd flattened your feet and broke both your ankles." He disappeared into the darkness, chuckling.

Kit smiled at Milt's departing figure. When she turned back to me, she leaned closer and said very quietly, so I was the only one to hear, "Darnell's acted like a concerned father all day. Luke's been a worried brother. But Milt's been like a fluffed-up broody hen. He thinks he's your mother, Ward. Nothing I did for you was good enough. He's been more of a pest than a jealous mother-in-law."

Thackery walked over and looked at the ground beside me. When I glanced down, I found Kit's blankets spread beside mine. He stared at her until she said, "I'm still worried about him. My proper place is here."

He stood very still, staring at her for another long moment before turning his chilling gaze toward me. Even the fire stopped crackling in the dead quiet.

"Next time you catch Chintry wearing a gun, kill him."

He turned stiffly and walked into the shadows.

TWENTY-TWO

ALTHOUGH MY HEAD ACHED the next morning, I could see clearly again. Breakfast went down and stayed, but my legs still felt wobbly. The tight skin on my face told me that my head was swollen, making me afraid to shut my eyes too tight for fear my scalp would split.

I couldn't find my hat. Kit watched me poke around and search for a while before female curiosity forced her to ask, "What's wrong?"

"Nothing's wrong. I guess the termites got my hat."

"Oh, I have it." She trotted to her saddle and brought my hat to me with a strained smile. "It kept falling off yesterday, and you didn't seem to notice."

"You knocked it off three or four times to rub your head," Pa said from beside the campfire. "Kit kept turning back to pick it up and bring it to you. She was wearing herself out. I finally told her to quit, so she carried it for you after that."

"Thanks, Kit."

She shrugged, and the strain went out of her smile. "You reminded me of a kitten with a cut foot I had one time. I tied a bandage on him, but the little fellow nearly went crazy until he gnawed it off so he could lick the wound. I guess you were going to rub your sore head no matter what, unless we tied you up."

Milt, crouched beside the dying campfire wolfing down his bread and bacon, said, "He's always had a sore head, but he doesn't usually feel the need to rub on it."

I tried every which way, but that damn hat felt a couple of sizes too small. Again, Kit watched me fumble around for a bit before she asked, "Want me to carry it for you?"

Without thinking, I answered, "No thanks."

Then I stood there like a fool trying to figure out what to do with it. I never before needed a place other than my head for a damn hat. Where does a riding man with a swollen head put an almost new hat without getting it mashed all out of shape? Finally, I let it fall to my back, hanging from the chin loop around my neck. I despised having anything hang around my neck, but I didn't want to spend the whole day puzzling like a half-wit on such a silly problem.

Milt walked over and stood grinning at me while he stuffed the last of his breakfast down his neck. I sat back down on my blankets to rest my shaky legs, and my voice came out sheepish when I asked him, "How'd I do?"

The grin vanished, and he spoke solemnly, nodding like a judge while he did his imitation of a prissy preacher we heard one time back home in Louisiana. "In my opinion, sir, you did a fine teaching job. Your friend and guest, Mr. Amos Chintry, received a fast lesson on our vigorous Western culture. Your foot-stomping and eye-gouging were agreeable, although a bit restrained. The shin-kicking and groin-kneeing were more generous and congenial, but you did the biting best of all. No man, indeed no horse, in Montana Territory could have bitten him any better. Mr. Chintry, I'm sure, will display with modesty the charming scar he so surely will retain from it."

I saw Luke grin and wink at Pa, who had his back to me, so I knew they were both listening too. Mike Freere's head was tilted our direction, and his hand holding his coffee cup remained halfway lifted to his mouth, forgotten. Thackery was out of sight, so I guessed he was minding the horses.

Milt paused and stroked his chin thoughtfully. "No, wait, I must retract a part of my last statement. Regrettably, I spoke in haste. After more deliberate consideration, I think the head-butting, with its unquestioned sincerity, was the warmest demonstration of our unique Western social virtues. Every last man in the crowd flinched and groaned with true Western pride, if not outright vanity, when you would butt Mr. Chintry in the face. Yes, most assuredly, that was the most poetic and musically satisfying part, sounding like somebody dropping watermelons off a high wagon."

Kit, fighting back laughter, scolded, "That's awful. What a terrible conversation. Both of you ought to be ashamed."

Milt continued as if he hadn't heard her, but his voice dropped its prissy-preacher-on-a-pulpit tone. "I give you a low mark for buttin' his fist with the top of your head. That was a neat stunt, but I don't think it worked all that good, even though you broke a couple of bones in his hand." He cut his eyes toward Kit. "That trick might do for another man, but Ward's too soft in the head here lately."

Kit laughed and asked, "Does that 'soft in the head' comment mean what I think it does? Maybe I'm about to feel insulted. Maybe I'm going to get Ward to beat you up, Milton Baynes."

He slowly raised his gaze to hers and chuckled. "See there, you love him, but you still don't know him."

"Oh, really?" Kit no longer sounded amused.

"Ward doesn't attack people. He's never done that in his whole life. He's a defender. Makes them come at him, that's his way. Last time we had a scuffle, he was only half grown, but he scared me to death. I won out over him, but I woke up shivering in the night from thinking about it. I decided that very night I'd run before I'd fight my little brother again. Nowadays, I just yap and circle without getting too near."

I started to rise, feeling embarrassed, but Milt stepped close and laid a hand on my shoulder. I shrugged against his hand and protested, "Come on, Milt. Let me up. I got a horse to saddle."

"Not you. Pa said to treat you like a sick man for a couple of days. No lifting saddles. No work at all till he says so."

"I'm all right. I do my own saddling."

"Fine." He pulled his hand away and dropped his voice almost to a whisper. "I'll just watch while you go tell Pa he's wrong."

When I hesitated, Milt smirked at Kit and said, "See, he's getting better. His good sense is coming back."

So I squirmed like a tied puppy at a rabbit picnic while everybody else did my chores. Kit wouldn't even let me roll my own blankets. Nothing bleeds the pride from a man faster than feeling useless, but Pa was right, I guess.

By the time we finished that first day's ride, my head pounded like the hammers of hell, and my stomach was sour as a demon's breath again. I slid from the saddle, stretched out in my blankets, made a dying man's face when Kit offered a plate of food, and fell asleep while it was still daylight.

Normally, with me, to wake was to rise, but when my eyes popped open in the quiet darkness of pre-dawn the next morning, I realized I didn't hurt anywhere. I closed my eyes slowly, cautiously, and found the tightness had left my face. I feared to move, so I just held still for a while. Finally, my hand crept slowly to my head. The shape felt familiar. I sat up and put on my hat. It fit.

"Expecting rain?" Kit's whisper was a warm, teasing chuckle beside me. "Afraid you'll get your pretty hair wet?" When I looked down at the vague lump under her blankets, her face was hidden in the shadows.

"Not since my roof fits again. What you doing watching me every minute? A man needs some privacy."

"I took you to raise. Remember?" Her left hand came flowing out of the blanketed lump, and the coals from the fire brought light from her ring.

Without answering, I flipped back my blankets and pulled on my boots. Shivering in the night coolness, I looked around for my coat.

"It's right there."

"Oh, for heaven's sake, Kit. I can find my own clothes."

"You didn't answer my question. Do you remember?"

"I wouldn't forget asking a lady to marry me, no matter how many dents I get in my head. Stop teasing me or I'll pounce on you, and your old man'll wake up and shoot me."

"I'm awake, and I got him in my sights. I'll shoot him for you, Kathleen." Luke's whisper came from the trees behind us.

"Oh, no, not you too, Luke," I groaned. "Everybody's against me."

Milt's blankets flew aside as he sprang to his feet. "I never heard the like of all the gigglin' and whisperin' in the middle of the night. Reminds me of the time down in Mexico when we . . ."

"Milt." Pa's voice was stern. "Don't tell that story."

"Heck no, I wasn't goin' to tell that one, Pa. I was gonna tell the one where we . . ."

"Milt, hush up." Pa sat up and yawned like a hibernating bear. "Is that coffeepot heavy or light?"

Three weeks later, Luke turned to Pa and said quietly, "We're working for nothing."

Pa straightened and mopped his face, his gaze wandering down the empty creek line. The valley had been ravaged. Dotted and veined with trenches and ragged holes, grass and trees torn away except for forlorn stumps, heaps of garbage, worn-out tools and abandoned gear strewn about, it looked like a battleground for enraged, mindless giants. Now, it lay devastated, empty and quiet except for us. Animals and birds no longer came here. The miners who had followed us to the area had given up, one after another, and drifted away to search for another strike.

Thackery leaned against his pickax and agreed. "Luke's right. I hate to give up on it, but it looks like we've cleaned it out."

Pa lifted an eyebrow at Mike Freere. Mike had given up his own claim a week ago and hired on as a powder monkey at our place. He returned Pa's glance with a shrug and a grimace. "Not for me to say, Mr. Baynes, but I don't feel I'm worth my wages. We haven't found a speck of gold since I been working for you, but we've moved many a ton of rock."

"I never worked harder in my life than in the last couple of weeks," Pa admitted. "I guess it just seems harder when a man gets nothing from his labor. One day we're taking out the richest ore anybody ever saw. The next day, nothing."

Mike rubbed his hands together, his calloused palms grinding against each other with a sharp, gritty ras   silence. "I've seen it before myself and heard of it lots of ot   ..ies. That's the way it goes in some places. No mother lode ever gets found, just splatters and chunks with rich little pockets here and there. Makes a man wonder." He looked up with a grin at Pa and Thackery. "This here was a pretty good chunk though, while it lasted. You gotta admit that."

"You ready to quit, Joe?" Pa asked flatly.

Thackery moved both hands, palms forward, in front of his chest as if warding off further discussion, shook his head, and said, "It's finished for me. I'm through with it."

"We have a nice time of year for traveling," Pa said, looking at Luke and then at me. "We'll start packing. Maybe we can be ready by the time Milt gets back from his hunting trip."

"Where you folks heading to?" Freere asked.

"First, to a horse race. After that, we'll have to decide what we're going to do." Pa cocked an eye at me and added, "I have a son who's a gambler. We're going to see if he's a winner or a loser."

TWENTY-THREE

IN THE PROCESS of cleaning out their cabin, Kit found Luke's huge nugget. After I'd dropped it into a dark corner, Kit ended up stacking things on it, and nobody thought about it anymore. That nugget lay there unguarded and forgotten while we went to town last month. Actually, it wasn't that it slipped our minds so much as everybody thought somebody else packed it with the rest of the gold we took to the bank. That's one of those crazy things nobody believes can happen. It embarrassed all of us so much that everybody just shrugged it off and didn't talk about it. Even Milt never said a word, just squeezed his eyes shut real tight with a pained expression.

Our plan was for the Thackerys to ride in with Pa and Luke. Milt and I would separate from them along the way and camp a little distance out of town. Mike Freere would ride with Milt and me, so he'd know for sure where we camped, and then he'd ride on in alone.

When the times for the races were posted, Mike would ride out and tell us when we needed to be in town. That way I could keep Peepeye out of sight and out of danger. The day of the race, I planned to bring my horse in and run the race without even feeding or watering him in town.

After the races, we planned to ride on out without spending the night. Again, we didn't want to expose Peepeye to danger from a man who might simply be crazy. Thackery and Pa would have time before the race to sell all the extra stock, tools, and cabin furnishings we wouldn't be needing anymore since we were out of the mining business.

Pa said he'd never heard of an animal being ruined like that poor bay somebody mistook for Peepeye. Before he said that, I never dreamed there was anything Pa hadn't heard of that had to do with horses. He'd been raising and running horses a long time and taught us boys to expect most every mean trick that could be devised. He always wanted us to be ready for anything, of course, and he felt that things would be easier for us if we knew most of the gambits to watch out for.

Maybe that sounds like Pa made cynics out of his sons while they were still little boys, but being ignorant never seemed to me to lead to a state of grace. A man can't help being stupid. That's born into him, and he can't change it. But being ignorant comes from a shiftless attitude, from not reading, not listening, not taking the trouble to think about things and learn.

After we separated, Milt and I unsaddled and relaxed. For once, he didn't have the fidgets, didn't spend half the night prowling around. Pa said Milt was like a wild goose, unhappy anytime he couldn't see a mile in every direction. Our little campsite was such a place, and sure enough, Milt was easy and unconcerned.

The next morning, he scraped together a tiny fire of little sticks and put water on to heat.

"Want me to make enough coffee for you too?" he asked.

"No, I don't like coffee. Never drink it. I prefer mint tea, if you don't mind."

Milt winked at me and poured water into the pot. My brother knew I would neither eat nor drink today, not even a sip of water, until after the race was over. A dry mouth and an empty belly meant several pounds lost and an edge gained over heavier riders. I expected no sympathy from Milt when I fasted. Both of us regarded that as part of my job, and both of us knew I liked my work.

It never occurred to my brother that he shouldn't hang his head over the pot, inhaling the aroma of fresh coffee with eyes shut from the pleasure of it. He proved his mind wandered other paths when he spoke. "I never been so eager to get away from a place as I was that little valley."

"Why? We got a little bit rich there. If I win that horse race tomorrow, we'll be richer still. This isn't such a bad place, this Montana Territory. We've all done fine. I found Kit here."

Milt shrugged. "Did you look around when we left? Did you ever see such a mess? A piece of God's earth was completely ruined, Ward. That makes me feel uneasy. Maybe that's what's wrong with me, why I don't like to be around people much. People don't seem to be happy till they've made everything around them so ugly I can't stand it. Seems to me God might turn mean if we keep tearing up all His work."

"I don't remember you tearing up much. Seems to me you were always off hunting."

"Yeah, but I was in on it. I didn't want to be standing there trying to look innocent when God got around to looking. How can a place ever be fixed again when it's torn up like that? I see myself standing there with a sick grin, all alone, saying, 'Gosh, I'm sorry about all this.' Then God drives me into the ground with a bolt of lightning or something like that."

"It'll grow back in a few years, don't you think?"

"Not likely. Suppose a man tried to ride across that valley on a dark night. Be mighty lucky if he didn't lose a good horse and get his own neck broken."

"You want to go back and fill up all those holes and trenches, maybe plant a few daisies?"

He gave a derisive snort and shook his head. "No. I'm not crazy. That'd take forever, and shovels don't like me anyway. I just want to ride away. I'm like a little kid, I guess. I like grabbing the cookies, but I don't want to stand around the cookie jar waiting to get caught and spanked."

Milt poured coffee for himself without even glancing at my cup, which he'd set out beside his from habit. Neither of us spoke for a long time, being content to watch the sun climb into a wide blue sky and feel the grass-scented breeze warming from the morning coolness.

"Want me to kill Chintry for you? I wouldn't mind."

"Now why would you ask a thing like that? I figure he'll walk around us. In fact, I don't expect to see him again."

"You're wrong, little brother. He'll be in town waiting for you. You ponder on it. Your Kathleen's skittish about you shooting people. You got that to deal with now. I could shoot him. She wouldn't like it, but it isn't the same since she doesn't have the same feelings about me. Besides, she doesn't really know yet how mean you are. Best she not have to find out. Best for everybody."

When Milt looked up at me, I expected to see a wry glint of humor in his eyes. His perfectly serious expression startled me. "Why you calling me mean, Milt?"

"You remember when you pulled iron on Chintry and stripped off his hideout gun? I would have bet every single thing I owned you were going to shoot him then and there. Then when he said he was going to kill you, I would have borrowed money to bet again, but you still didn't pull the trigger. That girl's good for you, Ward. The only thing I could figure was that you didn't kill him because she was there."

"Hell, Milt, I never thought about killing him unless I had to."

Milt took a long, slow breath, and one corner of his mouth twisted into a sour smirk. He held up the fingers of his left hand and held his right as if ready to count. "Tell me how many times in your life you ever pulled a gun on a man without killing him."

He waited for what seemed a long time before he went on, "Once, Ward, once, and Chintry was it."

"I wasn't sure he had that little gun. Besides, he didn't really do anything to me. I just didn't like him. He talked to me in front of Kit like I was dirt. That wasn't enough reason to kill him."

"Well, maybe you're not as mean as I thought. If he'd talked to me like that in front of my woman, I'd have put him in boot hill in about two seconds."

Our eyes locked, and I shrugged before looking away.

Milt said quietly, "Take a minute to glance toward town. That may be Mike coming." It was, but he was still too far away to identify when Milt had me look for him.

Milt said, "I made you a new pogamoggan. Yours is nearly worn-out. I saw you practicing with that mangy, raggedy old thing of yours. Throw it away. A man needs good tools." He handed me the Indian war club and turned to watch Freere approaching.

He must have spent time on it. I never saw a prettier piece of workmanship nor a more wicked-looking weapon. Drum-tight rawhide covered two feet of slender wooden rod. About eighteen inches of beautifully plaited rawhide connected one end of the rod to a leather-covered, flat rock, slightly smaller than a man's fist. The ones made with a round rock were better weapons, but the flat rock hid better under my loose buckskin shirt at the start and end of a horse race. Most Indians preferred shorter ones, but the longer version suited me. I swung it about two times, and I was used to it. Milt knew what I liked.

A Mexican rider who'd tried to lay a whip across Peepeye's nose had lain quietly and peacefully for two days without opening his eyes after meeting my pogamoggan with the side of his head. Another rider, trying to unseat me in a race in California, saw trouble coming. When he threw up his arm to ward off my war club, he blocked the rod, so I missed his head. The plaited leather whipped across his arm, and the stone broke his collarbone instead. His appreciation for Indian weapons went sky-high about the same time his butt hit cactus.

Mike swung off his horse and looked hard at Milt and me. He lifted both hands, palm up, in front of him and said, "I got awful news." When we didn't answer, he said, "The damn bank's shut down, locked up tight. Everybody in town says the banker's done disappeared."

Without a word, Milt handed Mike my coffee cup and poured from our pot. Then he turned to me, shrugged, and said, "I saw it coming." He glanced skyward. "I was afraid He'd turn mean."

"Who? What're you talkin' about?" demanded Freere.

"Milt's just joking. What'd Pa have to say?" I asked.

"He didn't say nothin' much, come to think of it, at least nothin' I heard. I guess, by the time I saw him, he must've got over the shock. When I rode in, your pa had that big nugget of Luke's laid out in the middle of the street. The whole road was clogged up with people crowding around to get a look at it."

Freere blew on his steaming coffee and cautiously took a noisy sip. "A fancy-dressed Eastern-looking feller offered your Pa three thousand dollars for that big old nugget. I thought, what the hell? So I offered five hundred more."

Mike's grin broke out, and he winked at me. "Wasn't none of them folks knew I was broke, that my boss's money to pay my wages went down with that bank. Anyhow, that Eastern feller give me a grim look and said he was ready to pay four thousand cash. I thought, in for a penny, in for a pound. I says four and a half. He says five thousand. I give him a hard look, see, like this here, and says five five. He hesitates for a minute, just long enough for me to shit my pants, before he says he'll pay six thousand. I shut my mouth, so he ran off to that other bank down the street. About five minutes later, he paid up right there in the middle of the road. Anyhow, your Pa ain't broke, boys. He done give me one thousand dollars for my part in the game, so him and Thackery still has five to split."

I turned away. It didn't take pencil and paper for me to figure I'd better stay out of town. In fact, I'd better hustle myself out of Montana Territory. With four in my family, my share of Pa's half of the nugget didn't come anywhere near the thousand I'd need to get in the race. Everybody in the country would soon know that Kid Baynes was a big-mouthed four-flusher who talked everybody into a big-stakes race and then didn't show up. Worst of all, my plans for Kit and me crashed around my ears.

Freere's voice jerked me around again when he said, "Don't go wandering off, Kid. Your Pa said for me to get you to town by three this afternoon with a fresh racehorse or he'd have my hide."

Pa must have decided to loan me most of his share. My eyes started stinging, and I stood there blinking like a fool. Maybe, if I could win, I might have something. I might have enough to make Kit comfortable while I got started. Maybe I could buy the land I needed with a little bit down and pay it out on time. There might be a chance yet. But if I lost, I wouldn't have a dime. Even worse, I'd owe money to Pa.

Milt, using his prissy voice, said, "Look at your pretty watch, Ward. We don't want to get our hair mussed hurrying to the party."

On the way into town, he said in a low tone so Mike couldn't hear, "Don't take a loan from Pa. You remember, he spoke against this deal from the start. I'll give you my share. If you win, keep it all. If you lose, forget it."

"I can't take your whole share, Milt."

"Do it as a favor. You need it and can use it to do good things. I'd just throw it away anyhow. I don't like thinking about that dead valley. Sometimes money can be a burden. I think it'd be bad luck for me. I'd be obliged if you'd take it. I started feeling better the minute the notion came to me."

TWENTY-FOUR

MILT RODE THROUGH TOWN ahead of me about two horse lengths, carrying his rifle across his chest. Mike Freere fell back about the same distance, the butt of his rifle resting on his hip. Peepeye had stopped acting snippy about me riding the sorrel and walked quietly along behind. I thought he'd never quit trying to yank me out of the saddle by jerking on his lead rope. My racing saddle only needed last-minute tightening, and Peepeye'd be ready. A boost into the saddle for me, and we'd both be primed to run.

Jesse rode, butt forward, in my holster on Milt's left hip. Nadine's smooth stock showed from his rifle boot. Milt looked natural and comfortable as could be packing two rifles and two pistols, and I felt stripped stark naked. Tight pants without a belt, soft racing boots, and a long, loose buckskin shirt closed in front with rawhide loops hooked over big bone buttons, that was my racing costume. I'd unhook a couple of loops once the race started, letting me pull the hidden pogamoggan if needed.

I wore no hat and no guns. Jockeys didn't wear guns, even in a raw, rough-and-ready race such as this. If a rider pointed a gun, a hundred men who'd bet against him would try to blow him out of the saddle. Then a hundred men who'd bet for him would shoot at the first hundred. Montana Territory would be half-emptied of white men before the shooting stopped.

My racing cap and silk shirt hadn't been removed from my saddlebags since I left Louisiana. I never wore them anymore. The cap would bring hoots and insulting comments from the crowd. The silk shirt would bring whistles of appreciation but wouldn't hide a pogamoggan. Besides, although I hadn't tried it on, I knew the silk garment wouldn't stretch to fit my shoulders anymore, although my racing tights gave me no trouble at the waist.

Hard as I'd worked and light as I'd been eating over the last two months, I doubted if my weight had dropped much below 130. I carried too much weight to ride in a high-class race now, but I knew I couldn't lose another pound without starving myself into a weak-kneed wreck.

We rode down a main street as empty as that of a ghost town. Even the saloons sat quiet and vacant, while dust devils played idly along the edges of the sun-cracked board steps. But the roars and cheers from the nearby track echoed through the silent buildings like a call to battle. Foolishly, I found myself listening for the clash of swords against shields and the screams of dying men. I remembered telling Thackery that the Roman Coliseum had come to Montana, gladiators and all. Soon I'd be in the arena.

A turn in the saddle and I found Peepeye watching me with head high and wide, calm eyes, the eyes of a veteran campaigner. The deep-throated growl of a packed, excited crowd and the lightweight saddle on his back told him all he needed to know.

I turned back to the front just in time to see Milt stop, pull my watch from his pocket for a quick look, and give me a nod. Mike rode up close to take the sorrel's reins as soon as I hit the ground. By the time Peepeye's saddle was cinched tight, Milt stood ready to give me a quick boost. When we came around a corner and rode down the street toward the crowd at the edge of town, Milt's horse drew close to my left stirrup and Mike's to the right.

At sight of us, the crowd churned like a frightened bee swarm. A hundred or more of them ran part of the way to meet us, half of them cheering, half booing and shaking their fists. Damndest noise I ever heard.

"Thought we weren't coming," Milt shouted over the din, white teeth flashing in his dark face when he laughed. "Hell, we got two more minutes till it's three o'clock. Just ease along, Ward. No hurry. None at all."

"Two minutes? Two minutes! My God, Milt, you had no call to cut it that close. If I don't win this race, I'm ruined. Why'd you do that?"

His head moving in tiny jerks as he scanned the crowd, he never once glanced my way, but I could see his delighted grin. "No call to be early. More time here would just mean more risk. What you worried about? Afraid your girl gave you a cheap watch?" Then he laughed fit to fall off his horse, acting like he'd pulled the world's finest funny. Anybody else in the world would have been stony silent with tension at a time like this. Not Milt, he was born to laugh and spit in the devil's eye.

My heart was in my throat, choking me to death, until I saw a row of horses prancing restlessly at the starting line. I walked Peepeye to a stake with a ten painted on it, my number, and wondered why two horses stood to my right. How could that be? There must be twelve horses in the race. No way to find out anything now.

Cooper's voice boomed through the shouting behind me. "Quiet! Quiet! Everybody shut up!"

When the din lessened, I glanced back to find him holding a fist above his head. Cooper bellowed, "This here is my watch, and it's the official time for this here race. The time is about fifteen seconds before three o'clock."

A roar of cheers and boos drowned his next words. He waited patiently for the noise to diminish before he started again. "This here is the last race today, and I ain't gonna start it till it gets quiet around here. If you men what come to argue and yell will stop, the ones what come to race can start. I'll just stand right here till you bastards get tired of hollering. We'll start a horse race just as soon's I can hear nothin' but peace and quiet."

The noise dropped quickly, but a man in the crowd shouted, "I still say Kid Baynes was late and shouldn't race."

The crunch of a solid blow came plainly in the sudden silence. Another voice said smugly, "He's done decided to keep quiet now, I think."

I couldn't help laughing with the rest of the crowd, but I had to tend to business. A quick glance down the line showed the big Chintry black in position eight. The two straw-headed brothers Coop warned me about filled positions seven and nine on both sides of the black. The one at stake nine beside me sent a contemptuous grin my way. Relaxed in the saddle on a powerful, heavy, blanket horse, he pulled his quirt suggestively across his cupped left hand, stared at me with icy blue eyes, and grinned some more. I found the horse at stake eleven to my right had a slight young rider with scared eyes. That one could be dismissed as a spoiler.

My attention came back to Strawhead at stake nine. I couldn't remember the name Cooper gave for him and his brother. His horse was too heavy for a mile race. A good sprinter, perhaps, but too thick-boned for distance. No horse like that had raced last month. A veering collision with such an animal would knock a lighter horse like Peepeye off its feet and out of the race, maybe inflict great injury.

And the best time to try that was at the start. Just at the time when the horses were surging to reach stride, a solid bump could send a mount down in a tangle. Or, failing that, the staggering horse, knocked completely off stride, might well dislodge its jockey. Would they try that trick at the start, right in clear sight of everybody?

I decided they would. Then they'd try to pass it off as an off-balance, veering start by a heavy, awkward, poorly trained animal. The horse would be disqualified, but it couldn't win anyway, couldn't keep up with the field. To be effective as a spoiler, that horse had to be used early, before it fell hopelessly behind.

Chintry would love that, seeing me knocked out of the race just ten feet from the starting line. He'd love to see me dumped on my butt and, maybe, my neck broken and my horse injured right in front of the crowd.

Another man yelled something, and from the sound of it, got himself popped in the mouth, starting another roar of laughing approval from the crowd. As seconds ticked by and Cooper stubbornly waited for quiet, I decided to hold Peepeye to a late start. If Strawhead veered at the starting gun, he'd simply miss me. Besides, I couldn't risk Peepeye before he got himself strung out, before his natural agility could come into play. I'd lose a second, at most a second and a half. Remembering the poor finishing times in the races I'd seen last month, I decided to sacrifice a little time, to gamble on a slow jump at the gun, rather than risk Peepeye getting a broken leg at the start.

Resisting the urge to rub the pogamoggan rock I held under my arm, I narrowed my eyes, imagining that big lumbering horse in front of Peepeye trying to swerve into us when we tried to pass. If I was wrong about my guess about a planned collision at the start, that horse looked like a sprinter who could grab a quick lead. In that case, I'd have to pass him.

Strawhead clearly showed me that he was right-handed in the process of fooling around with his whip, trying to scare me like he was dealing with a rube kid. I'd pass him on the left, so if he tried to use his whip he'd be wrong-handed. That would, at least, make it more awkward for him to try to hit Peepeye with that damned quirt.

I had to force myself to remember that I mustn't delay passing Strawhead if he got ahead of me, mustn't waste an extra second or two simply to break the man's head. My job was to win a race, not to punish a spoiler.

Coop's voice came clearly from behind me. "Now, riders, I'm gonna say 'one' and then 'two' and then I'm gonna say 'bang' with this here pistol. If anybody jumps the gun, he's done finished his race, and all the cryin' and bitchin' in the world ain't gonna change nothin'. Is ever'body ready? Here goes."

While Coop counted slowly, Peepeye sensed the other horses and riders getting set and shook his head irritably when he felt my firm hand on the reins. He knew the signal for a hold-back start, and he never liked to do that worth a damn. But we had practiced every kind of racetrack trick at least a thousand times. At the crack of Coop's pistol, the line started forward, except for Peepeye. He sprang forward just a second late, allowing Strawhead to cross about two jumps ahead of us and crash into the scared kid coming out from lane eleven.

As we charged past, the kid's horse went down, and the boy's scream, as high-pitched as a girl's in his terror, followed us down the track. But the big Appaloosa had staggered almost to a stop before Strawhead's quirt put him to rearing instead of running. Strawhead had missed his chance and would never catch Peepeye now.

"Hi, hi, hi, Peepeye."

He stretched out fine, and we passed three horses in the first two furlongs, but I could feel him sulking. Dust was already stinging my eyes so bad I kept them shut except for the tiniest slits I could manage. By then I had my buckskin shirt open and my pogamoggan in my hand, fingers holding the rod and stone both, so the stone wouldn't swing free on its plaited leather thong until I wound up to strike with it. When ready to use it, I'd put the base of the rod against my hip, release the rock, and slide my fingers down to the base. Thus, when I swung, I'd have the longest reach with the weapon that could be had.

"Hi, hi, hi, Peepeye." He was going good. We passed two more riders, but he was still sore about that slow start. Peepeye was outrunning the slower horses, but his stride had no joy in it. He was telling me, "Ho-hum, I'll run along, but I don't care much."

"Damn you, Peepeye, hi, hi." Just when I thought he picked up that extra spring, like he'd decided to get interested, he eased off again. By now, I couldn't tell whether it was the dust filling my eyes with tears or fear of losing. "Aw, come on, Peepeye."

Before I thought, before I even knew what I was doing, the pogamoggan rose and started to fall. I stopped it inches from Peepeye's rump. A scream came out of me like it had a life of its own. I had almost hit the best friend a man ever had, the tame, gentle friend of my boyhood. Now I knew what caused tears to gush from my eyes, streaking my face with stiff lines of mud.

The post! Peepeye wasn't quitting. He was slowing to round the post. I had no idea we were so close to the damn thing, but Peepeye knew exactly where it was. How had he found it in that cloud of dust?

His spin almost hurled me out of the saddle. While I should have been getting set for the turn, I'd been busy losing faith in my horse when he slowed, had almost struck my oldest friend, and thus had nearly lost my seat. That damned dust was so thick, if I did fall out of the saddle, it'd probably take me a half hour to find the ground.

Peepeye caught fire. He passed two more riders in the first hundred yards after the turn. We were still riding through dust so thick I couldn't see the crowd at the edge of town, but the air was clearing. My face felt like a stiff mask of dirt and streaks of mud, my bare chest was caked, and my open buckskin shirt had caught what felt like a shovelful of dry, grainy soil. My nose closed up and I rode with my mouth open now. A spinning clod came from nowhere, smashed me square in the teeth, and split my lip. I knew I'd spit grit and taste blood and horseshit through the rest of the race.

I wondered if I felt slippery blood under my shirt. Sharp, packed, sandy dust was cutting me to pieces at the elbows and armpits, but I had to continue to move the reins in time with the movements of Peepeye's head. This must be the way it feels to work with a layer of broken glass packed under both arms and in the bends of both elbows.

"Hi, hi, hi, Peepeye."

Dimly, I thought I could pick out two sources of dust not far ahead. We had a quarter of a mile to go, at least. I laughed in Peepeye's ear. "We got 'em, stud. Nobody finishes faster than you."

Arab Fair Winds loved to sprint the final quarter at the end of a mile race. He was a rare runner, seeming to grow stronger with every stride up to ten or maybe even twelve furlongs. Pa once said, "He looks like his legs get longer toward the end of a race."

We passed the first of the two sources of dust in about four strides, with me blinking my eyes desperately trying to see better. I couldn't be sure, but that horse looked like Chintry's black, running flat-out but without zest, a tired horse. The little jockey rode with the same lack of enthusiasm. He didn't even glance our way when Peepeye flew past, but I thought I saw a streak of blood across his face.

"Hi, hi, Peepeye, one more to catch."

When his two lengths of lead shrank to one, Strawhead's brother hung his chin on his shoulder and swerved his blanket horse to cut us off. This animal, clean-limbed and light-footed, was an aristocrat compared to the heavy horse his brother tried to run over Peepeye with at the starting line. Having run a fine race, the spotted horse showed a sprinter's distress at a distance just a bit too long for him. He'd win a lot of money at six furlongs or less, but he couldn't hold the pace for a full mile against Peepeye's class of horse.

I feinted to the right and swerved Peepeye to the left, figuring Strawhead's brother would likely be right-handed too. Passing on the left would match my right hand full of pogamoggan against his left hand full of quirt. I laughed out loud at the prospect. He looked back into my broad grin, and his eyes caught a flicker of the lazily wheeling stone when I started my windup. Just as I made a final spin before trying to knock a big, ugly dent in his head, he reined away with a panic-stricken expression, and Peepeye burst into the lead.

I tucked my pogamoggan away, feeling cheated, and hooked the front of my shirt back together with a furlong remaining in the race. With Peepeye in front and feeling good, I figured there hadn't been a horse born into the world who could catch him. All Peepeye wanted to do now was to get so far ahead he couldn't even hear hoofbeats behind him. He wanted to run clear out of the country, so his dust would settle and grass would grow before the other horses came along.

Laughing, I yelled, "Go ahead, do it. Let's fly, Peepeye."

Pa said later that we crossed the finish line with Peepeye at a dead gallop and me screeching like a drunk Indian with his tongue stuck in a hot bottle. I figure he was teasing me again, trying to make me feel like a pinhead.

I might've been screeching. That's likely, since I was feeling mighty good, but he couldn't have heard me. Nobody could have heard anything in that commotion. That crowd must have been a thousand strong, and everybody who bet for me was waving and cheering at the top of his lungs. And the ones who bet against me were shaking fists and squalling like scorched mountain lions. Luke told me later that the winners were throwing their hats into the air and the losers were shooting at the sailing hats.

But even with all that noise, I heard the shot that knocked Strawhead's brother off his horse just after he crossed the finish line behind me and reined up. The crack of a rifle was that much different from the pistol shots of the hot-tempered crowd, it snapped my head around just in time to see the hurt man slump from his saddle.

What saved me was that I never reined up short after a finish, and Peepeye must have decided he felt like running today, after all. Maybe he wanted to show me he was sorry about sulking earlier, so we hardly slowed at all at the finish line.

Anyhow, the shooter wasn't so good at moving targets. He missed me clean the first time, but he burned me before I ducked Peepeye and myself between two buildings. I slid out of the saddle and made sure Peepeye hadn't been hit. Then I leaned against a urine-stained wall and froze, huddled into a half-crouch in that filthy, stinking alley. I just cowered there, unable to stop shaking, dirty and frazzled as a hard-used field hand, scared near unto death, and feeling helpless as a newborn puppy without Nadine and Jesse.

It humbles a man to watch his own blood drip down amongst garbage.

TWENTY-FIVE

A MAN PLUNGED into the alley so fast and at such a sharp angle he crashed against the wall before he could slow down. The bore of the old flintlock pistol he pointed at me was bigger and blacker than some mine shafts I've seen. Deliberately, he thumbed back the massive hammer on that small cannon. Cursing myself for crouching in an alley like a sniveling coward and even forgetting to pull my pogamoggan, I straightened and braced myself, figuring I might as well go out like a man.

Blue eyes flashing in a square, hard-planed face, the man's expression was rigid with murderous fury. "By Gott," he shouted, "a hundred dollars I bet. You goot rider, so I vin. Now robbers my money take and yours too." He turned his back to peep around the edge of the building at the entrance to the alley. Scattered shots still echoed down the street. The crash of broken glass told me somebody couldn't resist a chance at the big window I'd seen on one of the saloon fronts.

Weak from relief, I stood leaning against Peepeye, holding my legs stiff and straight so my feeble knees wouldn't unlock and dump me on my face. My mama taught me it was rude to turn your back to a person, but she didn't have a case like this in mind. I'd never been so glad to look at another man's backside. Nobody shows you his back when he's meaning to kill you, so I felt mighty pleased with this big fellow's manners.

He shifted the huge pistol from one hand to the other while he rubbed sweaty palms across his rough miner's clothing. Then he glanced back and said, "Ach, the bullet cut your cheek only. Lot's of blood, ya? But no real harm. In *Deutschland* the rich men cut faces vorse dan dat ven dey mit der sabers play."

I looked down at myself and found the front of my buckskin shirt slick and bright with blood. My pants and boot tops were splattered, and both hands were covered with a blackening mixture of dust and gore. While I'd been crouched in a helpless funk, glassy-eyed with fear, I must have been feeling my wounded face, getting my hands wet with my own blood, and not even being aware of what I was doing. Now, I could clearly feel the flow down my right cheek, and the wound was starting to hurt like a hundred wasp stings. My first gunshot wound felt more like I'd been quirted across the face.

The bullet missed my nose, cut my cheek, and then must have flown harmlessly past my right ear. Or maybe it went the other way. I couldn't even figure which direction I'd been shot from.

My hand kept straying up to check my ear. For some reason, I felt enormously relieved to find the bullet hadn't clipped off a chunk of it. Stupidly, I kept pinching my blood-sticky nose and ear to be sure they were still part of my face.

"Ward, I'm coming in." Milt yelled from somewhere out in the street.

"Come on," I yelled back. "The man with me's a friend."

Milt came skidding in and slammed against the wall the same way the big miner did. Then Milt walked straight to him, shifted his pistol to his left hand, and reached out to shake hands. After the briefest handshake I ever saw, Milt turned toward the alley entrance and said, "You watch the back end of this alley, and I'll watch the front. I'm Milt Baynes, this little feller's brother."

After a quick glance at me, Milt went on, "Damn, Ward, I've seen deer gutted and hung to cool that looked better than you." He unbuckled my belt from around his waist and pitched Jesse to me, holster and all.

I said, "Thank you," and started feeling like a man again. I don't know which I was more glad to have close at hand, Jesse or Milt. I buckled my gunbelt and stopped feeling naked.

The miner said, "I am Gustav Schmidt."

"Your name is Lucky," Milt said flatly, scanning the street by leaning forward for a quick look and snapping back before anybody could get off an aimed shot. "When you ran into this alley, I figured you were after my brother. If a fool in that crowd hadn't bumped my elbow when I fired, you'd be a dead man right now. You're lucky as hell."

Flashing big, square teeth in a broad smile, Schmidt said, "You can call me Looky. *Das ist gut.* After today, my name is Looky Schmidt."

Milt snickered in his own nasty way and said, "You got two friends, Ward, one named Peepeye and one who calls himself Looky. Neither one of 'em speaks English too good."

Schmidt shrugged off a joke he obviously didn't understand, and his smile turned grim when he said, "Ya, ya, Looky Schmidt joost bet two months pay on a horse race. I vin, by Gott, at five to vun. I'm a rich man mit five hundred dollars. Then robbers off mit my money ran and try to my rider shoot. I run to help my rider, and his brother try to shoot me. Das ist me, Looky Schmidt."

Milt's brows went up about an inch. "Robbers? So that's what it was all about. I missed it all. Seemed to me everybody out there went crazy all of a sudden. Every damn fool who owns a gun was shooting all over the place. Not one of them knew who the hell to shoot at. I must have seen ten or twelve men drop."

All of a sudden, it hit me what the big German was saying. "Robbers? What did they get? Who got robbed?"

Schmidt edged his way cautiously toward the other end of the alley, talking as he went. "By Gott, dey all da bets got. All da prize money dey got. Everybody's money. Four or five men around der tables dey shot."

I loosened the leather thong securing Jesse in his holster and rubbed my hands on my pants. Nothing causes a gun to rust faster than blood, and my hands looked like a butcher's. More than anything else, I had a grim desire to reel around and howl like a hit dog. The bank closed, so our money was lost just when the mine came up empty. Then I won a big-stakes horse race, and the money was stolen, even our entry fee. Everything was crashing down on me at once. How long does a man have to face losing at everything he tries?

A sullen thought came to me. Ever since I'd won Kit, every single thing I tried went sour. Before I met her, money meant little to me. Now, when I desperately needed a stake, my only desire being to look after my woman and start a peaceful business, everything I touched turned rotten for me and my whole family. Something deep and ugly inside me stirred and started to grow. Meanwhile, my cheek felt like somebody was holding a branding iron to it.

"I'm tired of people stealing from me." My comment came out like the groping wisdom of an idiot. It sounded dumb even to me, but the simple truth can sound scatterbrained sometimes. I stepped out into the street, Jesse coming into my bloody hand. My voice echoed oddly off the buildings when I yelled as loud as I could, "I'm Kid Baynes. Anybody wants to shoot at me, have at it."

The wild shouting and gunshots stopped. The silence held for a moment or two. Then men began to appear, slowly coming off the ground and from under and behind every kind of cover. They all wore shifty expressions of both fear and embarrassment.

"You silly bastards lay around shooting at each other all you want, but I'm going after the thieves who took my money. Does anybody know which way they went?"

Two or three of the men, on their feet now and wandering toward me, motioned in as many directions. Behind me, Schmidt said, "Thieves that vay go."

I turned to see him pointing to the north with his oversized flintlock pistol. When he caught my eye, he reddened and shrugged, waggling the old weapon. From the corner of my eye, I saw Milt shift nervously, disturbed by the wavering old gun barrel. Pa would have taken a strap to any Baynes boy handling a weapon like that.

"Too far avay for this old gun ven I see them," Schmidt said apologetically, lowering the flintlock at last. "Many people try to ride avay from vild shooting and angry mob, so dos men confused about who does stealing. Dos men not der thieves see." He paused and said emphatically, "I der thieves see."

I started toward Peepeye, and Milt said, "You going without a working saddle, no water, no food, no rifle, no blankets?"

When I stopped and stared at him, not feeling friendly about his sensible advice and the way he read my mind, he went on, "I'll put things together, get spare horses and such. You get cleaned up and get a patch on your face. Meet me at the stable in about an hour. We may have a long ride. And look around for Pa and Luke. I haven't seen them." He took Peepeye's reins and moved away with his long stride, not trying to mount. Milt and Peepeye were old friends, but my brother never tried to ride my horse.

Ordinarily, my brother didn't try to do my thinking for me either, but I guess he saw I was about to go berserk and let thoughtless rage turn me into a fool. Stepping out into that open street and yelling a challenge to the whole town was a crazy thing to do. I had to get myself under control. Big, powerful men might get away with bulling their way through trouble. Runts like me get squashed when they lose their heads.

"Kid! Kid Baynes!"

I spun and watched a tall, skinny town boy skid to a stop with his hands up. It took a moment to realize he was looking down Jesse's barrel. I had drawn and cocked Jesse without even thinking. I eased down his hammer and holstered him. "Sorry, youngster. You want me for something?"

The boy stood frozen for a moment, swallowing and looking sick. Finally, he gulped and stuttered, "Sheriff Dodd sent me to get you, sir. He's got a man down there by the tables, uh, those tables they set up for the races." The young fellow couldn't take his eyes off Jesse, looked like he expected Jesse to jump out at him.

"You can put your hands down. I'm sorry about pulling iron on you. I'm a mite nervous. Thanks for coming after me."

"Uh, nervous. Yes, sir, I can see you might be. Yes, sir, I understand. Think nothing of it. I'm just glad to be of service." Now the boy seemed unable to pry his attention away from my bloody face. "You, uh, you know you're bleeding pretty bad there, Mr. Baynes?"

For some strange reason, this awkward town kid's confusion seemed to settle me down and make me feel better. I didn't dare try to give him a reassuring grin. If I did, my cheek would burst wide open again. Actually, I could tell the bleeding had almost stopped. So I kept what was left of my face straight when I said, "I bleed like this every time somebody shoots me." I glanced down at my spattered clothing as I started back toward the racetrack. When I went past him, I added, "Sure is untidy isn't it?"

"Yes, sir, uh, no, sir, uh."

I stepped around the stuttering boy and walked down the center of the street toward the edge of town. For purely contrary reasons, I took the center of the street, walking slow and trying to mark every window, every door, every crevice from where a man might try a shot. If anybody wanted a crack at me, I figured now was a good time. Maybe I needed to do something crazy, so I could wipe out the shameful memory of myself hiding in an alley, shivering like a whipped dog. Halfway to the racing tables, it came to me that this was the first time in my life I wanted somebody to shoot at me—I wanted to shoot back that bad.

When I walked up to the tables where all the horse racing business took place, two men carried a blanket-draped body past me on a door somebody had ripped off its hinges. A clean-shaven man walked along behind, carrying a black bag.

Sheriff Dodd stood, grim-faced, looking down at three dead men laid out side by side. Dodd glanced up at me and asked, "You agree to uphold the laws of the City of Bannock and Montana Territory?"

I shrugged and said, "Sure, Sheriff, why?"

He reached out and pinned a badge on my bloody buckskin shirt and said, "Good. You're a deputy now." Casually, he wiped my blood off his fingers onto his pants. "Where's that shifty brother of yours?"

"Shifty brother? I don't have a shifty brother."

"Come on, come on. I don't have time to mess around. Where's that Indian-looking brother of yours?"

"Oh, you mean Milt. He's gone down to the stable to get some extra horses. We heard somebody stole my prize money, so we figured to go after them."

"Good. You go get him, but instead of riding off on a wild-goose chase, here's where I want you to meet me as soon as you can get there." He drew a quick diagram with his finger in the dust.

I asked, "That close to town? You think the thieves are still hanging around that close to town?"

"Damn right. They blasted all four of the men officiating at these tables because all of these men would recognize them. The only one not already dead was old Cooper, but he was shot to pieces. He talked to us some before he died. That was him they carried past you on a door when you came up. Coop and the Crager brothers were in on this deal somehow, but they did a double-cross or got double-crossed. I ain't sure about all of it. Anyhow, the Crager brothers are both dead. Coop told Frank Jopson who the crooks are and where they planned to split the loot."

"Why did you wait for me? Why didn't you deputize a bunch of the crowd and go get those people?"

"Jopson is down there now watching the building them crooks is hiding in. Your pa, Mike Freere, and that other brother of yours, the great big one, they're all down there already. Your girl's daddy is with them too. I don't figure that gang is about to get away, but we have to be careful. We can't have no mob running down there and raisin' hell. We gotta handle this one real careful."

"I don't understand. Why don't you just get some men and arrest that bunch?"

"First of all, there's supposed to be six of 'em, near as we can put it all together. That might be a hell of a shoot-out, maybe, to have so close to town. I'd like to avoid that. Another thing, them men didn't just get a bunch of money we want to get back."

"What else did they take?"

Sheriff Chip Dodd shifted his weight and looked away, grimacing mildly as if any movement at all tortured his tender feet. "Your pa said we better wait till you come along. He said we'd better ask you about everything and get you to agree before we did anything or said anything to those crooks. He said it'd be a shame if there was a mistake, and you upped and killed a couple of honest lawmen."

"Me? Why would I do a thing like that? That'd be crazy. I don't believe my pa would say such a thing."

"Well, uh, you see, Kid, it's like I said. Those men didn't just take a bunch of money."

"What else did they take? What're you talking about?"

"Your pa said we'd better check with you, don't you see? It's mostly your family's money they got anyhow. He seemed of a mind you'd be more dangerous than those six crooks if we make a mistake. He allowed as how you'd set out to kill everybody involved if this went wrong. That feller Thackery, that cold-faced daddy of hers, he didn't say a damn word, just nodded to agree, nodded like a hangin' judge."

"Kit? They got Kit?"

"Yeah, they got your girl too, Kid."

TWENTY-SIX

THE PLACE where Cooper told Sheriff Dodd the crooks would be hiding out wasn't all that close to town. It was a ramshackle, boarded-up shack about a mile and a half from the center of Bannock, but it turned out to be after dark before I was to see it.

Marshal Frank Jopson met Milt and me. He stepped out into the middle of the road with his left hand upraised to stop us. His searching gaze lingered on my face for a long moment before he spoke.

"Hold up right here, men. There isn't any hurry. You sure you're up to being out here, Kid?" I just stared at him without answering, seeing a flicker of amusement in his eyes when he squinted at the badge shining on my chest. "I figured you'd be wearing a shield one day. Glad to see it."

"Just for this. After this, I'll give it back." My speech sounded hobbled and strange. My cheek was stiff with dried blood, and I spoke without moving my jaw, like I'd heard men speak when they had sore teeth. The doctor was busy with other men in town who were hurt worse than I was, so I rode out without waiting. I hadn't even taken time to wash the blood off my face. "I don't figure a badge is going to take root on me."

"Yeah, I know." Jopson nodded and winked at Milt. "I accepted a job as a Deputy U.S. Marshal, thinking I'd be through with a badge in about six months. That was ten years ago."

Impatiently, I started Peepeye forward, but Jopson stepped in front of him. He had iron in his voice when he said, "Pay attention to me, Kid. As long as you wear that badge of mine, you obey orders. I told you there's no need to hurry. Things are under control, and I plan to keep it that way."

"Badge of yours? Dodd gave it to me. I'm his deputy."

"Nope. That's my badge. I just had Dodd hand it to you. It lets you swing a wider loop than just being a deputy sheriff in a town. If worse comes to worse and we have to run any of those men down, you'll have authority anywhere. You're an officer of the federal government."

He took another badge out of his pocket and sailed it to Milt. "Put that on and obey my orders or ride like hell away from here."

"You think it'll help me with the girls?" Milt asked with a straight face.

"I guarantee it," Jopson said, without cracking a smile. He motioned for us to dismount and follow him. A few steps away, in the dirt beside the road, he'd made a little map of the place the crooks were holed up.

He pulled a pencil from his vest pocket and pointed as he spoke. "Old house, corral, stable where they have all their horses hidden, road goes by right here, little creek, woodline." He pointed to sticks standing upright in the ground. "Your pa's here. Thackery's with him. Luke's here by the road with Freere. Luke and Freere are stopping anybody from getting in our way by coming up the road from that direction. I'm turning back traffic from this direction and stopping the deputies Chip Dodd sends from town. I tell them what to do and where to go. We don't even want those crooks to know we're all around them. I got four other deputies out here already on this job, good men from town, and they're posted along here." He pointed to his dirt map.

"Now then," Jopson said, straightening to his full height, "the doctor will be coming out here as soon as he's finished in town, although I hope we won't need him. He'll be coming with Chip Dodd and a posse. Cooper told us the crooks' plan was to hide out here until after dark. Then they plan to ride out in six different directions."

"Cooper didn't seem like a crook to me," I said with my soretoothed man's voice.

"He got close to the Crager brothers, and they told him the whole plan. Chintry bet a fortune on Wicked, that big black of his. The Cragers were supposed to be Chintry's guarantee that Wicked won again. Coop and the Cragers framed it up for Lonnie Crager to win instead and bet a pile on him. Lonnie was to beat Wicked, and Ronnie was to take you out, Kid.

"If something went wrong and another horse won, then Chintry planned to pull the holdup. Chintry, or one of his men, was up on top of one of the buildings. Evidently, he saw Lonnie put a whip to Chintry's jockey and run past Wicked, so Lonnie caught a bullet at the finish line."

"What the hell did he shoot at me for?" I asked.

Jopson spat carefully to the side and shrugged. Then he gave me a mildly amused look and said, "Rumor around town is Chintry has a dislike for you, Kid. Since the plan was to shoot up the place and cause confusion, why not pick a target or two to even a score while you're at it? Killing you was just a bonus, seems to me."

"Why bother with Kit?" My feet wouldn't hold still. Standing beside the road for all this talk was driving me loco.

"Nothing personal, Kid. The scheme was to take any woman who came to hand, just insurance in case anything went wrong. They plan to ride off and leave her behind soon's it gets dark."

Milt asked, "If Cooper knew about everything, how come he let himself get shot during the holdup?"

Jopson nodded approvingly. "Good question. Damned if I can figure it. Only thing I can think of is the old man figured he could stop 'em some way. Maybe it happened so fast some other plan of his didn't work."

"You're asking us to sit around for a couple more hours while they hold Kit in there?" I asked.

Jopson nodded again. "With any luck, we can pick 'em off real quiet when they ride out one at a time in the dark. That's better than trying to shoot up that hideout with your woman in there. Maybe we can pull this off without anybody getting hurt."

Milt said quietly, "Good plan, Marshal. Soon's it gets dark, Ward and I, we'll just sneak up into that barn."

"Yeah," I agreed. "That way we'll be close enough to get to Kit quick if anything goes wrong."

"Absolutely not," Jopson said flatly. "Too dangerous. It might ruin everything."

"Marshal," Milt said quietly, "we understand your concern about the robbery and all, and a bunch of that money is ours, but this is a family matter to us, and that's a more important thing than money. That girl belongs to my brother. All of us would feel bad if you got in our way and got yourself killed. Fact is, it would make us all sad as hell." The click of a cocking pistol came just as Milt spoke his last word. Maybe Milt felt that the sound of a cocking weapon went together with the word "hell."

Jopson stared at Milt's pistol, which he'd sneaked out while he was talking, then at me. After a moment, he said disgustedly, "Damn." He looked away for a moment, evidently thinking fast. Finally, he asked, "All right, maybe we can talk this thing out so we can work together. What do you want to do?"

"First thing," I said, "is for us to sneak over and talk things over with our pa. We'll let you know what we decide. Seems to me it's up to us, really. We have more at stake than anybody else. My idea is for Milt and me to get as close to the house as we can. We'll let those men ride out to fall into your traps out here as long as Kit's all right. Otherwise, we go in the house and read to them from the Book. What do you say, Milt?"

"That would be my idea too. Let's go talk to Pa. We'll let you know, Marshal." Milt wasn't exactly pointing his weapon at Jopson. He was holding it just a bit off to the side.

Frank Jopson shrugged and turned away, so we mounted and rode a roundabout route to get to Pa without being seen from the house. Pa shook his head when we told him what we planned to do and said, "We'll all go. Milt, you and Ward go to the stable first. If there's a guard there, do what you have to do. Luke and I will wait a bit and follow you in. Then you two can try to sneak up beside the house and listen to what's happening inside. We'll let those men ride out as long as Kit is all right. The posse can catch them or lose them. Our job is to get our girl out of there safe."

Thackery asked, "What do you want me to do?"

I waited a second or two. When Pa didn't answer him, I said, "Papa Joe, we're used to working together in the dark. I think you better stay with the lawmen. You aren't half wild like we are."

As if to prove my point, Milt took that moment to pull his six-inch snickersnee from the top of his leggings, lifted one foot to stroke both sides of the wicked blade across the soft leather top of his moccasin, and tested the edge cautiously with his thumb. No man alive could watch Milt go through that little act and not feel a chill.

"Kit will want to see her daddy as soon as we get her back. I'll either yell for you or bring her to meet you right here," I added.

Thackery said in a matter-of-fact tone, "No moon yet tonight. That'll help you. Maybe our string of bad luck is over." Then he added, "Too bad there's no water handy. Just looking at you will scare Kathleen to death."

Milt said, "I have water. We brought canteens on the horses."

"Never mind," I said, "I don't want to start my face to bleeding again. We can tend to that later."

After that, we sat around waiting for dark. Time never passes slower than in a situation like that, with nothing, not a single thing, to do but wait and worry. Milt came to his feet and I said, "Not yet." He started pacing back and forth like one of the big cats I'd seen caged in New Orleans.

A walking horse quietly moved in the oncoming darkness behind us. A voice spoke softly. "It's Jopson comin' in." When he dismounted, he asked, "Anybody come this way yet?" When nobody answered, he said, "The boys on the other side, by the creek, they got one already. He had a thousand dollars in cash on him. I got this place surrounded with deputies, and every one of them's a damn good, picked man. How's that for quiet work?"

It was too much for me. I said, "Let's go." By this time, Luke had joined us, so I turned to him. "Luke, when you hear a barn owl hoot three times, come on up to the barn." His nod was barely visible in the darkness.

Milt moved into the lead and set a hell of a pace at first. When we came into sight of the black bulk of the old barn, though, he stopped and motioned for me to wait while he moved on in closer. I knelt down and kept still, knowing that men can see motion even in almost complete darkness. Then I heard leather creak, amazed at how loud it was, and I knew it to be the sound of a man hitting the saddle.

A low but clear voice in the windless quiet said, "So long, boys. Enjoy bein' rich."

Another voice growled, "Shut up and git."

The walking horse headed right for me. I crouched as low as I could, trying to catch the outline of the rider against the sky. The shuffling hooves came closer and closer. Out of all the directions that fool could ride, was he going to come straight over me? I pulled Jesse and then changed my mind. Jesse went back into his holster, and I pulled the pogamoggan out of my buckskin jacket.

Grimly, I remembered Thackery's comment about our luck changing. He'd spoken too soon. Of all the bad luck in the world, why did this damn fool have to ride right at me? If I moved, he'd probably see me. If I didn't, his horse would shy away, and the rider would know I was there. I wished for him to turn his horse away; I wished so hard I think my cheek started bleeding again.

The dark outline of horse and rider loomed over me, and the horse shied and reared. The smell of the blood all over me must have scared the poor animal half to death when I lunged to my feet, ran forward, and jumped to swing the pogamoggan as high as I could stretch. The awful crunch of stone against bone sounded as loud as a gunshot in the evening quiet.

The rider came out of the saddle limp as a half-empty sack of grain and fell right on top of me, driving me flat. The man must've weighed two hundred pounds. I struggled to get out from under his lifeless body, gritting my teeth to hold back a gasp when my cheek ripped open again. The frightened horse galloped away.

A voice said quietly, "I can't believe it. I think that damned Jensen fell off his horse in the middle of a flat field. Did you hear that awful thud? Sounded like he fell on his head."

Another voice said, "Tough titty. He's a good man with a pickax but a clumsy bastard in the saddle. It's just like him to break his neck after the biggest payday of his life." Saddle leather creaked again. "You might check. If he broke his neck, you can have his share. If you find him alive, go ahead and strangle the awkward numbskull." The sound of a slow-moving horse diminished into the distance, heading away from me.

I was afraid to move, not being sure whether or not the man could see me in the darkness. There was a tiny ripping sound and a nasal grunt. The same ripping sound came again, then again. Dead quiet returned for a minute or two before a barn owl hooted. I kicked and squirmed the rest of the way out from under Jensen's body and moved to the barn. There need be no concern about him. The swinging stone of my pogamoggan had cracked his skull. His sleep was permanent.

Milt's whisper greeted me when I crouched against the wall of the barn. "You get one out in the field?"

I whispered back, "Yeah."

"That makes at least four then. We got two and we know two rode off. Barn's empty except for the one I just got with my little snicker-snee. Should only be two more." He gave his barn-owl hoot three times to call in Luke and Pa, and we both crept into the barn.

"I'm going to the house," I said.

"Let's go."

"Wait."

The sound of rusty door hinges was unmistakable. Milt's whisper was almost a chuckle, "Come into my parlor."

Boot heels crunched on the rocky ground and a darker shadow appeared in the wide barn door. The man said, "Christ, it's dark in there, Sam." The pogamoggan struck him squarely on the top of his head, again making that distinctive crunch. I had to jerk the handle twice with all my might before the stone came loose from the dead man.

Milt's chuckling whisper came at once, "You don't need to hit 'em that hard. You act like you're mad or something."

I dropped the pogamoggan and started toward the house, walking briskly and not trying to be quiet. Milt came along behind, but as usual, I couldn't hear any sound from his movement. The front door opened directly into the yard, there being no porch. I marched up to the front of the shack like I owned the place and pushed on the door. Now that I was so close, I could see a trace of light around the edges.

The door rattled loosely against an inner bolt but didn't open, so I kicked it with all my might.

The latch ripped free, and I could see a spray of splinters and dust fly through the air when the door swung open and crashed against the inside wall. Kit, perched primly on the mud hearth, looked up at me and screamed. I saw movement on the other side of the room, so Jesse naturally swung that way and fired before I could think about it.

Chintry fired at the same time, and the bullet hit the door facing right beside my head, spraying splinters into my wounded cheek. Jesse banged again, driving Chintry back against the wall. He crouched there, glaring at me with such a look of malignant hatred it seemed the most natural thing to shoot him again, so I did. Slowly, he slid down the wall, collapsing with his legs spraddled out but still sitting upright. My cheek hurt me so bad I had to blink back tears. I took four or five steps across the room and aimed carefully.

When she screamed, "Don't! Please don't!" I swung my eyes to Kit. Pressed against the far wall, she stared at me with such a horrified expression, I eased Jesse's hammer down before I thought.

"Don't be afraid, Kit. You're safe now."

"Ward?" Her eyes were unnaturally wide and her face was the color of old book pages. "Ward? Is that you?"

"Yeah, Kit, it's me."

"Oh, Ward." She glanced wildly around the room for a second, then bolted for the door. I hesitated a second to look at Chintry again. Still sitting upright, his eyes were blank and fixed, empty of life. I could hear her retching outside, so I ran to help Kit.

But when I came near her, she moaned a protest and moved away from me, still bent over, still gagging.

TWENTY-SEVEN

THE RIDE BACK TO TOWN was mighty quiet. Pa and Thackery rode ahead with Kit. After Thackery shook his head and waved me off, I stayed away from her and rode behind with Luke and Milt. The moon was out now, and it seemed almost as light as day after the earlier darkness.

We pulled up so as not to overtake them when Pa and Thackery met riders on the road. We could hear the voices clearly, so it was no trick to learn it was the doctor coming from town. Pa told him to turn back, that the only men who got hurt were beyond his help.

Then Pa added, "Except my son. He needs his cheek sewed up, but he's right behind us. He'll wait till we get to town so you'll have a good light."

Milt asked with a very low voice, "Did they hurt your girl, Ward?"

"Don't think so. I think looking at me made her sick. That's the way it seemed to me. Went right out the door and threw up."

Milt chuckled. "True love."

I was too tired to get mad. Pain made a tough saddle partner, and it wore me down fast once the excitement of gunplay wore off. Besides, looking forward to getting stitches in my cheek had me scared to death. If I had a choice, I intended to back out of that misery. I'd watched it done and didn't see how anybody could stand it. The idea of a doctor sewing me up like a damn quilt gave me the shudders. In fact, my stomach was feeling pretty skittish just thinking about it.

Luke said, "Not funny, Milt. This isn't a good time for teasing."

"Why not? We got Ward's girl back and all the money. We caught all the crooks. It's a good thing we got that money, what with the bank closing up and all. We had enough hard luck when we lost all the money from the mine."

"What bank closed up?" Luke asked. "You talking about our bank?"

"Sure, what other would I care about?"

"Closing for one day because of a late currency shipment doesn't mean anything."

"Mike Freere said the bank was locked tight and the banker'd left town," Milt said. "Was he just joking?"

"Funny, we had lunch with the banker. Freere must've picked up a bad rumor," Luke said placidly.

"You mean we didn't lose all the money from our mine, after all?" I asked.

"First I heard of us losing anything. The banker offered to open the bank especially for Pa if he wanted to withdraw raw gold to pay the entry money in the race. Pa told him not to bother, and he agreed with Thackery to sell my big nugget. They decided to pay the entry fee out of what they got for the nugget and bet any that was leftover on Peepeye."

"Luke, you telling me Pa went and bet all of that money? Freere said Pa and Thackery had five thousand dollars." I couldn't believe it.

Luke chuckled. "Pa said you were right this time. He sure didn't think much of those other horses. I believe he got five to one for most of what he and Papa Joe bet. No wonder Chintry shot his way out of town. He was taking all comers and giving odds. He must've lost enough to buy a railroad."

"Ward, next time we see Mike Freere, let's thump him till he squeals like a pig under a gate," Milt grunted.

"Let's put it off for a few days. I'm feelin' kind of pale," I said, hoping my stomach would settle down. I couldn't stop thinking about getting my hide sewed up like a boot sole.

When we rode into town, a bunch of shouting and cheering men came rushing out into the street. The saloons hadn't lost any business, evidently, from the day's events. Our bunch rode up in front of the hotel and dismounted. I stepped off Peepeye, and that smooth-looking doctor walked up and grabbed my arm. "Your father is arranging for you to have a bath, Mr. Baynes. I shall meet you in that establishment yonder when you are ready." He pointed down the street to a saloon. "They have the best lights in town."

Pa and Luke practically threw me into a tub of hot water, and Milt came drifting in with clean clothes. The doctor passed something to Pa. I think he said it was laudanum. Anyhow, Pa made me drink it, and I started to feel better. In fact, with about ten pounds of dirt and dried blood washed off, I started feeling pretty good. I forgot all about needles.

We walked over to that big saloon, and they sat me down amongst a bunch of bright lights and mirrors before I saw the white towel on the table with a needle and black thread. I said real quick, "We don't need to be doing any of that sewing. No, sir, that isn't necessary. I'm just fine."

"Sit down." I swung around, and my mouth fell open like the village idiot when I found Kit standing beside me. What with no cursing and all the men standing around grinning like split melons, I should have known something was up, but I never thought to see Kit prissing around in a saloon. She put such pressure on my shoulder I had to sit down or get in a scuffle with her, which would have brought fifty men down on me. Wearing a clean dress with a white apron, she looked as fetching as they come.

"Look, Kit, you got no business here. This is a place for men."

"Dr. Anderson said I could help him fix your cheek."

"You don't need to do that. You'll just make yourself sick again. Besides, my cheek's fine. I think it best to leave it be."

"I got sick earlier because you were so messy I thought you were killed. You scared me to death. Then I couldn't stand to have you staring at me while I was, uh, indisposed. This is different. Oh, here's Dr. Anderson now."

She sure seemed eager to get on with it. I had no stomach for any of this, but when I tried to stand up, I found Luke's hand resting casually on my shoulder. Trying to stand up with Luke leaning on me was about equal to lifting a meat wagon.

Dr. Anderson, smiling like a jackass with a feather up his nose, lied in his teeth when he said, "This'll be over before you know it, Kid. You'll hardly feel it."

Lightning should strike men dead who murder the truth like that. The first thing he did was soak a towel with alcohol and start rubbing my cheek like he was polishing a doorknob. I wanted to give my famous wounded-panther scream so bad I nearly choked, but what could I do with Kit standing there and fifty men gathered around watching the best show in town. A man has to maintain some shred of pride and dignity, so I sat there pretending I wasn't dying while tears sprang out of my eyes.

"There now," Dr. Sadist Anderson lied soothingly, "you're past the worst part."

"All finished?" I croaked. "That's great. What do I owe you, Doc?" Luke had a hand on each of my shoulders now. I began to understand how Atlas felt, with the weight of the world pressing down on him.

"Just a few little stitches and we'll be all through. You'll hardly feel it," said the meanest liar I ever saw, stretching the black thread hanging from that cursed needle. "We'll need to pull the skin just a tiny bit to close the wound as much as we can," he lied cheerfully, and proceeded to try to stretch my face clear out of shape.

"See here, Miss Thackery, how we can't close the wound entirely? Sufficient skin was torn away that, if we closed the wound entirely, the remaining skin would be stretched too tightly on his cheek. That would pull on his eyelid, making it difficult for him to close his eye and distorting his facial expression. Thus, even though we do the best we can, he'll have quite a scar, but he'll still have a relatively normal-looking face."

While he went on talking to her as if I was a chair with its seat being patched, I kept my teeth locked as hard as I could. Dr. Sadist tortured me for what seemed like hours, prattling to Kit about smaller stitches making less of a scar, and that's why he needed to do so much sewing—and how she should note the tears running out of the patient's eyes and how his nose was running and how this wasn't really crying but the normal physical reaction to this kind of facial trauma, and on and on.

Then, gently, he strapped a pad soaked in alcohol against my cheek and I heard him say, "Of course, this patient is quite extraordinary. Few people can abide pain stoically like he's done. To have a patient sit motionless and quiet, affecting indifference, is very unusual."

Kit wiped the tears out of my eyes, and I found Dr. Sadist seated across the table from me. He said, "Change the bandage every day and soak the wound with alcohol. It'll stop hurting in a couple of days when the swelling goes down. I'll take the stitches out in four or five days. Or your lady can remove the stitches, if you like." He shifted his attention to Kit. "Just snip the thread and lift them out like you would when altering a gown, Miss Thackery." Dr. Sadistic's gaze came back to me. "That'll be five dollars."

I groped feebly around the empty pockets of my clean clothes until Luke leaned over and dropped a ten dollar gold piece into the doctor's hand.

Kit patted me on the arm and said, "We can go now."

"We going to get married before we start for California?"

Fifty miners held their breath in perfect frozen silence while she blinked and stuttered, "I, uh, we, uh, we shouldn't discuss that here."

"Why not? If this is a good place to get sewed up, it should be a good place to get married. Let's do it right here and now. I'm leaving tonight. Somebody in this town doesn't like my horse, so I'm riding out. If you're going to be stitching and altering on me, we should be married."

"No need to ride out in the dark. I have two deputies watching that bay horse down at the stable. I figure to join them men myself in a little while." Sheriff Chip Dodd looked so comfortable when he was seated and off his feet, I almost didn't recognize him.

A smiling young man jumped up from a nearby table. "I can go get the license and bring it here, ma'am. I'll just bring the recording ledger over here too. Won't take five minutes." He trotted out the door without waiting for an answer.

Another man cleared his throat and came ponderously to his feet, pulling a black book from inside his coat. "Reverend Jefferson James, at your service, ma'am. I never take a step from my bedside without the Book. Emergencies arise."

Kit turned and directed a smile at Thackery. "Well, I guess it's all right for me to go ahead, Papa Joe, since Ward has overcome your last objection."

I swung around in my chair so I could face him. Joe Thackery's rigid face was turning bright red. The old man was actually blushing furiously. The expression he directed toward his daughter was one of thin-lipped poison.

"Objection? You have an objection, Mr. Thackery?" I asked.

Kit's laugh brought my attention back to her. "He told me it wasn't seemly for a girl to marry a man prettier than she is. I guess his scar will take care of that for Ward, don't you think, Papa Joe?"

Thackery showed every symptom of horrible embarrassment, shifting nervously from one foot to the other while he muttered, "A feeble jest, sir, but in poor taste, very poor taste. I apologize, sir, most humbly and sincerely." He turned his venomous stare back to his daughter. "A regrettable poor joke, but one intended to be kept private."

Kit, ignoring her father, turned to Milt and said, "Milton Baynes."

Milt drew back a step, uncomfortable to be the center of attention. "Yes, ma'am?"

"Since I shall soon, as a wife, assist my husband in the stewardship of his property, I think you have something which belongs to him?"

Milt straightened, blinking, with a puzzled expression for a moment before he laughed and stepped to my side. "Yes, ma'am, I do. You are quite correct."

Milt slowly and deliberately pulled my gold watch from his pocket and placed it carefully on the table in front of me.

•   •   •   •

Actually, we started out for California a week later. Everybody wanted to help guard Peepeye. He was the town pet for a while. Kit took out the stitches. Didn't hurt me. Didn't hurt me at all.

My firstborn son always shrugs off the question when people ask him how he came to be called Stitch Baynes.

JOHN S. McCORD is a retired lieutenant colonel in the U.S. Army. He served tours of duty in Vietnam, Korea, Japan, and Iran. He later taught economics at Richland College in Dallas, Texas, for eight years before turning full-time to writing. His first novel, *Walking Hawk,* was published by Doubleday in 1989. *Montana Horseman* is the first in the Baynes Gang trilogy. In addition, he and his wife, Joan, are active in the D.F.W. Writers Workshop in their hometown of Bedford, Texas.